Basket Baby

a novel

Kelli Donley

Published by Asymmetrical Press, Missoula, Montana.

This book is a work of fiction. All characters in this book are completely imagined.

Library of Congress Cataloging-In-Publication Data
Basket baby / Kelli Donley — 1st ed.
ISBN: ISBN: 978-1-68287-010-5
eISBN: 978-1-68287-011-2
1. Adoption. 2. Bolivia. 3. South America. 4. Motherhood. 5. Grief

Cover design by Colin Wright
Formatted in beautiful Montana
Printed in the U.S.A.

Publisher info:
Website: www.asymmetrical.co
Email: howdy@asymmetrical.co
Twitter: @asympress

To the women of the world who have selflessly given a child to another through adoption.

And to those who are waiting, with arms outstretched and hearts overflowing, for the newest addition to their forever family.

She named him Moses, saying,
"I drew him out of the water."

EXODUS 2:8

Basket Baby

1. RINSE AND REPEAT

Macy sighed with relief, sliding sore shoulders under the warm bath water, escaping behind the locked bathroom door. She'd used the last of her stash of American bubble bath, which filled the small tiled room with the smell of peonies and roses. The claw foot tub didn't hold heat well; she'd refilled it twice already, fluttering through pages of a dog-eared paperback while waiting for the return of heat.

"Macy, I'm home!" She heard her husband yell, throwing closed the heavy front door and tromping up the tile staircase. "Maceeeeee," he sang.

She slid further under the water, just covering her ears although she could still hear him and the pops of bursting bubbles.

"Macy Duncan! I have good news for you! But I am only giving you hints until you get your wrinkly ass out of that tub!" He now stood on the other side of the bathroom door, booming.

She sat up too fast, bath water splashing to the floor.

"Good news!" He repeated. He was overly cheery, like an annoying college mascot whose candor didn't change if the team was winning or losing. If this move to Bolivia was bothering him, Ben wasn't letting his wife know.

"I'll be out soon, honey," Macy said, throwing the paperback across the floor, where it came to rest at the base of the porcelain sink.

"Good. We are going out for dinner, and you'll want to see what is waiting for you downstairs."

She didn't respond, reviewing a list of items from home she dreamed of. Books—a new stack of anything to read. The few paperbacks and magazines they'd thrown in their suitcases when packing for their new lives in Bolivia had been without thought. It was remarkable they'd packed anything of use. Macy didn't remember participating. Perhaps her mother had completed the task, which then again would explain how an unrecognizable copy of *The Joy of Cooking* made the cut.

Ben knocked. "Hey, why don't you let me in there? I could use a shower too."

Macy squeezed the bridge of her nose. She knew her eyes were red from crying.

"Can I have another half hour?"

"I'm hungry, Mace. You said you'd come with me tonight. Steak. Booze. Remember?"

She heard his voice rise with anticipation—like a puppy waiting for another pat—one she didn't have the energy to give.

"I'm coming, just give me a few more minutes."

He sighed heavily. "You've read every book in this house by now while soaking in that tub." He knew her too well.

Her toes peeked over a cloud of foamy bubbles. White moons pushed an aging pedicure toward oblivion. She'd gone to the salon the day before giving birth, two months prior. The outing had been a last minute treat from her mother.

"Well, if my pathetic begging isn't enough to get you out of that tub, I will give you another hint. When I came home a few minutes ago, I tripped over something left for you outside on the doorstep."

"For me?"

"Yep."

"How do you know it was for me?"

"It has your name on it."

"Mail? Really?" Her voice rose with excitement.

"Ha! I thought that might get your attention. Maybe . . ."

"From whom?"

"Guess."

"My mother?"

"Bingo. And of course it's gigantic. Obscene, even. I'd bet she got the entire town to put a little something into her first South American care package."

"Oh, God." She sighed dramatically, patting the delicate tissue beneath her eyes, hoping to reduce swelling.

"Do you care to know what's hidden inside? What gems she's sent from the hinterlands of Flagstaff all the way to the backwaters of Bolivia?" She could imagine him standing there with a grin from ear to ear, making her guess before pulling each item from the packaging. "I'm not going to open it and drag it upstairs for you. Get out of that tub, Macy. Meet me downstairs."

Two months ago in Flagstaff, cards, email and flowers arrived by the dozens. Even folks they'd considered strangers sent notes, trying their hardest to express sorrow at their loss. Macy struggled just to breathe those first few days. The grief settled like an elephant on her chest. She'd never known such pain.

Macy couldn't understand why the stillbirth of her first

child would be of concern to so many others. Social alarms rang with panic; their friends and family did what they could: baked casseroles and kept a close eye on the beloved couple. The dishes were delivered warm, frozen, and nearly every state between—one Pyrex arrived missing a scoop of crunchy onions and green beans and came with a note from an 8-year-old taped on top. The girl had thought it was for dinner and her mother hadn't had time to make another.

The gossip whispered by friends over lattes in the morning and over pints at the local brewery's happy hour became simple in its sorrow: the loss of the Duncans' child was tragic and nonsensical, especially for those who knew of the previous miscarriages. There was no playbook for graceful navigation of such circumstances. An awkwardly worked obituary, once intended as a birth announcement, ran in the *Daily Sun*:

> *It is with great sorrow Macy and Ben Duncan share the death of their son, Jacob Teller Duncan. Born 7 pounds 12 ounces May 1, 2006. A private service was held. In lieu of flowers, the family requests privacy.*

Eventually, the well-intentioned folk of Flagstaff ran out of dishes and lost focus. There were other tragedies in town, newer versions of second-hand heartache worthy of their mourning. The news lede shifted. A baby drowned in a bucket at a Route 66 motel. The mother, a Guatemalan maid, fled the scene, worried about deportation.

During the darkest hours of those first nights, Macy felt something deep inside fall away. She couldn't imagine ever being able to laugh with abandon again.

Macy stopped responding to her own name a few days after returning home from the hospital empty handed. The nursery was brimming with gifts from a recent baby shower. Eventually her mother came and took the presents away to the crisis nursery, some still wrapped in pastel teddy bear and hot air balloon paper.

This pregnancy had been different. This one they celebrated—after the cursory six-month mark. This one had a heartbeat, until he didn't.

Macy Duncan would not be pitied. It was Ben's alarming threat of hospitalization that finally stirred the return of her voice, a week after returning home. He'd taken her by the shoulders, shaken her gently and gotten her attention.

"I need you, Mace. Please."

She simply nodded, said, "Okay" and went back to bed. A few days later, seeing her husband crying into the empty kitchen sink when he thought she couldn't hear him, the dense fog of loss broke temporarily.

"Oh Ben," she whispered, burying her face into his chest. They stood, wrapped around each other, feeling the guilt, sorrow, and disbelief wash over their tired bodies.

"Love? Come on. We *are* going to dinner tonight. You have 20 minutes, more than enough. I mean it, Mace." She heard his words get softer as he descended the stairs, calling back at the locked door. He hadn't bothered to try the handle.

"I'm getting out," she muttered. Her curiosity piqued by the parcel, wondering if her mother had once again known what her only daughter needed in a pinch: dark chocolate peanut butter cups, a bar of her favorite French soap, a new set of soft cotton pajamas. Books. Help.

* * *

The last package she'd opened from her husband was a catastrophe. Two weeks after returning home from the hospital, she'd shuffled into the kitchen looking for Ben and a cup of coffee. A note on the counter said he'd gone for a hike. Ben always found solace in nature.

There, not far from the note was a small, eggplant purple velvet bag. She'd smiled before opening it, thinking of the many times Ben had surprised her with small tokens of his love. Expecting a piece of blue glass for her collection, or a bottle of perfume, she stuck her hand into the soft bag.

When Ben returned an hour later, he found Macy collapsed on the kitchen floor among the debris of a broken coffee cup, eyes glassed over, two fingertips silver with ash.

"Oh fuck. No!" He screamed throwing his arms upward. "No! You weren't supposed to find that. *Him.* No!"

After the outburst, Ben cleaned the kitchen calmly, brought Macy back to bed, and then placed his head in her lap. From one breath to another, he became a different man. She watched his chest heave with grief. Like a hurt child, he sobbed, shuddering as he drew deep gulps of air, surrendering.

"Careless," he'd muttered again and again that ghastly afternoon, as the sun set red over the San Francisco peaks. "Stupid. Careless. How could I?"

She'd never forget the lightness of their son's remains, pebbly and soft gray. Feather weight. How with a delicate whisper of wind, they could blow away into nothing. Without thinking, she'd brought her ashen fingertips to her nose upon discovery, breathing him in, dumbstruck by the void of scent.

She had wanted to breathe in sweet baby powder, sour breast milk, even the pungency of a diaper needing changing —some normal baby smell.

"Mace," he shouted up the staircase, "I don't hear the water draining."

"Damn it!" Her words echoed off the tile walls. "I said I'm coming. I'll be down in a few minutes!" She heard the coldness in her voice.

Months later, she was still leaking, making the bathwater a milky and confusing mixture of relief and heartache. Her physician promised via email it wouldn't be much longer; it was rare for a woman to lactate this long without being able to breastfeed.

"Exercise and a healthy diet always help. Be kind to yourself." He had even had the nerve to include, "Have some sex with your husband. God knows that always makes someone feel better."

She hadn't replied.

Sitting in the tub, Macy had looked at Ben's old-fashioned metal razor and blade more than once. Rubbing it over her wrists, she heard her heart pound as the cold steel tickled delicate flesh. Dark blue and green veins threaded the surface.

It was a way out she wanted to reserve as an option, but not something she could do now. The images of Ben finding her lifeless body, his screams and unending pain—she couldn't do it to him. She couldn't add to her husband's sorrow.

She removed the blade and threw it away, blaming the housekeeper for her fastidious cleaning. She tucked the now empty razor under the bathroom sink and let the hair grow on her legs and under her arms. The soft, dark tufts were something she'd never let go before. Her underarms smelled of a garden after a spring rain—like the patchouli-scented women of Flagstaff she'd long chided as "dirty hippies."

Ben hadn't noticed. Or if he had, he hadn't said anything.

There were rays of light that came through the fog, moments when her notorious sarcasm bubbled to the surface. A flash of light. A keen sense of focus. A curiosity pushing her to peek through different windows, examining the day's light. That morning, she had awoken feeling rested. And tonight, she was actually hungry.

"I'm cracking a bottle of that local Malbec while I wait," she heard Ben shout from downstairs. "Please don't let me get drunk alone and feel like an American stereotype."

Macy let out a snort.

"I heard that!" She could hear the smile in his voice.

The housekeeper's romance ballads played from a tiny radio above the kitchen sink. Ruth would likely be preparing another vat of her albondigas soup. Macy was convinced the maid thought all woes could be cured with food. Some remedies were international.

In Flagstaff, Macy won her first photography prize climbing in the Grand Canyon. She'd been in the right spot with both blind courage and great equipment. Today, she was an American ex-pat housewife living in Bolivia. Macy suspected Ben's interest in the forestry position with a US government outpost in the South American country was an attempt to remove them from their hometown-turned-fishbowl. To protect his wife from the gossip. To save their marriage from the statistics. Few couples who lost a child went on to see their partnership thrive.

The change in scenery meant little in the first few weeks;

she'd spent the majority of her time with her nose in a book in that old tub, or flat on her back in their four-poster bed, watching the light and shadows play on the ceiling as the days passed.

Grabbing a long peach silk robe she'd received as a wedding shower gift two years prior, she quickly ran a comb through her mop of hair, tugging at tangles. Macy pulled the garment free, staring hard at the figure in the mirror. Her wet auburn hair was still thinning, falling out in clumps. She had the extra to spare; her thick hair had always been the envy of her friends.

Macy cupped her heavy breasts, noting the purple stretch marks beginning to ease to a soft pink. Moving downward, she tugged at the ribbon of weight woven around her waist, pinching the bulge at her hips. Gently, she let a finger brush where she'd been stitched back together, cut from the episiotomy. The tenderness no longer made her wince.

She avoided looking at her face in the mirror—the small chickenpox scar above her right eye brow, the tiny hole that never healed from her college nose ring, the small brown mole near her hairline, none of this would have changed. What Macy didn't want to see were the new lines around her eyes, or the bags beneath. She was also nervous about the silver strands she found in her comb. The aging she would manage like any woman, with annoyance. But the eyes of this woman, she couldn't bear to see.

Jacob's fingertips had been perfect. The arch of his nose. The curve of his cupid bow. The blond, barely-there eyebrows. He was perfect. The weight of his tiny bottom that fit perfectly cupped in her hand. If he'd only filled his lungs with air.

* * *

The smell of cardamom, pepper and adobo filled her nose. Macy's mouth watered as she dressed for the evening.

"God, something smells wonderful."

Ben poked his head out of the kitchen, the edges of his lips stained purple. Macy stood in the entryway, shaking and examining what was indeed a large box from her mother.

"Look at you. If I wasn't so hungry, I'd take you back upstairs."

She glanced toward their bedroom to see Ruth quietly on her knees on the staircase, drying up the trickle of water Macy trailed from the bath.

"I'm getting a bit too used to her doing that for me." Macy's cheeks flushed. She hadn't wanted house help, but Ben insisted. It was culturally appropriate in Bolivia, and he'd told her they were doing their new community good, providing an otherwise out-of-work single mother with a salary.

"I'm sorry Ruth. I should have been more careful." Macy bent down to the woman, pulling her up by her round, dark arm. "Whatever you are cooking smells incredible."

"Gracias, Señora." Ruth nodded, taking the wet towel and Ben's boots, recovered from upstairs, and returned to the kitchen.

Macy was unsure if the woman actually understood, but she did appreciate her presence. Not having to cook, press Ben's shirts, or worry about the market was a delight. She hadn't done those things well in Flagstaff. Mercifully, in Bolivia there was no expectation. They never asked Ruth to cook; the housekeeper made a dinner whether they were there to sit down and eat or not. Macy didn't bother to ask what happened to all the leftovers.

Ben was halfway through a bottle of wine and the evening

newspaper. Somehow these tiny towns supported not one but two editions of their daily news. She thought of her old friend and editor Sam, the newsroom and the countless stories they'd reported about their dying art. Print journalism in Flagstaff—and everywhere else—was going the way of the stone tablet. "Thank you, Al Gore and your internet," the newsroom staff bemoaned.

"You look great, babe."

"I'm wearing dirty jeans."

"Your favorite."

Ben coyly raised one eyebrow and tossed back the remainder of his glass.

He'd teased her for years that those jeans would get up off their cramped apartment floor and walk away on their own to the laundromat. Jeans and a thrift-store sweater were her uniform, and exactly what she'd been wearing the night they met.

"Thank you, B. Any news from home?"

"Nothing worthwhile. The President, good old Evo, still hates the US. The US still hates the coca growers. No one wants to budge and no one will talk about the fact that if Americans didn't lust for cocaine, we wouldn't be interested."

"I meant *home* home."

"Flag? Sweetheart, what are the chances of hearing about anything from northern Arizona in a small community newspaper in southern Bolivia?"

"Well, we ran articles about Bolivia occasionally."

"I'm sure Sam will pick up a wire report the next time there are protests. We can't count on the Tarija Times to do the same if students skip class for an early ski season."

She smiled. October in Bolivia was spring. They'd completely missed winter this year by the timing of their move. Two summers might be just what her soul needed. She'd longed for the changing aspens on the San Francisco Peaks and her community pumpkin patch, but a year without black ice and off-white Phoenicians clogging the highways at the first sight of snow would be a reprieve.

"Fair enough. I can imagine the headlines anyway. 'German Falls off Grand Canyon Edge: Suicide?' 'Freshmen Test Scores Lowest Yet.' 'Lumberjacks Ranked Last in Big Sky Conference.'"

"Sam would call you a cynic, you know."

Their crew started a bet with friends a few years back. Each New Year's Eve they'd pick a date in the calendar, a pool that predicted the first international visitor death at the Grand Canyon. The story was routine to Flagstaff and had heartlessly lost its sense of tragedy in the newsroom. More than a dozen people died in the canyon annually, and Macy had been the photographer on call for most. She'd become friends with the rangers and even quietly petitioned the county to consider funding additional railings. Sam would have been irate if he'd known of her support; the tenets of journalism kept her from being vocal about opinions outside of her home.

Macy grabbed Ben's hand and squeezed, ignoring the itch of homesickness. "I believe I was promised a steak."

With a huge smile of purple teeth, he wrapped a hand around her waist.

"Don't you want to open that box first?"

"It can wait. I've got a hot date with a piece of meat."

He let out a hearty laugh and carefully kissed her neck. Macy let him spin her toward the front door, soaking up every moment of this ray of happiness. It was a brief taste of normalcy.

They stepped outside into the brisk spring evening. The uneven cobblestone streets of Tarija wove pedestrians and sputtering, overloaded motorcycles and taxis toward one of the many city squares, each with an imposing Catholic church standing sentry. Café umbrellas sprinkled color across the otherwise dusty taupe canvas. The streets, buildings, and people all seemed to have the same olive-skinned hue. Macy breathed in deeply, trying to center herself. Some tree she didn't recognize was in full bloom, casting pink flowers to the street and making the walk seem like something from Candy Land.

Ben rambled mindlessly about South American politics, familiar with the broken sidewalks and rough, patchwork streets. She followed cautiously. The sidewalks were wide enough for one person. Chalky white tree roots reached upward through the concrete and cobblestone. She missed the bright, pungent smell of pine. The familiar stink of skunks.

They reached the small restaurant and were immediately poured generous glasses of wine. Ben reached across the table and took both her hands, just as he'd done on their first date. She felt the twinge of butterflies.

"A Boliviano for your thoughts."

His words slurred a touch and she realized, with both annoyance and envy, he was tipsy. Macy considered the question. Where to begin? She pulled her hands into her lap, recognizing she had complete power to set the evening's tone.

"Well, that doesn't seem fair." She motioned toward the door where a dark skinned Bolivian couple sat, waiting empty handed.

"The locals?"

"They were here before us. We spent two minutes in the entryway and have something to drink before they were greeted."

Both looked over, unexpectedly making eye contact with the woman.

Ben smiled. "You used to love when I could sneak us ahead on the list at the brewery."

"Among our own."

"Well, yes. But I didn't say anything."

"You didn't have to. I'd guess they all know you by now. We are the Americans. Look at us. We don't look like locals."

The two looked around the room. The native Bolivians on this side of the Andes and at this altitude were petite and most had dark features. In a restaurant of this caliber, the Bolivians inside were the rare few—those who had extra pocket money for a meal out at a restaurant with linens and, as Macy noted gratefully, a considerable wine list on the menu.

"Of course. My love, Macy Duncan, will be the champion of the Bolivian underdog." He reached under the table and grabbed her hand back. "I love it. This is exactly what you need, a cause. A project." He spoke in a deep, announcer voice that always made her giggle.

"Right." She smiled. He always believed in her.

"No project too big. Avenger for all!" He threw up a fist and did his best super hero impression. They both laughed, their familiar senses of humor slowly beginning to reemerge.

"It is just too perfect that your first time out in this country and you observe what I haven't been able to see for two months. It isn't that I don't care, but that I don't see it, Mace. You know, that's exactly what makes you a great photographer."

Macy soaked in the praise. It felt good, even if she knew what he was trying to do.

They nibbled, dipping the bread into the spicy salsa, sipping wine and enjoying the patio, the cool weather and the noise of a busy restaurant. Ben rambled about the festivals of the week and the different things he'd seen in the square. Macy rolled the wine around in her mouth, feeling the tension in her shoulders dull with each sip.

"It feels good to be here with you," she relented. It did feel good. And she certainly missed feeling connected to her best friend. When was the last time they had sex? She couldn't remember.

Macy let her hand explore momentarily above his knee before something caught her eye. Just over Ben's shoulder was another Flamboyant tree in full bloom.

"God, look at that. I should come back here in the daylight and take a closer look." Macy nodded at the heavy limbs hanging sensually like a bejeweled dancer.

"Maybe you should come back with your camera."

"Maybe." She looked hard at the pink blooms.

"You do remember that tool attached to your hand since the day I met you?"

She took a deep breath.

"I'm not ready."

He pulled his hands away, shaking his head. "I know I'm pushing you. But you need it. We need it, Mace." His tone softened.

"Can we just make it through dinner first?"

"I was so happy to finally hear your laugh tonight. Mace, you aren't ever going to be ready if you keep hiding underwater. Do you want an underwater camera? I suppose I wouldn't mind photos from that bathtub."

She could tell by his bravado he'd had enough to drink. If they were at the pub in Flag, he'd be sliding his hand up her dress to see if she was wearing underwear.

"Ben, I can't. Please? It's just too fast. All of this is happening too fast."

"You can't?" He threw his hands in the air with a soft laugh. "Bullshit, you can't. You are Macy Duncan. You climbed El Capitan. You snuck into a castle in Ireland to get the first sunrise photo from the turret. You make the best homemade carrot cake in the world. There is very little that you cannot do."

Squeezing her eyes tight, Macy lifted her glass. She was either going to have to catch up with him or leave.

"Ben." She sucked in air as quickly as she could, feeling the pressure of a sob building in her chest. "I don't wake up every morning and think, 'How can I stay in the bathtub all day and piss off my husband?' You realize that? Do you know how badly I want to go back? How I wish I could make this all different? How I wish I didn't fail?"

"No, I don't know." His voice lowered and he stared at her. She noticed new, faint lines around his eyes. "Stop with the 'fail' bullshit. You didn't fail. We didn't fail."

The pair sat in silence for several minutes, neither willing to budge.

"You have a choice. You get to pick how you are going to treat me. It's me, Mace."

She let out a slow wail. "I just want to get through dinner. This day. This moment." The hum of the restaurant immediately stopped. All eyes focused on the new foreign couple, those who should have known better than anyone that such public emotion was inappropriate.

"Okay," Ben's eyes searched hers. He grabbed her hands and squeezed them tightly. "Okay. Not here. Please. I'll drop it."

Macy brought the cloth napkin to her face with one hand, and pinched her leg with the other. She could tell by the flushed tips of his burning red ears that she'd embarrassed him.

"I can't just go back to the way it was." She whispered it, but they both heard the struggle for control in her voice. He'd pushed too far.

He drained his glass, stuck another piece of bread in his mouth and raised both hands, palms up.

"Fine. I hate to see you cry. I hate feeling like this is my fault. I am doing my best here, Mace. I thought bringing us here—" He stopped, running his hands through his hair as he did when he was annoyed and didn't want to say the wrong thing. "I just thought we could figure this out together away from everyone. That we would help each other."

Macy stared at her plate, feeling her stomach burn from the spicy aji.

"I sat at my desk this afternoon trying to figure out how to get you out of the house tonight. I'm so glad you are here, that I can still woo you with red meat and wine." Ben smiled weakly. "Mace. I am right here. I miss you more than anything I've ever missed in my life. More than good beer. More than ESPN."

She let a laugh escape, allowing her bubbling disappointment to cool. Their life in Bolivia had come without many of the luxuries they'd taken for granted in Flagstaff, including access to Ben's first love: *Sports Center.*

She hiccuped once, and patted her cheeks, trying to regain composure.

"I hate that you know how to do that."

"Do what?"

"Make things better with a quick laugh."

"You used to love that about me."

"I still love you, B." She flashed a wry smile. "And please stop telling people I climbed El Capitan. For God's sake, I hiked around Yosemite. On the ground. I didn't even camp."

He was still laughing when the waitress arrived with plates popping and snapping, begging for the steak and grilled vegetables to be savored. She picked at the food.

"Woman, I love that body. I mean, I love your body and I miss it so much. We have to figure this out, Mace. Soon." His voice was soft, but he made sure not to take his eyes off her. Macy had known this man long enough to understand he was about to deliver bad news. "Look," he said, taking a deep breath. "I have to leave tomorrow morning. There is a meeting in Santa Cruz and I'll be there for several days."

"You're leaving me? Now?" Her heart pounded.

They hadn't been apart more than a few hours in the last few months. She'd never thought she'd be one of those women who clung to her husband, but Ben on a plane without her made her sick. She swallowed hard to keep down the acidity in the back of her throat.

"Macy, I am not leaving you." Ben said the words slowly. "I am going to work. I'll be home in three days." They finished their meal in silence, him picking at the steak she could no longer eat after he'd finished his own.

"In case you change your mind about seeing the city." He pulled out a Holga from his sweater pocket. She'd long wanted one of the cheap cameras, but had never put the effort into tracking one down.

"Oh Ben, how did you?" She fiddled with the camera,

feeling regret wash over her for her inpatient tone. The inexpensive black plastic wouldn't hold up for long, but she would need a few hours and one roll of black-and-white film to make it worth the purchase.

"eBay," he responded. "Can you believe they even *have* eBay here? I can't get a good basketball game, but shopping is apparently international. I was trying to get you to open this little package before we left the house too."

Macy smiled sincerely, taking another gulp of the Malbec, the tension falling away as the warmth of the wine finally settled into her limbs. Her legs were heavy and relaxed. Her mother had asked if they'd have the Internet in Bolivia, as if the World Wide Web were a misnomer for northern Arizona web.

"Ben, thank you."

"Oh, and one more thing." He fumbled with a tiny Spanish-English pocket dictionary. "You will need this. You are going to have to learn Spanish because after these weeks with Ruth, she is barely managing 'Hello Meester Duncan.'"

"Damn my mother for being right about the frivolity of French. Bon, Monsieur Duncan, je suis Meeses Duncan?"

"Oui, oui, ma cherie. Voulez vous . . . Wait how does that go?"

"You'll come home?" She grabbed his hands. She needed him to remember her insistence, whether they'd both had too much to drink or not.

"Of course I'll come home." Ben raised an eyebrow and stared hard at his wife. "Mace. Take walks, get out of that house, avoid your mother's phone calls, and find something here that makes you feel alive. Go shop and send her a giant package in return. When I come home, have a reason to greet me. At the door. Dressed. We aren't going anywhere and I can't come home to find you crying alone in that damn tub. Promise me."

Something stirred within her when he spoke so forcefully.

"Promise me."

Raising her glass, Macy toasted her husband's optimism. "I promise you Meester Duncan. You will not come home to find me crying, alone in the tub."

"I love you, Mace."

There it was. Macy sat back, feeling the words settle and her own stubbornness begin to ease. She waived the waiter over and motioned for an additional bottle of wine. Draining another glass without considering how her husband would have to carry her home over the fragmented sidewalks, Macy gave her very best reassurance, hoping to convince herself too.

"Camera. Dictionary. Wine. Avoid my mother. Reason for living. Don't worry, B. I'll be fine."

2. BLUE

Luz stood in the modest kitchen, separating honeycomb, licking sweetness from her fingers to satisfy the never-ending hunger. The bees gorged after an unpredictably wet summer, producing a hearty harvest; bits of pollen gathered at the bottom of the jar. She tapped it gently, marveling at Mother Nature's power to create gold liquid from fields and insects.

One moment she was separating honey, preparing jars for market as she'd done countless times prior. The next, Luz stared at the floor, her face burning hot, wondering how she hadn't made it to the latrine in time. A puddle spread on the dirt, which she could feel on her bare feet, but not see over her ripe belly.

"Mija, es tiempo. Venga, querida."

Her mother knew. Luz guessed it was the scent that brought La Doña inside their modest mud and stick home.

"Mija, it's time."

She'd been preparing for the birth of the next grandchild. Word was sent: rally the other women of the village. Luz's baby would be born. Finalmente!

Luz felt her braids unravel a bit with each blinding contraction. Her lean legs were pushed backward by las doñas, her mother ready with a clean knife to cut the umbilical cord. They all knew the first birth was the hardest. By the tenth child, you barely had to stop working.

She suspected these women, who'd raised Luz and countless others in Entre Rios, had long solved the paternal riddle. The clue she'd been unwilling to give. Within earshot, las doñas didn't spread gossip, more than likely out of respect for her mother, Doña Maria. One was wise in Entre Rios not to let la Doña Maria hear you say anything about her family, even praise. Luz knew her mother valued discretion nearly as much as the fields of potatoes that kept the family fed.

When the infant, blue and covered in afterbirth, finally emerged with a wracking, bubbly scream, las doñas wept quietly.

Luz knew. Immediately, she knew.

It was the gurgle. This child did not sound like the many others she'd witnessed birthed on the same dirt floor. The dead ones didn't make a noise. It was their mothers' cries you had to endure. The live ones eventually hiccupped a deep, angry, surprised whelp after a good slap on the ass.

This baby did neither.

Las doñas swept the infant away to clean her, looking to Doña Maria the entire time. Luz followed their gaze.

Please don't drown her. Please don't leave her out for the animals. Just give her to me!

Warm tears flooded Luz's face. She was overwhelmed with more emotion than she knew was possible, including a profound gratitude for her mother's gentle help. She looked into her mother's eyes.

"Damela, por favor! Por favor, mami!"

Please. Do not let them take her.

Doña Maria sighed.

Luz couldn't wait another moment to feel her child's skin. To count her fingers and toes. To see the color of her hair and the arch of her back. She felt so different without a child inside of her—full of renewed purpose.

"Damela! Damela!" Luz began to scream.

"Give her to me, now!" Luz cried.

Carefully, one of the elders placed the infant in the young mother's arms after receiving the surprising nod from their respected friend, Doña Maria. This child would die the long way, leaving everyone wounded.

"Pray God will take her soon, my child," Doña Norma whispered.

"Give me my baby, vieja bruja," Luz growled.

The elder snapped back as if slapped. Luz smiled; she was riveted by the most beautiful creature she'd ever seen.

"Mija, eres perfecta," she sang, sweeping the baby's dark hair to one side. Ten toes. Ten fingers. A perfect arch to her back that swept downward to a perfectly formed round bottom.

Luz was in love.

Eventually, she let her eyes creep upward, over the infant's chin. A purple canyon sliced through the babe's mouth, carving a highway into a deformed nose. Her breath caught.

Luz continued moving upward, slowly. The moment she met her wawa's dark eyes, she knew there was nothing she'd ever be able to create as perfect as this child. She rocked the little girl, newfound joy spreading with each heartbeat.

"Ahhh!"

Luz screamed again, even louder, with elation. The elders swayed at her side. She could see the grief on their tired faces. How wrong they were! This child was perfect!

The last of her modesty fell to the floor with the placenta, after her mother carefully pulled her legs back, inserting a finger to make sure the afterbirth had been expelled. She felt her mother pushing her here and there, tenderly examining and determining if she'd need stitches. It was as intimate as the two had been since Luz had been delivered on a similar night, nearly 15 years prior.

As the night passed, her breasts were massaged by aging, gentle hands that also placed warm cloth laced with healing herbs on her wounds. Their tears fell on the girl as they worked.

Luz found sleep, with the infant in a small basket next to her. She woke only once in the night.

"God hasn't approved of this. That is why the baby will die," a voice hissed.

"You are not welcome in my home. And if you are not careful, I will see that you are no longer welcome in Entre Rios." Doña Maria's voice was tired, but still threatening.

Luz listened to her mother growl like a cornered puma, reminding everyone who was in control. She kept her eyes closed tight, but could feel the women standing in the doorway of the house, impeding the breeze.

"My daughter's baby is none of your concern. And if I hear of you spreading lies, I will see you are punished." La doña's foot tapped in the dust. "How dare you tell her the child should die soon? Imagine if these were the first words you heard after the birth of your mangled twins? No one said such things to you Norma. Remember that. Remember, I know your secrets."

"This is what happens when young girls are secretive. When they lay down with men when they were supposed to be working. When God doesn't approve!" Doña Norma was unfazed by the warning.

Luz jumped when she heard the slap. She smiled, rolling over to touch her infant daughter, who gurgled with each breath, but slept as only newborns can.

Luz had no idea a baby's eyes could change color. She'd spent most of her childhood tending the hives, watching the bees grow each summer. Queens and drones working in harmony, marching along in nature's regimen. She understood the worker bees best. Spending much of her formative years alone in the golden highland hills, she herded a small flock of sheep and made sure no one stole the family's prized honey.

As such, Luz didn't have any idea she was pregnant until her older sister caught her one morning, changing clothes after a quick wash.

"Por Dios! Estas embarazada?" Carmen whispered, shocked. "You are glowing! How could this have happened? How could I not have noticed?" She paced.

Pregnant? What?

"Carmen, stop looking at me." Flushing red, Luz quickly pulled down her shirt. She had been ill, but had mistaken morning sickness for a gallbladder attack. The water, heavy in minerals, caused most in Entre Rios to have occasional bouts of such illness. Pregnant? How could she have not known?

Luz's hands fumbled over her belly, equally protective and confused.

Carmen stared at her, the youngest. Luz knew what her sister thought. She was "la chiquita."

Carmen often confused Luz's last place in the birth order for something fragile and naive. In truth, Luz saw the world for what it was: golden hills, honey, and hunger. Men, as her mother had long shown her, come and go. Sometimes children did too. But the hills were always there. And without the right weather for honey, or if the potato harvest came short, the village's hunger intensified—like coffee left too long on the fire, boiled down to an angry, thick, dark mess.

"Ay, what have we allowed to happen?" Carmen had raised Luz, along with a handful of older cousins. Doña Maria oversaw the operation, much like the potato farm and llama pens. There were younger hands with more energy to raise the baby. Luz didn't mind. There was always someone pinching her arms when she spoke out of turn, or when the seasonal harvests didn't produce enough honey. Those same mean fingers also stroked her head, teaching her to braid her own long, raven hair; they placed warm cloths on her stomach during her first cycle, carefully explaining the bees she so loved in their hive weren't the only ones to consider.

Luz and her friends were fed contradictory stories about the beginnings of life at the small, mud-walled schoolhouse. The boys were sent outside to play soccer. The girls were told to sit tight and pay attention; their eternal salvation depended on it.

The schools, funded by Catholic gold and silver, told of angels impregnating the Virgin Mary. Such miraculous pregnancies from brown indigenous girls were unlikely. Souls were lost in pleasure-seeking behavior. Legs crossed tight, they labored through countless lectures on the consequences of chasing an ecstasy their young minds couldn't yet fathom.

"My soul will be lost if I feel pleasure?" Luz repeated the lesson to a girlfriend on their walk home from school. "Do you believe that?"

"You must."

"Why? Doesn't that seem strange?"

"Didn't you hear the nuns? Hell, Luz. We will go to hell."

Luz laughed. "It just sounds too simple to me. Like a way for those constipated nuns to feel good about their choices. We are pretty. We are young. We don't have to become them."

Luz watched the girl run off, her braids bobbing as she did. Luz made the matter worse when repeating her doubts in class. The head mother saw she was whipped in the school yard in front of all the students, as a lesson to all.

Sin, even in thought, was not allowed.

The girls at school didn't speak to her after that day. The boys made kissing noises any time she got too close.

Carmen, however, stroked her ears and told her it would all be okay.

Soon enough those silly children would know the truth. The real truth. Not the story of angels and virgins.

Village elders, fueled by centuries of South American ancestral adventure, whispered creation stories of the jaguars. The hunt, prowl and mating dance. The glory of catching what you want for a manic moment, only to discover another soul could never truly be your own. Instead, the mothers would murmur over their children at night—the joy of life is finding love by intimately knowing our own soul.

"My sweet sister, you will love one day. It will hurt as much as it delights. And if you are very lucky, you'll always remember to love yourself."

Doña Maria caught wind of her youngest's public punishment and made a visit to the school. After, Luz was told to stick to her hives; she could learn plenty in the fields as her mother and sisters had. She was not to return to school, never mind that she could barely read—a skill that would need more practice than tending bees allowed.

Neither Immaculate Conception nor poetic folklore prepared Luz what to expect when an older, charming man took her by the hand one afternoon to a quiet pasture. She'd watched him for months, wondering what it would be like to touch his skin. To smell his neck. To feel those soft, foreign hands on her waist. In her hair. Running his fingers down her sides.

That night, she dreamed of swallowing bees. Their coupling had stung, swelling her flesh with discomfort and desire. The bees returned weeks later, as she climbed the hills to the hives, her now broken heart thumping with each step. Her foreign man departed Entre Rios and the outlying villages, leaving behind more than either realized. The bees tingled and swam in her stomach for months, making her ache for another afternoon in his arms.

"You'll have to explain eventually, but until you are ready, just say it was bad water. You've been sick from the well. No one will know otherwise." Carmen walked over to her sister, pulled up the shirt, and placed a palm flat on Luz's stomach.

"But you must tell me now. I won't repeat it. Who did this?"

"I. I don't know." Luz stared at her flat, thick feet. She'd never worn chanclas.

"You don't know? Ay, hermanita. Como? How couldn't you know?"

"Please don't."

"Don't?"

"Don't tell Mama."

"Ha! Mama's going to find out. This isn't a secret you can

keep! You'll be much bigger in the next month. I'd guess you are four moons already."

"I didn't know."

"Did someone hurt you?" Carmen took Luz by the shoulders, her voice suddenly softer. "Luz, querida, did a man push himself? Oh God. Oh God! You tell me right this moment. Tell me who hurt you!"

Luz shook her head. Her long black braids swished against the middle of her back. He didn't hurt me. I wanted more. I miss him.

"Oh! You are in love!" Her sister's voice clung desperately to the possibility their youngest hadn't been victimized. "Oh, Luz. That must be it. Tell me!" Carmen's smile brightened. Love would mean marriage and a celebration. Everyone in the village knew the first baby didn't always take nine months to arrive.

"No."

"No?"

"No. No, I was not forced. No, I am not in love." Luz felt the warmth climbing her neck. Her ears began to burn with timidity.

I couldn't love him. He'd left me. I wouldn't love a memory.

"Then who? I promise I won't tell Mama, but you must tell me if someone did this to you. If someone took you . . ."

Luz squirmed.

"No one took me."

These were the last words she'd mutter for months about the father of her wawa. Doña Maria begged, perhaps for the first time in her life. Carmen threatened to line each young man in the village up and call in a curandera to cast a spell. Every man for five golden hillsides was considered a suspect.

Norma spread her theories. Luz and the baby's pending birth were discussed at the village well, around the evening fires, on the main road. By the time her water broke, she was certain even the llamas roaming the Andes had heard of her youthful stubbornness.

It took the wawa's arrival—the babe gulping for life through a cleft palate—for the village to fall silent, but only after making their final judgments. The gossip moved with the cooking smoke from one small home to another.

"The baby probably won't survive the week."

"There was no way for her to latch."

"No bother finding a doctor in Tarija. They can't even afford the bus ticket."

"Stupid girl. What did she expect?"

Others whispered it was a blessing. Luz was young. She'd have more babies. She'd find a husband and start over. The wawa wasn't meant to survive. All of this nonsense made its way back to Luz those first few weeks, even though Carmen tried her fiercest to protect what was left of her sister's innocence. Luz simply clamped her jaw shut, unwilling to spit back. She stared at her wawa in awe.

This was a child to be celebrated. This was a child to be loved. Gossip and disapproving judgments would not take her from the joy of her beautiful daughter.

The curanderas also visited Doña Maria's house, providing the family consolation that the child's spirit would return to the earth. Next time, the child would arrive a warrior. This babe would always be a part of their village, watching over their well-being from the next life.

"You're just as bad as the nuns! OUT!" Luz pushed at the women with a broom, keeping the baby protected with the other hand.

Doña Maria, more suspicious and tactful, simply thanked them for coming.

"Please let me pay for a sachet of herbs. My daughter could use strength and peace."

It was a traveling missionary, visiting the outlying village, who stoked a fire of rage. The young man from La Paz approached the house after an earful of Norma's news.

"Señora, there is still time to baptize, to teach your daughter repentance." His shoes were dusty from the long walk, his tie as crooked and out of place as his presence. "Perhaps we could also speak with the father? He should confess. They should both recognize this deformity, this unnecessary death, as a sign from God."

This time it was Doña Maria's turn to pick up the broom.

"The baby's birth was a sign. Entre Rios should see God was watching. Sin is never rewarded!" He screamed these final proclamations, running as fast as he could muster away from Doña Maria.

How surprised the curanderas, Catholics and everyone in between were when the beekeeper focused her renewed obstinance on the infant's survival. Doña Maria watched her daughter with curiosity. She insisted Luz not name the baby; it would bring bad luck to a child soon to be buried. Luz could keep her alive as long as the babe wasn't in obvious pain. They wouldn't register her with the local health ministry post or bother with compulsory immunizations. No need to let anyone outside of their protective village know about their wounded bird.

Doña Maria cared for her grandbaby as necessary, although unwilling to bond with a "fleeting soul." Luz watched with a sick sadness in her chest as her mother refused to look at her child's face.

"Mija, we will see this child to the next life, whatever that may be. Losing a child isn't simple. I . . . I know this pain. I am sorry you must taste it with your first, querida." Her mother took a deep, ragged breath. "There will be others."

Luz stared ahead, unwilling to acknowledge her daughter's birth defect.

"She is stamped for death, hermosa. Do not hold hope otherwise, my love. Or you will make the loss worse." Her mother spoke softly.

Luz left her bowl untouched, tucking herself in to the small cot with one hand on her precious child's basket. She closed her eyes, considering her mother's words. When Carmen arrived hours later, she overheard the two speaking outside.

"Carmencita, our beekeeper will return to work in the hills soon enough. La tragedia will not kill them both." La Doña's firm voice had returned with the dark of night. Enough coddling.

"Si, mami. I will see she returns to work soon. We'll protect her."

"Better than you did last time, mija."

Carmen sighed. "This will all be over soon, mama. Lo siento."

Luz rocked the basket, holding on for their lives.

Her breasts, heavy and aching, anchored her body as she swept, bent at the waist. Methodically and as a quietly as possible, she used the handmade broom to sweep yesterday's dust out the tiny front door to its source: the altiplano. She heard her baby bird's voice, a sweet cooing from the cradle in the corner.

The child wasn't thriving. The split palate would need surgery. But if Luz rocked just so, if she stood just right, the baby would find her nipple, relieving the pressure that built in her chest, fueling them both with a moment of hope.

How can we get to the city? How can I pay for a doctor?

Luz's mind never stopped creating new, wild plans of action. Even in her sleep, she dreamed of nurses handing her a healthy toddler, with a perfect smile. By day, Luz held her baby girl close, fed her as much as she could, and kept her warm from the whipping winds of the altiplano and the stinging welts of village gossips.

As Luz swayed her hips beneath the large pollera skirt, the morning light caught her daughter's eyes. Overnight, like a deadly Chagas' bug creeping from the thatch above, life changed in a simple moment of delayed biology. Her daughter's long, curly lashes now framed bright *blue* eyes. Six weeks after giving birth, with a flicker of light, Luz's fate changed.

"Ay, por Dios!" She whispered, examining the baby, turning her from side to side.

Luz was in serious trouble. Those blue eyes! Of course at birth, her baby bird's eyes were a dark coffee brown. They were the complementary rich shade of the Bolivian high plains, where the wawa had come screaming into the world that starry, warm night.

Luz yelped; her stomach twisted into a hive of anxiety.

How had her eyes turned now? Had she truly angered God? How could her secret be revealed so easily?

Yesterday the wawa could have been anyone's daughter.

Today, the baby was Henry's.

3. REBIRTH

Ruth walked through the central market of Tarija, examining the wide rows of noisy butchers. A vendor with long gray braids hacked at meat with a small machete. She had adorned her hair with bundles of black yarn at the ends to make it appear longer. The braids moved rhythmically as she raised and lowered the long knife. The liver was so purple, Ruth initially mistook it for an eggplant.

Ruth watched as the woman sliced the organ meat into sections, weighing each one and taking mental note before tossing them to waiting pieces of old newspaper. The butcher wiped her hands on a yellowed apron and speedily tied the packages with twine.

"Qué quieres?"

What did she want? Ruth scanned the table and the chunks of meat hanging above on hooks. Ribs, stomach, tripe, and a section of prized, overpriced steak for the gringos in town who didn't know how to cut up a less expensive roast. She stuffed her hand in her skirt pocket and jingled the few Bolivianos she had left to feed her family.

With four mouths to feed, eight feet to shoe, and countless teeth that always seemed to need attention, Ruth couldn't catch up, much less buy herself that much needed new bra. She could have put her boys in the state-run school, which would have allowed her to work far fewer hours, but she saw what tontos came out of those schools. Her children were no fools. Working for gringos was her way of ensuring a proper private education for her boys, whether Andres helped or not.

Sighing, she pointed to a knotty piece of leftover beef and a tiny portion of liver.

"Molido, por favor."

She watched as the woman twisted her neck left then right, shooing her braids behind her shoulders and placing the meat in the old heavy grinder. Ruth smiled, watching the meat grind together, mixing with her cleverness. Her boys would never know how iron in the liver made them strong, how so many children in their neighborhood weren't tired, but anemic. Nothing made the housekeeper feel wiser than finding new ways to extend the money she earned each week to provide for her barones. She'd die before she and her children would join the growing number of hungry indigenous Bolivians. Too many could be found wrapped in brightly woven blankets, playing cheap, imported, made-in-China "Andean" flutes, begging before the city's cathedrals.

Ruth was okay with the occasional lie, even though she knew Jesus Cristo wasn't terribly fond of her reasoning. So she had to fib to her boys by sneaking vegetables and liver into their meals. There were worse sins.

With an indigeno in the President's office, her four boys had a better chance. They would need to be healthy children to grow into strong men.

She handed the vendor all of her coins and placed the pitifully small package in her pocket, replacing what remained of her earnings. Meandering through the other stalls, she kept her head down to escape the carnival of fruit, vegetables, and breads. Ruth placed a hand over her growling stomach when she walked by the chicken feet vendor.

Oh, what she wouldn't do for a steamy plate of fava beans and fried chicken feet.

Ruth whispered prayers over the noisy calls of customers, farmers, bakers, and shepherds—prayers for all of them, not just her own crying belly. The market was even busier Friday afternoons. Families may not eat well all week, other than a good meal after mass on the weekend. She'd come not just to buy liver for her boys, but to replenish a few staples in the kitchen of her new jefa. The woman didn't know how to cook. Then again, she didn't eat much either. And yet, there was Señor Duncan each morning to hand her money for more groceries.

The boys' father had never provided for her this way. Ruth ran her tongue along her back molars, worn from nightly grinding, feeling the aging bone wearing away as her anxiety only increased.

"Ruth, please take these Bolivianos. Make sure we have bread and fruit. And thank you, Ruth. Keep an eye on her for me."

She could barely understand his broken Spanish, yet the smile on his face, the way he gently placed the few bills in her hand and always used her name, she knew he was a good man.

What Ruth didn't understand was how he could love a wife who rarely left the house. La Señora didn't bother to change out of sleeping clothes. As the neighborhood maids could spy, little else ever hung from the laundry line. No lingerie. No spring dresses. No baby clothes. Ruth could only imagine the gossip. Her Americano bosses were either newlyweds who rarely got dressed because they so enjoyed each other, or someone in the house was desperately ill and didn't leave bed.

Bolivians had a touch for the dramatic, inhaling the latest telenovelas from Mexico City and Buenos Aires with gusto. She knew few would guess the truth: the young woman was burdened by demons Ruth hadn't yet uncovered. There was evil weighing Macy under that bathwater each day, Ruth was certain. A pecado so large, Señora Duncan couldn't remember happiness.

Thankfully, Ruth was certain her employer's lack of energy worked to the housekeeper's benefit. To earn a bit of extra income, Ruth had quietly approached the Spaniard's maid next door. The ambassador's family had a handful of children. Their lines were always heavy with freshly washed soccer shorts and the official's white button downs, his initials embroidered on each French cuff.

Happily, their maid agreed; Ruth's path to a much needed new wardrobe would be paved in washing those of others.

Her growing boys loved the jefa's lack of appetite. They often ate the uneaten bruised fruit and crumbly buns. Ruth snuck them home in her bag in lieu of placing them in the trash. She and her children weren't beggars, but they certainly weren't too proud to eat leftovers, either. Jesus Cristo appreciated her frugality, she was sure. Somehow these ripe discards seemed sweeter. She cut out the brown bruises on the fruit before serving them sliced. Her children never were the wiser.

Andres, dónde estás ahora?

Where was her lover eating dinner this evening?

Her back tensed as she considered the options, none of

which led back to her small kitchen table, under the roof where he'd fathered four boys.

Ruth's feet shuffled along the aisles of vendors in worn leather sandals.

"Oh Ruth, nevermind. Don't think about it. Don't think about him."

But she couldn't stop herself. She envisioned the basic ivory wedding gown she'd wear in the church square. They wouldn't be able to marry inside, but she was sure the civil ceremony would make her boys delighted all the same. She'd carry a bouquet of yellow roses and yarrow. He'd have a shiny silk tie and a smile and he'd finally tell her how happy he was to pick her.

He'd pick her. He'd pick them all.

Finally.

Deep in thought, the housekeeper didn't realize she was speaking aloud until an indigenous woman resting on her heels, selling bread from a handmade basket yelped, startled. Ruth had nearly walked into her, deep in her daydream.

"Perdon, perdon."

She felt the prickle of embarrassment spread from her neck. Ruth picked up her pace, exiting the market and walking quickly toward the Americans' house, switching the heavy basket from one hand to another. Shaking her head, reality flooded her vision. The housekeeper was just another indigena running errands — using the time to escape to fantasize.

A bouquet? A lace dress? Who did she think she was?

She'd imagined a life together a hundred times. Christmas mornings. Birthdays. Being so comfortable with each other, they'd argue about household responsibilities. These dreams never manifested, after more than a decade of berating herself for their sinful relationship. Did he ever really love her? Would God forgive her for what she'd done? Her life was just another set of lies she'd said so many times, they rolled off her tongue like the truth.

Would his wife ever find out about the boys? Would he ever really leave her and join his family?

Thankfully, Ruth had been able to get out of the village and find work. Her boys did so much better in the Tarija schools; they could disguise the fact that they didn't have a father by living in the city. In the village, chisme and gossips ruled with wicked tongues. The children who were particularly cruel typically came from one of the many homes led by a threatened, fat housewife who worried her even fatter husband was the next to be lured into Ruth's arms. These children called her boys hijos de puta—sons of a cunt.

Puta was a word you didn't say to Ruth or her children. Puta was a word that made you pack up your things and leave without glancing over your shoulder at the place where you were born. Puta was the word that made you wake up in the middle of the night with a stomach ache like you'd been punched by regret. A word so damning you sobbed yourself back to sleep—careful not to let the eight ears sleeping by your sides have any idea things weren't exactly as they were supposed to be.

She wasn't certain of many things in life, but there was one thing she knew for truth: Ruth Leona Castro was not a puta.

She swung the basket back and forth as she managed the crooked cobblestone streets, her shiny black hair cut in a neat, efficient bob whispering back and forth passed her ears with each step. Finally arriving at the casa de los Americanos, Ruth set down her wares. She was built like an egg, with the large, round stomach of a woman who'd had four big children in quick succession. But it was her biceps that were noticeable, strong arms that had rocked those babies, swept the floor, made the soup, washed the laundry and pushed them all, albeit slowly, upward in life.

She'd been caring for homes in this neighborhood for a decade, but these were the first Americans she was hired to cook and clean for. Ruth was used to delegates and working families from European and South American countries. This family was stranger than any other.

Family.

If you could even call them that. They were two scrawny white folks who seemed to only rarely speak to each other. There weren't even any children to care for. At least the pair was sleeping in the same bed. Ruth held out hope, genuflecting each time she looked in the guest rooms to see the linens still crisply pressed, tucked in the way only she could master.

Ruth let out a deep sigh, swung open the heavy front gate, entering reality.

"Señora, ya regresé."

I've returned.

4. AWAKENING

"Señora?"

"I'm in here!"

Macy threw a pan into the large ceramic sink, noticing how sweet the kitchen now smelled. Ruth rushed into kitchen after Macy heard a crash in the entryway.

"Señora, qué pasa aquí?"

"Oh Ruth. It's okay." Macy wore a tired smile. "I was just hungry and I couldn't find you. It's just simple oatmeal."

Macy pantomimed for the housekeeper to come to the stove. The two looked over the pot, bubbling with cinnamon and sugar. A box of matches were scattered across the kitchen table, the tricky pilot light eventually lit.

"Really, it's the only thing I know to make, other than carrot cake. I lived on it during the winters in Flagstaff," Macy whispered. She felt her neck grow warm with insufficiency.

Macy suspected Ruth had prepared meals daily since their arrival, many of which she hadn't bothered to come downstairs to eat.

A lone orange on the floor caught Macy's eye. It must have dropped from Ruth's basket on the way in. She carefully took the bewildered housekeeper's hand and led her into the entryway. Down on her knees, she helped put the few errant items back in the basket.

"Ruth, I need to learn Spanish, and how to live here. I know you don't understand a word I'm saying, but just saying it out loud somehow makes it better. You must think I'm crazy, but I promise you . . . It hasn't always been so bad. You want to hear a secret?" Macy cleared her throat, then continued in a whisper. "I don't even like to take baths. When you think about it, they are gross. Sitting there in your own filth."

Macy laughed, shaking her head.

"Ben says I have to leave the house and I think he's right." She took a deep breath. "He's right. It's time."

Ruth stared at her with wide eyes, remaining silent. Macy stared back. The American was at least a foot taller and a decade younger. And while she may have prided herself on her lack of domesticity in the United States, she felt entirely inept in Ruth's presence. The house was spotless. The meals warm. The laundry pressed. Everything moved in a perfect household choreography Macy had always thought was only possible on the pages of women's magazines.

"Let's have some breakfast. Come with me." She led the two back into the kitchen. Ruth swung open cabinet doors to pull out a bowl. Macy easily leaned over her and pulled out a second, motioning for the two to sit together. It took Macy pushing on the woman's shoulders a bit to get Ruth passed the social barrier of joining her employer at the small kitchen table.

Carefully, Macy ladled two bowls of oatmeal and poured steamy mugs of coffee. Macy added generous pat of butter to each bowl and then closed her eyes at the first bite, letting the richness and familiarity flood her senses. The pair sat at the small prep table, normally used for crushing spices and chopping vegetables, instead blowing on a spoonful of oatmeal. Ruth twitched with obvious discomfort.

"Yo soy Macy."

Ruth looked up. "Sí, señora. Yo soy Ruth."

True to her Andean heritage, Ruth came out "Root."

"Tu eres Root."

"Sí."

Several hours later, they'd progressed to colors and numbers.

"Señora, que gusto!" Ruth had washed the dishes, tidied the kitchen and refilled the matchbox when she returned from the bathroom. Macy noticed a good bit of laundry she didn't recognize blowing gently outside on a long clothesline. It was the observer's curse—everything seen behind a camera's crosshair.

"Ruth, do you have children? Niños?"

"Si, señora. Cuatro barones."

Macy searched her dictionary. Baron: commonly used in some South American countries to refer to male children. She had four sons. Four!

Macy felt new tears gather in her eyes. That explained the laundry. This poor woman was working herself silly to keep this giant house clean and raising four boys. Oh, to have four sons.

Macy's brain was tired from the intense language session. She couldn't help but feel the same awkwardness of junior high school French lessons. Words were not her forte.

"I need a break. And believe it or not, Root, going outside for a walk sounds easier than trying another set of conjugations." Macy wiped away her tears, excusing herself from the kitchen. "Thank you for your help. Gracias por todo."

Todo came out like Dorothy's dog, not the native "totho."

Macy sighed. The maid nodded and smiled, with her polite poker face, never revealing what she could or couldn't understand. "Eventually, right Root? The bird makes its nest one stick at a time . . ."

Smiling, she raced up stairs to get her new camera and put on some running shoes. Maybe she'd get lost and see how much of that newly acquired Spanish she could remember. She could imagine the conversation:

"Who are you?"

"Casa roja!"

"Where are you from? How can we help you?"

"I have 31 years!"

Her stomach was queasy from the previous night's hangover and a gallon or so of the housekeeper's strong coffee. She'd eaten like an only child does—slowly, without worry. There would be plenty. Now, she wished she'd eaten more.

I can do this. I can take a simple walk. I can take photos. I love taking photos. Leaping down the staircase with forced optimism, Macy ignored the tightness of her skin after the unexpected tears. She put one hand over her stomach, summoning courage.

"Adiós, Root!"

Grabbing her sunglasses, she swung open the front door. How long had it been since she'd worn these glasses? For that matter, how long had it been since she'd been outside in sunlight? Grief had made her a vampire.

Blinded momentarily by the bright sun, Macy reached to close the door behind her. In an instant, her foot caught on something, pitching her forward, toppling down upon the stone veranda. Smacking her knee hard on the ground, she tumbled to the earth.

"Son of a bitch!" She felt a cold, sharp chill run from head to toe, raising goose bumps on her arms and forcing her jaw to grind. A crimson pool of blood rose quickly through her torn jeans. "Ouch," she moaned, shaking. A broken tile on the walkway had sliced her leg and knee.

The sunglasses were in pieces from her stumble, but the Holga was fine.

"Root! Root? ROOOOOOT. Help me!" The heavy door was shut tight, and her cries rendered useless. Slowly, Macy pulled herself up, whimpering, testing her leg to see if anything was broken.

How had she managed to fall? There were just a couple of steps. Then Macy heard the noise.

"Waaaaah!"

She scanned the courtyard. Birds perched along the exterior gate, mindlessly chirping their afternoon concerto. A fuchsia bougainvillea craned toward the sky. Noisy cars burped leaded clouds of exhaust, and people puttered down the busy neighborhood streets.

"Waah!"

Macy found the sound coming from a bundle resting on the top step, placed before the entry. This had caused her fall. At closer look, the obstacle wasn't a simple package, but a basket. A shiny green hand-knit blanket escaped one corner, cocooning the precious contents. In that brief moment, blinded by sunlight, she'd tripped over the basket, rocking the inhabitant inside.

"Waaaah!" The basket rustled.

Macy held her pulsing leg, staring at the basket with disbelief.

Go away.

"Waaah"

Oh. God.

Dizzying specks clouded her vision. With the spring sun on her face, and a brisk wind in her hair, Macy shut her eyes, trying fruitlessly to prevent a torrent of unwanted memories from a hospital 6,000 miles away. The sounds of healthy babies born in rooms nearby. The cries of hungry infants lined up in identical basinets in the nursery. The happy tears cried by new grandparents, peering over their progeny.

Her stomach tightened into a knot, and Macy swallowed hard, trying unsuccessfully to keep the dreaded memories tucked away.

Tethered to a tower of beeping machines at Flagstaff Medical Center, the room smelled of rubbing alcohol, Pine sol and bleach. Like she'd sucked on pennies, her mouth was full of bitter copper. She heard her heartbeat, banging like pots and pans in her ears.

"I'm so sorry Mr. and Mrs. Duncan, your little boy didn't make it through birth. I am so very sorry. Ma'am? Ma'am, we've called for help. The chaplain will be here soon."

"Waah."

The blanket's edge fluttered in the wind. Birds continued to sing. Traffic sputtered. Vendors weaving wheelbarrows full of produce rolled by. A catastrophe unfolded at Macy's feet.

She struggled toward the door, grabbed the handle and plopped on the top step next to the basket. Opening the door a crack, Macy bellowed, "ROOOT!"

Quickly the raven-haired woman appeared. Her eyes grew wide as her bushy eyebrows gathered in shock. "Ah, por Dios!"

Wrapped tightly in the knit bundle, a perfect set of bright

blue eyes peered up at the women from the center of the basket.

"Guurrg." The child made wet, sucking noises, not quite a cry or a laugh.

The housekeeper didn't think twice, reaching with instinct as she'd done a thousand times with her own fussy babies. She scooped up the child, raising the tiny heartbeat to meet her own. Immediately her wide hips swayed to the rhythm of her breath. Ruth looked, with apparent confusion, cradling the child.

"Señora?"

Macy stood; blood ran down her leg underneath her torn jeans. She took several paces backward, successfully navigating the steps this time.

"I . . .I . . ." She took a deep breath, her tongue heavy in her mouth. "No."

She felt the beads of sweat quickly come to her brow.

"No." Macy said it again firmly.

This wasn't happening.

"No!"

The housekeeper's face was pained. She kept calling, "Señora? Señora?"

Macy raised her palms flat and continued backing away; she could see the maid's head shaking back and forth and see Ruth's lips moving, but she could no longer hear anything but the pulsing in her ears.

"We are so sorry."

Macy stood, shaking her head at Ruth.

"He looked fine at the last ultrasound."

She felt her sunglasses crunch underfoot.

"We can do an autopsy if you'd like, but we wouldn't recommend it."

She flung open the gate's latch.

"This, well, this just happens sometimes. There is no one at fault. We are sorry for your loss."

Macy ran aimlessly into the arms of a city she did not know.

5. EPHESIANS 5:14

Macy ran through the city with her fists pumping and legs moving as fast as they could take her. Away, away, away. She did't feel the open cut on her knee or the cool breeze on her cheeks.

Was it a prank? A gift? Who would leave a baby? Especially at her door?

She ran.

Past the zoo, with broken sidewalk underfoot, where a lone panther turned her way from his street-side cage. Macy smelled of fresh blood.

She ran.

Past the spice market with baskets woven from golden reeds, cradling pungent fragrances she'd never tasted. Vendors looked beyond her to see who was following in chase.

She ran.

Finally, she arrived in front of a small Catholic church with its bell wailing. The church was nothing like the behemoths in the square. The stucco was missing in some spots, revealing red brick. The metal roof dipped curiously on one eve, pushed downward from the overgrown limb of a nearby timpana tipu tree.

It was the bell that got her curiosity and brought Macy to a stop. She turned her head, watching while a young man with Down syndrome pulled the heavy rope. He pulled the rope with a smile spread across his face, giggling as it rang and shaking his bottom, dancing to the noise. The ancient bell's timbre rang over her, as she gasped at thin air. The blood from her cut leg reached her shoe. Her view narrowed, blackness growing around the edges.

I cannot pass out here. Oh God, I cannot faint in the street!

Macy threw her head between her legs to catch her breath, quickly sliding down to the cracked curb. Within a few minutes, she was able to look up, still puzzled as to why the boy was still ringing the bell, now at least 30 times tolled. The young man smiled and giggled as he pulled and pulled. She smiled in return without thinking, his joy resonating.

The bell's ringing matched the pounding thump in her shin and the wush wush wush of blood she felt in her ears. The beat copied the manic spasms of her lungs as they searched for relief from the thin air.

These were the first sounds she'd noticed since the baby's wail.

Clang! Clang! Clang!

The bell continued, the boy's smile widening with each tug. Finally, an older man rushed from a tiny office next to the church, waiving his hands overhead with exasperation. He had a mop of gray, curly hair that bounced as he ran toward the boy.

"Francisco! Basta! Ya dije diez veces, no viente! No más! Por favor, Francisco. No más!"

Another man wearing an apron came out of the bakery

across the street. He shook his broom at the noise before returning inside, wagging his head in annoyance, his face drooping in a grimace.

The boy dropped the rope and skipped away, still grinning, oblivious. Macy took it all in before lowering her head between her legs, sucking in air.

"Good grief," the man said, staring up at the bell, unaware of his audience. His accent was distinctly American.

Macy snapped to attention.

A New Yorker! What was he doing here?

She heard his footsteps approaching.

"Hola! Estás bien?" Pushing herself up from the curb, she noticed his clerical collar out of the corner of her eye. The sight evoked memories of the last time she'd seen a priest.

When Macy awoke to a priest leaning over her bed, he muttered something like, "My child, I am here in your time of sorrow." A sedative fell one drop at a time into her IV. She remembered sleeping with the call button in her hand, summoning the nurse for more the moment she realized the bag had emptied.

Vaguely, she remembered the priest praying for a few minutes, eventually whispering, "God, too, lost His son."

Ben was in the cafeteria fetching coffee. Her mother slumped in the corner in an orange upholstered chair, snoring. They were all exhausted.

"Leave me alone." Her eyes shot open, teeth bared. She clawed out of the fog for a moment, anger surging. "My child was real. I am not your child. Get out of my room!" In her head, there were another thousand words she wanted to shout. Expletives were on the tip of her tongue when she fell back against the pillow, exhausted from the brief outburst.

"Oh. Well. I apologize," he cleared his throat. "I did not mean to upset you in this . . . this fragile time." The priest withdrew his hand from her arm. With a deep breath and a condescending shake of his head, he tried again. "I'd like to offer you peace in this trying time."

Macy drew in a deep breath. "I am not fucking fragile. Fuck. You."

Her voice rose with each syllable. Macy gripped the metal bed rails. Woozy from sedation, she was the most surprised at the surge of anger. She growled at the small man, staring at the small white square of fabric covering his Adam's apple.

He began to slink away.

"God doesn't exist. If He does, he let my child die. So don't for a moment think you can make this better with your holy bullshit. What do you know? My baby boy is dead!"

Macy choked on the words, then moaned the low guttural howl of one in mourning. Ben, waiting in the hallway, sobbing quietly into his coffee cup, would tell her later of the nurses who cried at the station. Of the new mother in the next room who squeezed her healthy newborn, every time he walked by. Of her own mother, who couldn't bring herself to hold her dead grandson.

Ben's pleadings hadn't been able to rouse her grief—but the priest's thoughtlessness had tipped the first domino.

Macy's mother sprang to attention at the eerie groan, throwing her body over her child's, snarling at the interloper. The priest scurried away, passing Ben in the hallway; they all listened as his dress shoes click-clacked down the tile corridor.

"Fuck off." These were the last words she'd said to a priest, and the first she wanted to say to the next.

"Hello? Are you injured? Is that blood? Hello?"

Macy looked at her pants, dark with blood.

Suck it up. You can do this. Get up and get away from him. Get away from this church.

Her sock was sticky, blood dried along the elastic edge around her ankle. She loved these running shoes. They hadn't seen daylight in months, and now one was stained crimson.

Damn it.

"Hola!"

Macy imagined his thoughts. Was she American, European, or perhaps South African?

Macy nodded acknowledgement and backed away from the church.

The last thing I need now is another priest.

She limped a few steps and then picked up the pace. He followed closely. She guessed he was middle aged and he had the round stomach of someone who loved bread, but hated exercise.

"Señora, qué pasó? Puedo ayudar. Soy Padre Pedro."

Macy waved him away, feigning misunderstanding.

Do not follow me. I will outrun you, injured or not. She cracked a thankful smile when the bell once again began to chime.

"Oh, Francisco," he muttered. Macy was several paces ahead. Nonetheless, she heard his heavy exasperation as he turned back toward the church to prevent more off-hour clanging.

Macy moved as quickly as her leg would let her. Not a quarter mile away, she let out a yip when she saw a trailhead. Cruz Hill cast a fat shadow over the church. It was a brief and steep climb, with decaying cement statues honoring the Stations of the Cross along the winding path. There was little vegetation, other than a few oddly placed eucalyptus trees, their trunks the same dusty white as the church in the distance.

Macy sighed with relief reaching the top. She stretched her arms overhead and then again swung her head between her legs, feeling the thin air fill her tight chest.

When night fell, reality returned. Shivering on a metal park bench, covered in sweat, her leg ached and teeth chattered.

Where is Ben? God, where am I? What am I doing? Her thoughts and worries cast a fog.

A giant cross made of fluorescent bulbs came to life behind her, popping and crackling. She jumped, startled. Macy looked down at her exposed arm, now tinged blue.

Bathed in the light of Christ.

Macy squeezed her hands into fists.

"Stupid symbolism. Stupid town," she mumbled toward the sky.

She huffed, feeling her chest rise as tears dripped down her chin. This was Ben's fault. Pressing her fingers against her eyebrows, Macy considered her options.

"Really, God? Really?" She screamed at the sky, her voice echoing off the crumbling statues of saints.

Macy wiped her face, remembering the many times she'd felt alone in her young life. This was the loneliest. Worse than the father-daughter dances of her youth she pretended weren't as hurtful as Father's Day. Worse than the first miscarriage, when she couldn't understand what was happening, why there was so much blood. Worse than spending the last two months hiding from her husband in a rusty bathtub that couldn't keep warm.

Staring out over the dusty South American city, church bells rang from more than one cathedral. Their chorus was off beat, but even Macy begrudgingly found the beauty of their songs. The pungent scent of warm, roasting meat from parrillada stands caught her nose. A hummingbird buzzed by —a flash of emerald green and bright red extravagance. Under other circumstances, she'd dream of such a setting for the golden hour—the perfect time to photograph. It was odd to see such an dazzling creature at this time of day, but nothing that had happened since she had walked out the front door seemed to make sense.

Macy flexed her jaw, gripping the camera with one hand and the bench with the other. She debated whether she had the energy to find her way home.

Leaning her head back against the cool metal bench, she closed her eyes for a moment, shivering. She thought of the neon cross and wondered how far away it was visible. On the eastern edge of the city, the rows of yellow hills seemed to continue as though they stopped only when reaching the Atlantic.

Macy ignored her growling stomach, rolling over on her side, away from the cross, her eyes shut tight.

6. YANKEE FAN

Ruth paced the length of the first floor, listening as the boards creaked in the same spot each time. The baby had finally fallen asleep after she'd used a makeshift bottle filled with warm rice milk. It was too late in the day to go to the market to find a real bottle, or a nursing mother to help.

Where was la señora? Could this broken child be nursed?

She'd never come home. Her patron was expected to return tomorrow afternoon. She'd have to find a way to contact him if Macy didn't return soon. He wasn't answering the cell number he'd left for emergencies. Ruth called again and again.

Ruth listened as the line rang until it didn't. There was the message.

"You've reached Ben Duncan, division of forestry for USAID. Please leave a message after the beep, or shoot me an email. Thank you. Gracias!"

He laughed quietly before he'd ended the message. Ruth listened to that message ten times, speaking every other time, calling on the half hour. She never knew what to say.

"Señor Ben, this is Ruth. Your housekeeper. Please come home. Your wife is missing."

"Señor Ben, this is Ruth. The maid. Your wife has left the

house, and we do not know where she is. The local priest has gone looking for her. Also, there is a baby."

"This is Ruth Campos, your maid. I am calling because your wife has left. Please return home soon."

"Señor Duncan, please. Please call. This is an emergency."

Ruth had no idea how else to contact Ben in Santa Cruz, much less what to do with another baby. It had been sheer luck her friend Mayra was able to watch her own boys for the evening. She'd wrapped the baby to her chest and headed home quickly to check on her sons at *la cena* after Macy hadn't returned by sunset. Her boys didn't need to sit in a dark home alone and hungry because of this silly American woman.

Por Dios. Who knew why the woman decided to run off at the first sight of a brown babe? Why had she agreed to work for these gringos?

The sun rose. The baby would soon wake and the mother of four knew rice milk would work only for so long.

Where could she be? Tarija streets weren't safe, much less for a foreign woman wandering by herself.

Ruth made coffee and rummaged through the pantry to find supplies for breakfast. She had a hand in a bag of sugar when there was a knock at the front door. Shaking grains from her hands, she rushed forward, opening the door.

"Padre Pedro! Usted, qué hace aquí?"

In broken Spanish, they gossiped. Who were these foreigners? What was Macy like? Did the Father know where the woman was now? She'd been missing since mid-afternoon yesterday. Why didn't they attend church? How were her boys?

Of course the priest knew of her decade-old affair with a married man. He was the only one she could confess to.

* * *

Macy squinted at the bright, early morning light.

"Ah! Who the hell are you?" Macy raised her hands into fists before her face. She'd awoken with a jump, feeling someone placing a hand under her head of long, wavy hair. Whomever he was had tried to gently rouse her, but her heart raced with the specific, disorienting fear of waking in an unknown place.

"Macy? I am Father Pedro. Peter. Just call me Peter." The same priest from the day before. He looked anxious until she realized her hands were still in a boxer's stance and lowered them.

He smiled, palms raised in front of him. "I didn't mean to scare you. I'm sorry to disturb your sleep. Although," he chuckled to see Francisco's handiwork, "I'm glad to see someone tucked you in."

She pulled back an unfamiliar, green plaid blanket to find her pant leg crusted with blood. The sight brought on immediate nausea.

"Ouch. God. Ouch." She reached down, touching her swollen leg. He watched, taking another step back.

"Here, maybe this will help a bit?" He handed her Ben's navy NAU sweatshirt, and opened a backpack to reveal a thermos full of black coffee. He quickly poured her a lid's worth and sat down next to her on the bench.

"How in the world . . ." Her shoulders relaxed and she opened her mouth, feeling her jaw pop. She swung her chin up one direction and then the other, her vertebrae cracking in turn.

"I stopped by your house this morning and spoke with Ruth. She is pretty worried. I hope you don't mind, but after I saw you yesterday . . . Well, I was worried too. I am glad I was able to find you."

"Shit! I mean . . . God. How did you find me? You spoke with Root? Ruth, I mean. How long have I been out here?" Her face grew red. "I didn't mean to sleep here. I remember watching the stars and then. Well." She rubbed the side of her face where indentations from the bench left lines running from temple to chin. "I'm actually surprised I slept. I can't believe after yesterday . . ."

"You mean the baby?" He looked at her with a curious smile.

She had her nose in the soft cotton of the sweatshirt, sniffing like a bloodhound for some trace of her husband. "Oh." She scratched her head. "You must know. You spoke with Root."

"Yes. I'd guess it was quite the shock to find her that way. That sweet little girl is still at your house." He reached into the bag and handed her a crusty chunk of warm bread. The bitterness of the coffee made the back of her mouth hurt.

"I heard there was a new American couple in town. I'd hoped we'd meet on different terms. The news in Tarija travels quickly. When I saw you yesterday and you didn't respond . . ." He took a breath. He ran his hands through thick, unruly gray hair. Deep creases under his eyes gave away time spent at brutally high altitude. He wore a simple Timex digital running watch and his own blue sweatshirt.

"I'd hoped you'd come to Mass. I haven't seen you at church."

"We aren't practicing." She cleared her throat. Crumbs clung to one corner of her mouth. She'd split the bread and offered him half.

He waved away the offer. "You look hungry. Doesn't Ruth cook for you?"

"Oh, yes. She's wonderful. I'm so glad she was there

yesterday. I should have stayed. I should have done something. I just couldn't. I didn't know what to do."

They sat there in silence for a moment, listening to the busy city below awaken. Roosters continued to crow long after the sun rose over the horizon.

"I should go home . . .to the house. I need to speak with my husband." She grimaced, pushing at the bridge of her nose. "I should thank Ruth."

"Are you okay?"

"No, I really just need to go home. I need a shower." She didn't open her eyes when she spoke to him.

"You know it's essentially a requirement that you come to church when you live in Bolivia?" He cracked a smile, which was missing a side molar. "It is social. Church, mass—it is what nearly everyone does. It doesn't mean they believe."

"It's been years, Father," she interrupted. "And to be honest, I haven't been out of the house much since we got here. Home," she took a deep breath. "I need home."

"You picked a great place to spend your first night on the town." He grinned. She could see in his gentle eyes he was trying to be friendly, not intrusive. She felt her guard lower for a moment, forcing a pained smile in return before snapping her eyes closed.

"Well, come on then," he said, pulling her up by the elbow. "I'll help you find your way. Is it a migraine?"

She cracked an eye and stared at him.

"Yes."

"I get them too. More so at this altitude. Let's get you back. Can you walk?"

She took a deep breath, pushing her fingers into her temples.

"I think so."

"You're going to need stitches on that leg. I can get you to the hospital."

"Home first. I need to call my husband."

"Where is he?" He grabbed her by the arm to help steady her.

"On some adventure trying to solve this country's coca problem, or some other social woe. Shit. Shoot! Where is my camera?"

Miraculously, the small camera sat tucked under the bench. Face reddened, leaning on one leg with her eyes pinched shut, she considered what a sight she must be. "Thank you, Father. And for your help getting me home. I can't believe I slept here. I sleep more in Bolivia—I'll give this place that."

He nodded. She felt his shoulders going up and down. Lowering his voice, he continued the conversation, which she suspected was his way of distracting her down the hill and back across town on one bad leg.

"What are you two doing here?"

"His job. Fresh start. All that nonsense. You're from the East Coast?" She struggled to string the words together, and was quickly reaching the point where she'd beg him for silence.

"The Bronx. Go Yankees." He punched the air above him and a large, sweet grin spread across his face. "And you?"

"Arizona. Go Cardinals." The pair wound down the hill, past the light-bulb cross, the statues, the bell tower at his church.

"You mean Diamondbacks?"

"Sure."

The priest laughed. "You guys beat us once in the World Series . . ."

"My husband is the sports fan." She clenched her hands.

"How long have you been married?"

"Two years."

"Children?"

She tensed. They'd reached that moment. "Can we not do this right now?" She stared hard at the cobblestones, trying to open her eyes as little as possible, speaking in a whisper. The migraine's strength swirled like a hurricane behind her eyes.

"Of course. Of course! I'm sorry. You could say I'm rusty at conversation with peers. And . . . especially Americans. I mostly spend my time talking to kids."

Peter soon took the hint and quieted, navigating the pair through the city streets, past the spice market, the zoo, the Lebanese grocery store and over the cobblestone streets to the American's rented home in the wealthiest neighborhood of town.

He was nearly carrying her by the time they reached the house's gate. Macy tried smiling through the pounding pain as he brushed away the bougainvillea bush to ensure she wouldn't absentmindedly take one of the vines to the face.

"Thank you," she managed.

Ruth was waiting at the doorstep, a tiny Bolivian baby girl wrapped tightly to her chest, waiting.

7. DETERMINISM

"Buenos días Root," Macy muttered, keeping her eyes down and hands gripping the priest's arm.

"Buenas, Padre. Buenas, Señora. Espero que todo esté bien?" Ruth patted the priest's arm.

Padre Pedro smiled wearily at the baby in her arms.

"Todo está bien, pero nos vamos al hospital." His voice was firm. He instructed Macy to grab a change of clothing. Ruth noticed a gray hair growing from a mole on his neck—the same one that distracted her during sermons. She shuffled her feet toward the kitchen, rocking the baby with each step.

They'd take a taxi to the hospital. He wanted Macy's leg stitched and to speak with a colleague, a friend who worked in pediatrics. This doctor would know more about the baby.

He told Ruth about finding Macy on the hill, between noisy slurps of hot coffee. She nodded, desperate for details that wouldn't be shared, swallowing her judgment.

Who runs away from a baby?

Babies need care. Husbands need attention. Dinners need to be both cooked and eaten. Contentment was black and white. Yet, each wealthy family she'd worked for made themselves miserable. Comically, they did so in ways they thought were unique to their own home.

Alcohol. Adultery. Apathy. Atheism. Abuse.

The five As. If only they'd listen to her. Ruth had cleaned up after each, nursing egos, and feeding souls. The source was simple: too much time. If Macy, or any of the others before her, truly knew hunger, they would stop this nonsense. Padre Pedro may try to fix la señora at the hospital, but Ruth knew what she really needed: a purpose.

"Ruth, ayúdame con un poco de almuerzo."

The housekeeper's moment of enlightenment passed.

"Claro que sí, Padre." Of course she would prepare breakfast; Ruth Leona Castro knew her purpose.

After more coffee and a plate of toast and fruit, he cleared his throat. Ruth swayed, the baby sleeping on her chest, as she danced around the kitchen with ease performing a dozen tasks at once. She was happy on her rightful stage.

The two spoke at a whisper. They could hear Macy opening and closing doors upstairs, making far more noise than necessary.

"Ay, careless." She clucked her tongue.

"Ruth, tell me about yesterday. Again. Slowly." Padre Pedro looked up from his empty plate. She flushed, hoping he hadn't heard her complaint.

Ruth repeated yesterday's story with more detail, her mood clouded by the sleepless night. She watched her boss run away from the home at first sight of the child. She tried to follow a series of blood drops until they eventually ran into a patch of dirt pathways, winding a dozen different directions through the market. She fed the sweet little girl rice milk overnight. Also, she had a theory as to why the baby's mouth had such a gaping wound.

"We will get back to your theories, Ruth. First, you are certain you didn't see anyone leave the basket? What time did you come back from the market? Do you know anyone who has given birth lately? Any of the other maids in this colonia pregnant recently?"

Ruth answered with as much patience and respect as she could muster. He was a priest. More so, he was her friend. Kindly she explained if she had known who the mother was, she wouldn't have spent all night feeding and soothing a screeching baby who wasn't hers. Ruth had done this four times with her boys. The very last thing she wanted was to have yet another fatherless child in need of an advocate.

Also, it wasn't fair to suggest this baby was a housekeeper's simply because her skin was also a darker, indigenous brown.

"You are right, Ruth. I'm sorry. I am just thinking of the women who leave children at the church with me. And, well, they are rarely women who can afford to live in houses like this. I'm not saying it is fair."

She nodded. He was right, though the truth stung.

"Ruth, this baby is blessed to have found you, of all people. I bet the mother knew you'd be here, that you'd be able to care for her. I would guess she knows you. And look! You've done so well. An inexperienced woman wouldn't have known how to care for a wounded baby."

Her neck and face flushed by the rare praise.

"It is strange," he continued. "A Tarija mother would have known to leave her at the church with me, with the others. Or at the hospital with Doctor Claudia. There is no shame in either; but a basket baby? I just don't understand. The village elders know of the orphanage, too. Strange, the secrecy with this one."

He shook his head.

"Father, it is because of her lip and the social services. Closed until Monday. Of course this mother thought we would just keep the broken baby. We'd find her care. Well . . ." Ruth let out a deep breath, "We cannot keep her."

"Oh, Ruth." He patted her hand. "No one expects you to keep her. She needs surgery. That palate is likely infected. She's lucky to be alive." He scratched the back of his scalp, staring hard at the child. "I will take her to Claudia. She will know how to help, if she can be helped."

"Por Dios."

"In the meantime, I can only hope my own children are behaving. God only knows how many times the bell has tolled off hour." They laughed. "I'm sure Don Campos is counting."

"Goo!"

Her sounds were muffled, escaping the slit starting just beneath her perfect button nose. Her palate, split like so many highland children, didn't keep the sweet girl's lips from curling upward in what Ruth would have sworn was a smile.

"Goo!"

"Oh, aren't you a sweet angel?" He cooed, taking the child from Ruth, and placing her in his lap. "You need a good Christian name. Teresa? Are you a saint?"

The baby's skin was the color of fertile earth. Her hair was a black mop with a cowlick that curled the entire bunch to the left in a swirl. Her eyes were a curious shade of blue.

The pair decided that in her own broken way, this was the most perfect child they had ever seen.

"Just don't tell my sons," Ruth added, laughing.

"God is so good. I cannot have children, but I get them anyway. Do you see that blessing?" He smiled widely. She noticed his missing molar. "The naming is one of my favorite parts. Will you help me?"

"Oh, yes!"

"She needs a survivor's name—like yours, Ruth. Naomi. Leah. Mary. Esther."

Macy walked into the kitchen, wearing a large gray v-neck t-shirt. Ruth noticed she smelled of lemons.

"Please don't name her. We can't. She isn't ours." She spoke tersely.

Padre Pedro cleared his throat. The happiness of the prior moment dissipated.

"Root, call my husband please. Have Ben come home immediately."

"Si, Señora. Ya llamé, pero . . ."

Ruth tried to call a dozen times during the night. She wasn't sure if he'd ever received her messages. She'd try again, of course. There was no bother mentioning her own children were still waiting for her. No one other than the Princess and the Park Bench seemed to have gotten any sleep last night. And yet here she was, ordering around a priest!

"How are you feeling?" He rocked the baby, who was starting to fuss, as he'd done many times before at the orphanage.

"Like I got hit in the head with a hammer. Right here." Macy pointed to her temple. "I'm probably dehydrated. I need coffee. Root, por favor?"

Her wet hair clung to her shirt, leaving dark pools at her shoulders.

"The central hospital is the best in the region. They will be able to help."

"I took a pill for my migraine. They are my saving grace, but the leg isn't looking any better."

"The pills are your saving grace, huh?" He let out a casual laugh.

Ruth listened as Macy sighed dramatically.

The housekeeper could understand every word of the conversation. Countless hours of watching "La Calle De Sesamo" while nannying employers' children had worn off on her too. Her spoken English was weak, but her secret knowledge was a jolt of power.

"I think I need stitches. And something for the pain."

"You both need medical attention. The hospital isn't far; unlike Cruz Hill, we will be able to find a taxi in this neighborhood."

Ruth rested against the counter. If she hadn't known better, she'd have sworn she was watching a married couple, exhausted by a recent birth. This is what it could have been like with Andres. Only he'd never held his boys when they were infants. She'd only imagined his gentle sway with their young ones.

Did Andres rock his children—the ones he had with her?

"Root, please find my husband." Macy raised her hand to her ear for the international sign of telephone. "Señor Ben?"

Ruth nodded, wanting to rewind time by a day. To be sitting at the kitchen counter with the kinder version of this same woman, teaching her Spanish, pretending to enjoy a bowl of oatmeal.

"Si Señora. Sin problema." Ruth nodded, but shook her head as she walked away, mumbling.

8. TAXI

Macy followed the priest outside, careful to land intentionally on each step from the front door down to the garden walkway. She noticed several bricks stained with blood. They hailed a faded yellow Datsun taxi. Macy placed her head against the cool car window. A thermos of hot coffee rested between her legs.

The baby began to fuss in the priest's arms as the car bobbed along the cobblestone streets. She noticed the driver had a lip full of something, reminding her of an Arizona rancher's chew. He wove the car skillfully around deep potholes.

"You must know how to do this better than I do." Padre Pedro looked at Macy, arms outstretched, a gentle smile across his face.

Macy grunted, curling herself into a question mark of unease. "Doubtful, Father."

He smiled. "Well, there is time to learn. I have. If this former New Yorker can raise dozens of children with special needs, you can hold one baby in a cab."

Macy looked at the man, eyebrows arched. "Dozens?"

"You saw the boy ringing the bell."

"You care for him?" Her eyes were wide.

"And many others. I was called to do so."

"Like, by God?"

"Ha!" He let out a hard snort. "Well, yes. But technically, I was called by the regional bishop. You know. On a telephone?"

She let a quick laugh slip. "Oh. Right." Closing her eyes, still she could hear the blood pulsing in her ears, the notorious soundtrack of pending disaster.

"I came here 20 years ago. They sent me to Peru first, when I was fresh out of seminary. I worked with a local tribal group. That post didn't work."

"What do you mean?" She opened one eye, with curiosity.

"It just didn't work. Priests do have a calling and mine is here. Tarija. With children." He motioned toward the thermos. "Drink some of that. The caffeine will help the migraine."

Uncharacteristically, Macy did as she was told, trying to take careful sips between the driver's lurches. She kept her eyes closed, and the light out, as much as possible.

"After Peru, I was sent to Bolivia. At first I was sure it was a punishment. This town is small and so little happens. There are nearly as many churches as there are people. Have you been to the squares?" He paused to look at Macy, but she didn't respond. "Each one has a giant beast of a church built by the Spaniards once upon a time. And inside each of those aging buildings, where we preach about Jesus feeding the poor, are altars made of gold."

Again, she raised one eyelid. She could see spit gathering in the corners of his mouth. He spoke in an excited whisper; the baby had miraculously fallen asleep to the movement of the car.

"Not gold paint," he continued. "Not fake gold. Real gold.

Gold that came out of mines in Potosi on the backs of thousands of Bolivian natives. In front of those churches sit women from the same tribes who are now starving. They hold babies out to passersby and beg. They teach their children to beg." The priest shook his head, his face in a heavy frown. "Do the priests in those churches feed the indios? No. They preach about the word, from gold castles, and use brooms to push those who need the most help away from the front steps. For goodness sakes, it couldn't be clearer in the scriptures: 'For I was hungry and you gave me something to eat, I was thirsty and you gave me something to drink, I was a stranger and you invited me in . . .'" He took a deep breath and looked up at her. "Where does it say, 'Use brooms. Ignore the hungry'?" Bracing the light, she watched his face as he spoke, the gray hair much more visible from his profile.

"I'm sorry. I guess I've been waiting for ears that understood English to hear that tirade for far too long. I've spent years working by myself, and with those who don't see things my way." He chuckled. "I know now my little humble church—sin oro—is a punishment. But I'm glad I'm here. The children need me. Tarija is a nice place to live, if you give her a chance."

Macy remained silent. She glanced out the window at a sea of people moving in waves. Farmers on bicycles laden with baskets of produce. Women with large bags of bread in their arms and babies tied to their backs. School children chasing each other in worn uniforms, patches on the knees. She tried not to notice the milk making her bra damp under Ben's old sweatshirt. Her body was in denial, if not punishing her. Or luring her to try again.

"Do you want to try?"

"Try?" She panicked. Could he know what she'd been thinking?

"Holding her. It might feel good."

"It won't."

"How do you know?"

"I know. Okay? I know. Plus . . . Christ! My head hurts and there aren't seat belts back here and why are you pushing me?" Her temper burst into the taxi.

"Waaah!" The infant wailed. Macy winced. She tasted the nausea before she could open the car window. Between one pot hole and the next, she was sick on her feet. The priest pulled the infant toward his chest just in time. Macy left her head between her legs, listening to her own gag.

This was the definition of misery. This exact moment. Macy would always remember it.

"Ah! NO!" The driver bellowed at the priest in Spanish. Macy could only imagine the conversation. It would be extra money. He wasn't cleaning this up. Before she could apologize, the small car pulled into the worn emergency bay of a towering gray hospital. Macy piled out of the car, shaking off the thermos, clutching her backpack and unwittingly praying for help.

"Oh, God. Oh, God." She shuffled forward. The acidic taste in the back of her throat made everything worse. In a moment, Padre Pedro was next to her, gently guiding her arm with one hand and clutching the baby with the other.

"Hold tight, Macy. This will be better in a moment, dear. Just a moment."

She took a ragged breath, trying hard not to smell herself.

He pulled her into the hospital, where she was swept away by nurses. She heard his booming voice commanding nurses before a pinch in her arm. The florescent lights above burned orange into her eyelids after she squeezed them tight. Macy's stomach cramped and her legs tightened for a moment as the medicine wove its way into her system.

Mercifully, the pain fell away.

9. ASSIGNMENT

The kitchen phone rang downstairs for 10 minutes before Macy recognized the noise. Groggy from pain pills laced with a sleeping aid, she carefully maneuvered the staircase, grinding her teeth and breathing through the sharp pain that shook each step. A handful of stitches ran along her shin, throbbing beneath the bandage.

"Hello?"

"Jesus. Mace?"

An echo rang on either end of the line, each speaker's voice repeating quietly.

"Yes. This is Macy." She was surprised to hear English, even though she'd answered the phone in her native tongue.

"Macy, it's Sam. I've been trying to get a hold of you all morning. Your mother said you had house help? I'm surprised you are answering."

"Oh Sam! Sam! It is so good to hear your voice. How's Flagstaff? How's the newspaper? Sam, don't hang up!"

She heard his deep, belly-shaking laugh reverberate across the distance. "Why would I hang up?" He laughed again. "Everything is just fine. We're all the same. Too many meals, too little exercise, too few scoops to be considered anything other than a regional hack paper."

Macy knew the thing Sam McDaniels hated most was the way the Phoenix newspaper treated those who toiled over the "inconsequential" news of sleepy Flagstaff. Their headlines were only important when the Cardinals were in town for summer training camp, when a foreign tourist died at the Grand Canyon, or when the occasional hunting accident happened on an otherwise slow news day in the bustling southern Valley.

"Oh, Sam." she sat down on a stool with a thump, taking care to prop up her injured leg. "You'd never believe life in Bolivia. They have two papers."

"Two?"

"Yes! A morning and an evening edition. Remember when we joked we wanted to move where the Internet hadn't yet taken hold? I found just the spot. You have job security in Bolivia. You should come work in Tarija, Sam."

"Funny, in a way, that's why I'm calling. But first, tell me doll—how are you? How are you really?"

"Other than a some stitches holding my leg together at the moment, I'm okay."

"Okay? What happened? Is your leg alright?"

"My leg is the least of it. There has been a 'development' as you would say."

"Spill, kid. I just poured myself a hot cup of coffee and the paper is out for the day. I've got plenty of time."

"A baby."

"Really! You're pregnant! I thought your mom said you didn't want another . . ." She could hear his voice change as he smiled. She imagined him rising to his feet in the noisy newsroom, swinging a hand to his hip and throwing the other into the air with a fist of triumph, all while cradling the phone under his ear. She'd witnessed this many times when he'd found a great news tip.

"No." She cut him off. It had been a mistake, she realized instantly, to mention the basket baby.

"Oh. I. Well, you said baby and I assumed. God. Listen to me. I miss you, Macy. There is no one here to call me on my hypocrisy!"

How many times had he screamed at reporters for such leaps in reasoning? Assume? She imagined him standing there with a palm to his forehead.

"It's okay, Sam. The maid. The maid found a baby. We have a baby in the house, but it isn't mine. I shouldn't have brought this up. I'm sorry. I don't want to talk about it." She took a deep breath. "It's just so nice to hear your voice. Tell me — tell me something good. Why are you calling?"

Macy stammered and her stomach clenched at the thought of anyone at home celebrating the recent discovery. The basket baby wasn't hers. Now that the Duncans weren't in Flagstaff, she hoped the word "baby" was replaced with "Bolivia" in gossip swapped among friends. She'd once slung such gossip herself, with a journalist's curiosity and gusto. It took imagining your own sorrow being shared and altered like a wicked game of telephone to see how ugly and painful such talk could be.

"Find another maid." His voice, suddenly paternal and protective. "No need having a little one wailing around now." Sam had been her boss and friend for years, but as a childless bachelor, he couldn't know what she or Ben felt during the last few months. She was always touched when he spoke to her with a father's love, including the talk he'd given her when she'd resigned. "Burgeoning career! Well-respected. Why?" She'd expected it to be worse.

"Anyway, what's this about your leg?"

Macy's attention snapped back to the call. "Ah, nothing big. I tripped. The sidewalks here are uneven and there is a German family in town that makes the most amazing wine. It hurt like hell, but the hospital is nicer than you think. Old, understaffed, but clean. The nurses wear these little hats like 1950s movies. I was entertained."

"Cobblestone streets and local booze at altitude. I can do the math."

"Don't get me wrong, I'd do just about anything right now for one of your beers."

"Ah yes, long live the legend of the McDaniels home brew."

"So, Sam—how is my mom?"

"She seems fine. She was in the newsroom the other day with loaves of bread . . .something about a bake sale at the Humane Society and not wanting the calories in her own pantry."

"That sounds about right. I owe her a call."

"She may have mentioned that."

"I'm just not ready yet." She sighed. Her mother. Few people understood their complicated relationship, but both Ben and Sam were wise enough to leave them be. Mother and daughter were two stubborn tectonic plates—as Sam once quipped. Little good came of them being forced together. They'd figure it out.

"I'm not pushing, kid. Promise. How's that husband of yours?"

"Ben's good. He's been traveling and brought home a sassy

Australian coworker you'd love. He's a drinker and his accent alone would encourage you to finally leave that dusty newsroom for some international adventure. The stories that man has to share. I can't tell if he's more funny or perverse. Anyway, you'd love him. And he'd enjoy your home brew too. They are at the office now."

Ben and Raleigh had arrived at the hospital just as Macy was receiving her last stitch. Her memory of the day was cloudy, but she recalled Ben holding her hand as the doctors fastened the bandages. She did not remember the 12 hours prior, when she'd slept in a noisy hallway on a gurney, comatose from a sedative. In her haze, Macy was briefly introduced to Raleigh, who reportedly wandered away to flirt with a handful of nurses.

Ruth had finally reached Ben; he'd gotten on the first flight back to the city, dragging his coworker with him in panic.

It wasn't until much later that night when Ben climbed into the tub with his wife that he learned about the catalyst for the fall, his wife's night on the hill, the "interloping" priest who, in his mind, sounded like more of a Good Samaritan. With her naked back against Ben's stomach, and her bandaged leg propped out of the water, she told him about finding the baby. How the panic made her run. She'd felt so foolish, but she thought for just a flashing moment it had been a cruel joke. She hadn't known what to do.

The next morning she'd overheard her husband in the kitchen explaining to his Australian counterpart that he wouldn't be traveling to Santa Cruz again anytime soon.

"We have a few legal issues to sort out."

"Everything okay, mate?" Raleigh's voice seemed sincere.

"It will be, yes. But I need to be here. With Mace."

"Tarija. Tarija. I wonder what the ladies of this fine city are like?"

"Something tells me it won't take you long to figure that one out.

She'd listened as they'd laughed, with wonder at how easy it was for them to communicate. Less than 100 words and they'd tucked away the last few days as "legal issues to be sorted," and made plans for Raleigh to stay in the guest room for a week or two until they organized the local office.

"Tell Ben the university boys miss him. I was on campus this week interviewing a professor, and no fewer than three tweed jackets asked me how you two were doing in Bolivia. It seems everyone's favorite tree man has fled town." Sam's voice was playful. "Although it's Flagstaff. So they weren't really in tweed. More like overpriced wicking fleece." He snickered.

"Those idiots wouldn't give him a teaching job when we lived there, and now they miss him?"

"Bird in the hand, darlin'."

"Sam, I've missed you." She wrapped her free arm around her waist, imagining her friend in his typical plaid shirts and puffy ski jackets. He was one of those men who nicked himself shaving and likely had a tiny piece of toilet paper stuck to his neck or cheek until lunch.

"We miss you too, kid. The photographers are scrambling trying to find any way of managing the schedule and field you handled with grace."

"How are they doing?"

"The wire hasn't picked up a photo from us in six weeks. But hey, I have faith. It's the digital revolution. At least I don't have to worry about them smoking dope in the developing room like I did a decade ago. That reminds me—I have an assignment for you."

"An assignment?"

"Well, I figure the extra cash can't hurt, and if that leg is good enough, you need to strap on some hiking boots. Looks like there is a bit of international drama taking place nearby and the wires are hot for the story." He paused. She knew he was enjoying dragging this out.

"Sam!" she cried.

He laughed. "Their Bolivian stringer is in Brazil covering a fashion week, of all things. Could you pick up a weeklong assignment? It sounds like something you'd love and when my friend Smith at the AP heard you were in Tarija, he called immediately."

Macy's ears perked. She loved wire stories. In Flagstaff, they'd been the rare exception. She'd once had two photos in *USA Today* in the same week, a feat by small town standards. While they didn't need the money—Ben's government checks were enormous for their Bolivian living expenses—she felt her curiosity rising.

An escape.

"I'd love it, Sam." She took a deep breath. "Tell me more."

10. BY NAME

"Absolutely, no way, not a chance, no."

"You're kidding me?"

"Mace, no! Yes, I'm glad you want to get up and get dressed, but no."

She laughed, packing her camera and lenses. "Since when do you tell me what to do?"

"I don't pull the husband card often, but I am. You are not, absolutely not, going by bus to the middle of nowhere in this country. Also, it would be nice if before you fled, we could at least speak about what happened this week." Ben paced the bedroom, his hands shoved in the back pockets of his blue jeans. This was his tell. Macy knew when he was aggravated or just hadn't slept enough, he'd cram his hands in his pants and pace until he worked out whatever was bothering him. Or took a nap.

"You know what happened. And you know my business. There's no time to sit and have a cup of coffee and gossip about the kid left on the doorstep. Ben, I've got to go. Now."

"Macy! Damn it. Of course I know your business. And better than anyone else in our lives, I've put up with it. How many nights did I wait for you to return from a midnight assignment?"

There had been countless nights he'd waited while she was in the Grand Canyon. Or standing over a roll-over accident, on an icy Interstate 17. Macy nodded in consent.

He slumped on the bed next to her suitcase and began unlacing his heavy work boots.

"My wife will not be traipsing across the Bolivian hillside in a public bus. You know these are the most dangerous roads in the world, right? Now, damn it! Sit down for a moment and let's talk about this." The hair fluttered on his forehead. Ben's voice had taken an angry, unfamiliar growl.

Macy threw her hands over her head and plopped down the other side of the half-packed bag. She was surprised. In their years of courtship and marriage, he'd never spoken to her with such annoyance.

"Now. Start over." He took a deep breath. "What are we going to do about this baby? And how is your leg? Why didn't you call me immediately?"

"My leg is fine. I asked Ruth to call you. She said she tried lots of times. I'd wanted you there to help with both, trust me. The very last person in the world I wanted to see me sick with fear was a priest . . .you know me and stitches."

"Do I know you? I mean, for fuck's sake, a kid was left at our doorstep and your immediate reaction is to run away and then somehow find work in another town? What's happening here?"

"I'm not having this conversation with you." She scowled, returning to her packing. She tossed items into the nylon bag.

He stood and threw one of the boots at the headboard, hitting the wall above. It smacked with such a force, bits of paint cracked and fell below to the quilt.

Macy froze.

"What the fuck?" she whispered.

Ben began to pace again, holding the other boot. She watched as his neck grew red.

"I just don't know how to communicate with you anymore. You fleeing is not helping. Do you hear me? We are in trouble, Macy. Trouble. I need you here to help me figure things out."

"But you don't. You're smart and you'll manage." She looked at him and tried to smile. "Just stop throwing shit. You're scaring me. And you're going to scare off that housekeeper and then really be in a bind. I don't think they have pizza delivery in Tarija."

He did not return the smile.

"Oh fuck that. I am not talking about pizza here!" His voice rose. "This is a kid. Someone left a kid on our doorstep in a foreign fucking country and you want to run away and let me figure it out?"

She gulped.

"Well?" He continued. "Well! That's it, isn't it? I'm supposed to fix this? Who the fuck ever asks what *I* need?"

He raised his hand to throw the other boot.

"Ben! Don't. Please don't. Okay. I am listening."

"I am not okay with you leaving. Are you listening to that?"

"You told me to go. You told me to pick up my camera." Her eyebrows arched, ready for the rebuttal.

"Yes! To the fucking market! Walk to the zoo. I didn't say get on a bus and take off for God knows where!"

"I understand. And I'm sorry, but I am going." She said it just above a whisper. "It will be good for me, and I'd guess good for us. I want to work again, Ben."

He let out a groan and slid to the floor in defeat.

"That's it. You're picking your career."

"No." She bent down and looked him in the eye. "I'm picking survival. If you leave me in this house with that baby, I will not survive. Are you listening *to me*?"

His eyes grew wide, and Macy saw how his shoulders slouched with the understanding of what she would not say: being around a baby now would be her undoing. She was so fragile, death might be easier than being forced to care for a child that was not her own.

They sat together on the floor for a few minutes in silence.

"And your leg? How does it feel now?" His tone softened as he reached for her.

"It's sore, but I'll be fine. It's starting to itch. I'll pull the bandages off in two days and reapply the salve they gave me. My leg is the least of what we should be wasting time discussing. Honey," she smiled and pointed at her watch gently, "International wire deadline."

He ignored her need for brevity. "And the baby. Where did she come from? Did you see anyone?"

"I don't know where she came from. Neither does Ruth. Ben," Macy was losing her patience, "I told you everything I remember." She replayed the bits of conversation they had in the bathtub the night he'd come home. She'd been drugged and he'd gotten few of the precious details he needed before possibly making sweeping custodial decisions that could forever change their lives. "We took her to the hospital. The priest dropped the baby off and then came to hold my hand while they stitched me up." Macy shook her head remembering the blur of emotion.

* * *

The migraine had upended Macy. After she'd awoken from the sedative, Padre Pedro was still there. Pedro rubbed her back and held her hair, while Macy leaned over the trash bin, watching the blood pulse from her leg. She'd misjudged, thinking the worst was over before becoming sick again, which the priest took all over his chest. Her neck, face, and ears turned crimson. She was flustered to show such weakness in front of a stranger.

"I puked on him. I remember that," she said, laughing with nervous embarrassment. "He left to change his clothes right before you arrived. You probably passed in the hall."

Ben sighed. "Did you hold her?"

Macy looked away, recognizing her husband had wanted to hear about the baby's well-being, not hers.

"Tell me. What does she look like? What did it feel like to hold her? Were you okay?"

"He wanted me to hold her in the cab. Padre Pedro—Peter —whatever you want to call him. He couldn't get her to stop fussing and thought somehow my ovaries made me apt. Little does he know."

Her husband's golden eyebrows gathered like he'd been hit.

"No, I didn't hold her. I got sick in the taxi too. Poor cabbie. I couldn't. I can't. I just saw her and my stomach twisted." Macy swallowed the lump in her throat. "He was just in our arms." She paused, dropping her head. "I can't."

"Okay." Ben nodded. "Mace. I want to help. We are doing this together. All of this. You can't just rush through it without me."

She grasped her hands. "Not now."

"When? When are we going to discuss him? Jacob. Our son. When are we going to talk about what happened?"

"Ben," she pleaded, stepping away. "Not now. I have a deadline. I am not doing this now. Of all times, not now!" He grimaced, and he ran one hand up the side of his head.

Her voice softened as she returned to her luggage. "I promise I will when I'm ready."

"What if I fucking need to talk about him? He was my son too." His voice cracked and she realized her husband was on the verge of tears.

Grinding her teeth, putting too much weight on her injured leg, she continued throwing things into her backpack. She'd double checked there was a bottle of pain meds at the backpack's front pouch. They were working well enough to keep the edge off the sharp leg pain.

"Stop this. Come with me to the hospital and at least help me figure out what to do next. I don't know how to handle this. We need to speak with the priest and the doctor. We can't just abandon a child left at our doorstep."

"Ben, she isn't ours. You don't have to do that. We wouldn't be abandoning her."

"Aren't you the least bit curious why someone left a baby at *our* door?"

She didn't respond for several minutes, letting the items she packed become damp with tears. He stood a few feet away, arms crossed, unwilling to comfort her, although she could tell he was sick with grief too.

"Look, I needed you." She tried not to whimper or whine, but her voice was undoubtedly a mixture of both. "You weren't there and I needed you. It is pretty fucking convenient now to want me at home."

"This is the one time in two months I haven't been by your side!" He held on to the other boot like a weapon.

"And it was the moment a child was abandoned at our home."

"Do you think I planned that? Give me a damn break. I've stood outside of that bathroom cajoling you day after day. You cannot possibly think I had anything to do with this."

"No. You were too busy drinking with your asshole frat brother." Raleigh hadn't hidden his love of women or booze since arriving in their home. His behavior, which was unremarkable in their previous American life, was a glaring example of a carefree existence they missed.

"You're being ridiculous. I am not doing this. You want to call names? Fine. But I'm not playing along this time. You can't continue to treat me like this."

She fought dirty. The few times they'd argued to this point, he'd always stopped it. Macy would come back to him in a few days and apologize and ask to talk. This was the routine.

She watched him grimace. She'd hurt him. Again.

"Look. I don't want to fight, as good as it feels to simply feel anything—even anger. I just needed you. And then Sam called and offered me this job and you told me you wanted me to get out of the house. This is the perfect opportunity. I took it without thinking you'd be angry."

"I don't want to be angry either, Macy." His tone softened. "I don't want to fight. But we have to talk about him. About us." It was the look he gave her that broke her obstinance. His eyes were pleading.

"I loved him so much," Macy conceded, whispering his name, sitting hard on the bed. "Jacob."

"I did too," Ben whispered.

"I know. And I know not talking about him has to be the wrong thing to do. I'm sure a team of shrinks would have a party with the fact it makes me want to puke to even have to say his name. To think about his tiny hands."

"Jacob." He grabbed her shoulders and turned her toward him. "Jacob. We can say it, Mace. JACOB!" Ben screamed at the top of his lungs. She jumped. He screamed again. "Jacob! Who cares what's right, Macy? God, I just want you to care. About me. About us."

She nodded and they found each other, tears running down their hot, angered faces. Macy sobbed into his chest, the sorrow always there, pulsing and flowing freely whenever she'd give it the chance. "Jacob." She continued muttering his name.

"We are going to survive this," he said into her hair.

"Can we?" She stepped back, wiping her face. "I don't know how people do."

"We have to. You are my family." He grabbed her again.

With their foreheads pressed together, she felt the warmth of his crying on her face. His sorrow.

"You are my family," he repeated softly. "And I love you more."

She pulled him, wrapping her arms around his waist with all of her strength, feeling true comfort for the first time in months.

"I love you too, B." They stood together, shaking and holding onto each other with force, when she realized the time.

"Shit! Ben! I'm going to be late. I promised Sam. I have to go. Babe, I have to go." She flailed around the bedroom grabbing her bag and stepping toward the doorway. "Sam said they'd likely run these photos in the big five. I've got to get going or my shots won't make it before someone else gets wind of the story."

Ben raised his fists above him, shaking them at the sky. He'd lost. "You'll take my driver Fernando and the truck. He's outside waiting for Raleigh and me. We'll figure something else out until you return. And he has a radio. You will use it to call me if something happens."

"I will?" Her eyes brightened momentarily at his protectiveness.

"You will. Come home quickly. We aren't done here."

"Okay. All you had to do was ask." She smiled and he accepted it like a hard-earned trophy.

"I'll be able to sleep knowing Fernando is protecting you. I suppose I'll go to the hospital and figure all of this out in the meantime. I'll get the details."

"I promise to be safe."

He walked her outside, shaking Fernando's hand and closing the truck door behind her. Macy pulled on another pair of sunglasses and buckled her seat belt. "See? Safe. Already." She tried to smile and he laughed, holding her hand through the open window.

"Go, before some other hack steals your story. And Fernando, bring my wife home soon, and in one piece." Ben shook his head, his shoulders hunched, and walked back inside before the driver nodded, shifting the old truck into gear and pulling away from the curb.

11. NOTCH

"She's lucky. That's what they should name her—Suerte." Ruth placed one finger in the baby girl's hand, watching as the tiny fingers curled around hers. She stood with the priest and pediatrician over the infant's hospital bed. The baby had an IV of antibiotics and a feeding tube. Monitors beeped nearby.

"Suerte? How about Blessing?" Padre Pedro fiddled with his running shoe laces. Ruth wondered if priests in the United States were allowed to work in jeans, sweatshirts, and tennis shoes. Bolivian priests wore suits. They were cheap, but they were still suits. Padre Pedro always had a stain on his t-shirt, by comparison.

These Americans were so confusing.

"Any luck, so to speak, in convincing your American friends to foster her while we determine medical treatment?" Doctor Claudia glanced at Padre Pedro and Ruth.

"I haven't. Not for lack of trying, I promise. The good news is, I've spoken with the husband and asked him to join us today. His wife has apparently taken a trip on the altiplano."

"La gringa is more courageous than you described. Her stitches must not be slowing her."

"Ruth is their housekeeper, and she is the one who cared

for the baby the first night. She knows Macy better than anyone, I'd suppose."

"Padre, I can't explain that American woman!" Ruth no longer hid her own frustration, throwing her hands in the air. "She is a runner! Life gets hard and she leaves! Sprints!"

The priest shook his head.

"Oh Ruth, dear. The desire to hide from our problems is not an American one, but universal. God made us flawed. He's got a sense of humor, as they say." He smiled.

Pedro always knew how to remind Ruth, albeit gently, of her own shame. Flawed. She too was flawed, and madly in love with a married man. She wondered how the priest was able to carry everyone's sins. She thought of Jesus on the cross, of the weight He must have felt.

Once, over café con leche in the central square, Padre Pedro confessed to her, for a change: the confessional provided an ample amount of entertainment. He never tired of hearing different versions of the same love stories, as his penitents trickled through the queue before weekly communion. If there was one thing he'd learned as a priest it was everyone had a story, and everyone wanted to be heard. He enjoyed hearing it all. Knowing what was happening behind closed doors. He couldn't decide if he was a busybody or if he was blessed by God to be so genuinely interested in his congregation.

Ruth remembered blushing at the admission. The priest was also human. And he got some joy from hearing her tell of her heartache. Of how Andres was never there. Nonetheless, she continued to seek confessional. He was the only one she could speak to, even if he was smirking behind the black mesh screen.

Ruth stuffed her hands deep into her skirt pockets, as

though she could find where she had stashed that extra patience. Ruth didn't have time to be at the hospital this morning. The house needed cleaning, and the Spaniard's children had gotten into a mud fight yesterday. There were baskets of laundry waiting for her on the kitchen doorway.

"Doctora, she left to take photos in the altiplano," Ruth said, moving the conversation along. "Some story for a newspaper in the United States. La señora Macy didn't ask me to help her pack, so I have no idea how long she will be gone. But her husband is wonderful. Señor Ben is a kind man."

"Let's hope so. This baby needs a kind family. Should we discuss treatment options?" The physician tapped her foot as she spoke.

"No. Just do what is best." The priest didn't look up from the child as he spoke.

"You know, Padre, I have babies brought in from the indigenous groups daily," Doctora Claudia said, hurriedly. "The childhood burns, the asthma. Those cooking fire accidents alone could keep a team of pediatricians in business —if there was money. You of all people know we have to discuss practical options."

"I am not going to let this one die. She's survived two months God knows where, only to be abandoned on a doorstep. You need money to make her better, I know. I will figure it out if the Americans won't help." Pedro's gray eyebrows joined in a furrow, and he pursed his lips.

The pediatrician put her hands on her hips. "Yes, Father. I know. You don't want to let any of them die. And you've said you'd find the funding before. It just doesn't work that way anymore. I've been asked by administration to remind you we do not have credit at this hospital. That you . . ." Doctora

Claudia stopped to clear her throat. Ruth could tell this was hard for the woman to muster. "Well. You do not have credit. I will need to see that surgery can be funded before we begin."

Padre Pedro scratched the back of his head. "Shit." He said it in English, even though both women understood perfectly well.

Ruth stared at her dusty feet. Her sandals were well worn; she'd sewn them back together herself several times with a thick leather needle. She weighed her options. If she volunteered to care for this baby, her own children would grow hungry. Then again, how could she let an infant die?

"I want to help," she added meekly. "I have my own boys. I have to care for them. But if there is a way I could work here a bit to help pay for her care, I will."

The priest remained silent. Doctor Claudia shook her head.

"Oh, for heaven's sake. We can't have you working another job to pay for her care," the priest said. "You are one of the hardest working women I know, Ruth! And when was the last time you spent an afternoon with your children? Lord, Almighty. I'll just figure out a way. But thank you, Ruth. You are a good woman—worthy of your name."

Ruth beamed, smiling and soaking in the praise.

The doctor growled. "Oh, you two. You are a team, aren't you? Well, it is working!" She threw her hands in the air. "I will deal with administration if I have to, but first we'll convince the Americans to open their wallets. They must have the money."

Padre Pedro's head snapped up. "Oh Claudia, you are the best!" He nearly sang the words, so overcome with happiness. "Just the best! You are such a blessing!"

"I'm sure Señor Ben will help," Ruth added, relieved she wouldn't have work even more hours. It was true: she was barely home with her current schedule.

A slight knock on the doorframe got everyone's attention.

"I think I heard my name. Ruth, good to see you." Ben and the tall, blond Australian appeared through the doorway. Both men stuck their hands out to greet the housekeeper.

"Hello. I'm Ben Duncan. Do either of you speak English?"

"Ben, it is great to finally meet you." Ruth had told him all about the Australian houseguest. "I'm Padre Pedro, or Peter. Your choice."

"Oh, yes. Thank you. I owe you quite a debt of gratitude for getting my wife to the hospital. I hope she wasn't too difficult."

Padre Pedro cocked his head. Ruth could tell he was waiting in silence to see if Ben would provide more detail.

Of course she was difficult. Ruth wanted to scream it. *That woman!*

"If she didn't thank you herself, it is only because we've had a challenging year." Ben grew quiet. The pause quickly became awkward.

Raleigh cleared his throat, breaking the silence.

"Excuse my poor manners." Ruth noticed Ben had been staring at the bassinet. "Father Peter, this is my colleague Raleigh Brooks."

"Gentleman, this is la Doctora Claudia Nagarette," Padre Pedro said. "She is the sole pediatrician for thousands of miles —one pediatrician for the entire Department of Tarija. She happens to be caring for that sweet bundle your wife found last week."

"Nice to meet you," the three mumbled courteously, with handshakes all around. Even though the custom was to lean forward with a kiss on one cheek, Ruth suspected Ben didn't have the energy for cultural competency, while Raleigh didn't want to get too close to Claudia's furry upper lip.

"Is that her?" Ben leaned against a wall, tucking his hands behind his back.

"Yes. I suppose we should also introduce this sweet child," Pedro said. The five of them leaned over the infant, as the nearby machines continued their cacophony. An underfed infant with a shock of dark hair and gorgeous blue eyes stared back.

"Does she have a name?"

"No, not yet." The priest stood with his hands on his hips. "Have any suggestions?"

"Oh, I am not sure that's my role, Father. I'm really just here to sort out what happened."

"I see. What's your wife told you?" The priest smiled warmly. Ruth noticed how kind his tone was, even though he had to be exhausted.

Ben sighed. Ruth watched the color in the man's face change. She couldn't tell what he was feeling, but it appeared he was both angry and deeply saddened. "The basics. I'd like to hear your account."

"Well, did you know there was a note left with the child?"

"What? No. I don't think Macy knows that either."

"There was. Ruth here found it after we had come to the hospital. It was tucked under the bottom edge of the basket."

"Well? What did it say?" Ben was growing agitated, Ruth could tell.

"It was a crudely written note on the back of a store receipt. Shall we go to my office to discuss?" Claudia asked. Her English was textbook, without a trace of slang.

"Mate, that's my cue." Ruth had a harder time understanding the Australian's English, but context clues helped. A line of new nursing graduates in pressed uniforms had just walked by. She tried not to laugh as they watched the foreigner excuse himself to comically follow the group in chase.

"You'll have to forgive my colleague. He's, uh, rather in love with Bolivia." Ben squirmed. "To your office then?"

Claudia rolled her eyes, then led the group into a large nursery. Her office was on the far side, past countless machines humming as two dozen tiny chests rose and fell. Nurses in white gowns and starched caps rushed in and out of the room with soiled diapers, bottles, and IV poles. The facility was trying to treat far too many medical conditions, with facilities and technologies decades past their expiration dates. The room made Ruth queasy.

"Good Lord, I didn't know there were this many sick children in Tarija," she whispered to the priest. Most of the infants were heavily sedated, more than likely suffering from respiratory illnesses. One was covered from head to toe in bandages, wrapped like a mummy.

"All of these children." Ben's voice had risen as though it was a question.

"Yes?" The priest stopped. Ruth knew he'd been in this nursery a thousand times. He must have forgotten the initial shock. The sharp smells. The incessant noise. The haunting shadow of death, waiting in the hallway for his next victim.

"I'm guessing it looks bleak," Padre Pedro interjected. "Don't be fooled. While many of these small bodies will go on to the next life, it is a sweeter one. And for those who remain? You'd be pleased to see how talented the Bolivians are at their craft. I've had two knee operations at this hospital. They were both done expertly well. While la Doctora Claudia doesn't have a plush waiting room or a Ronald McDonald house down the street like the hospitals you're used to, she does have a team of well-trained nurses and physicians."

"Are these children all abandoned? Orphans?"

"Oh, no. Some are. But most are here for treatment. This hospital treats all children for thousands of miles. If a family can afford to get their baby here . . ." He drifted off. "Look, it isn't America. But these kids do get great care."

The five reached the office, where an assistant, also wearing nursing whites, appeared with a tray of tiny butter cookies and steaming mugs of dark tea. The baby remained in her bassinet, wheeled by the doctor to the center of the group.

Ruth helped herself to the refreshments, thankful to be sitting. If she had to be away from the house, she might as well enjoy herself.

"She's so . . . Well, she's so small. How old is she?" Ben had many questions.

"The note said she is 10 weeks old. It's a miracle, really, that she's survived." The doctor had the infant's chart on her desk. "Her mother must have known what she was doing. I'd guess she's had other babies with the same cleft palate."

"More?"

"Cleft palates are often genetic." Claudia's English was likely British, Ruth decided. Less difficult to understand than Raleigh's but still not easy.

"Are there more here now?"

"There aren't any other children in this room at the moment, but clefts are quite common. Girls in Bolivia often start having babies when they are themselves still girls, and most of the rural women don't have prenatal care. We just don't have the same services you would see in the UK or New York."

Ruth knew this reality. She'd been 16 the first time Andres got her pregnant. She didn't know what "prenatal care," meant, but she did know the one government nurse assigned to her former village regularly found reasons to stay in the city instead.

"You've seen one before?" Padre Pedro said, scooping up the baby girl. "They aren't uncommon in the States. They are usually just fixed much earlier. American children rarely die of this defect."

"She's lovely, this one." Claudia stepped back. "But that doesn't mean she'll survive. She's terribly underweight, although someone took quite a bit of time to find a way to feed this little girl. She probably couldn't latch. I'm guessing by the color of her skin, she's indigenous. Her mother probably didn't have access to running water or a bottle. So, whoever cared for her had the patience to spoon feed this little wawa."

"That's how we fed baby birds when they fell out of the nest," Ben said. "How could someone love something so fiercely and then abandoned it at an empty door? And what is a wawa?"

Padre Pedro smiled. *"Wawa* is the Quechua word for baby. Many of the native folks here speak Quechua as their first language. As for the abandonment, your guess is as good as mine. Although basket babies aren't uncommon, unfortunately."

"Basket babies?"

A nurse knocked at the door before entering, bringing in medication for the baby. Her machines continued to beep. Her IV dripped steadily. She was soundly asleep.

The priest motioned to Ben to see if he wanted to hold the

baby. He nodded and the infant was passed from one set of arms to another, each person holding her as delicately as possible. Ruth couldn't wait to touch the baby girl again. She made sure her turn was last so she could stand in the corner, rocking the infant, still connected by tubes to the many devices, ever so carefully.

Ruth's eyes traced the baby's small face, the purple wound, the tiny bridge of her nose, the arches of her brow, the black hair burst from the crown in a wide swoop to one side of her gorgeous little head.

"She is a beautiful baby bird," Ben said, watching Ruth.

"She needs a home while we determine care options. We can leave her here, but she'd do better in your home." The doctor walked over and stroked the baby's head while she spoke, her voice soothing. "As you can see, one of our biggest issue is space. With this sort of crowding, we have a higher rate of hospital-borne infections. We have great surgeons in the region who will perform her first surgery, but her recovery will be swifter if she can do so outside of this nursery. We need someone to be her champion."

"Her what?"

"They need the baby to have an advocate," the priest interrupted. "It isn't a long commitment, only a few months. She'll need someone to get her to appointments, care for her after surgery and comfort her."

Ruth's voice cracked. Thick, unexpected tears gathered in her eyes. "Señor Ben, I will do whatever I can to help." The priest translated. Ruth thought of the days her sons were born. She could never express how grateful she had been to see each one was healthier than the next. Andres may not be around much, but she was lucky all the same.

"I haven't been in a hospital for a while. The last time was under tragic circumstances . . ." Ben paused. "I am sorry, but this is not an easy decision and certainly not one I can make without my wife."

His voice wavered. They watched with wonder as the man's shoulders began to shake. The priest reached over, placing his hand on Ben's back.

"What did the note say?" Ben found his voice, although it came out barely above a whisper.

Ben looked at the crumpled note. In the most rudimentary Spanish handwriting he read, "Please fix her. I couldn't. She is my greatest gift." Ten words that would forever change the trajectory of a life. Ben ran his fingers over the simple message as Ruth watched; he examined the receipt for more clues. On the back was scribbled, "Wawa,10 semanas." Child, 10 weeks.

Padre Pedro explained the basket had been purchased in a nearby shop, more than likely one of a dozen sold that day. Paid for with a handful of *Boliviano* coins, the trail came to a dead end.

"'Please fix her.' Could the mother have known we lived at the house?"

"Probably not. But she did know someone wealthy lived there. The gardens are well tended, and she could have seen Ruth coming and going from the market with food. It isn't unexpected that a wealthy or foreign family would live in such a home, especially in your neighborhood."

"Because we have nice gardens? This doesn't make any sense. Don't you have orphanages? Wouldn't the mother have family?"

Claudia pinched the bridge of her nose.

"With some increased frequency, unfortunately, women

are abandoning their babies. There is a custom in the rural areas. When a baby cannot be kept, because of incest or disease, the mothers, las indigenas, act out of survival. They leave the baby on the steps of a wealthy house, or at the gate, or with the guard, guessing someone inside will take pity. They know the social services will encourage those who found the child to keep the infant safe while custody is decided. We simply don't have a social safety net like you do in your country." The doctor spoke with frankness that cast no shame on abandonment, but hinted at her bitterness in having to ask yet again for a foreigner's help. "I am that social service asking for help."

Ruth noticed how crows feet gathered in the corners of Claudia's eyes, the liver spots on the back of her hands, and how her smile was bracketed with deep parentheses. This woman worked long hours for the children of their community. Ruth felt a surge of pride for her Bolivian sister.

"Otherwise they die?"

"Many, many do. Sadly, our country has a disgracefully high child mortality rate. Delivering a healthy baby in the altiplano isn't an easy feat. Only a handful of these children reach doorsteps like yours."

"Why?" Ben raised his hands as he spoke. Ruth swayed her hips, rocking gently and stroking the baby's head as she listened.

"Why? Because these people live on a just handful of grain each day. They don't get the right vitamins. Birth control is a luxury of city life. Babies are born deformed every day. There are few choices."

"I'm sorry. I didn't mean . . . Well, I can imagine."

"You can?" The doctor laughed.

"Well, not exactly. But I'm trying."

Ruth stared at the doctor. Her moment of pride was washed away; why was she treating Señor Ben this way? Before she could speak up in his defense, her jefe left them speechless.

"I lost a kid. The last time I held a baby, it was my dead son. Now my wife finds a baby someone has left us and we have to wonder why? It seems like a cruel twist, especially since this kid may die too."

This time the doctor and priest didn't bother looking down with shame. Ruth stared at them, not bothering to hide her shock. Her contempt for Macy came back like a heavy punch to the gut.

How wrong she was! How impatient she had been with la señora!

The revelation struck each differently, but left them equally embarrassed.

"We didn't know. I am so very sorry. I wouldn't have brought you here . . ." Padre Pedro shook his head.

"No one knows. We are dealing with it. It's just . . . Kids die in America too. For stupid reasons. And we are having a hard enough time trying to understand this, without having to consider caring for a sick child in a foreign land. I'm not saying no. We are going to have to ask a lot of questions before we make any move toward bringing this child into our home. I'm not sure it would be good for me or my wife."

"And the child?" The doctor spoke softly.

"Excuse me for speaking so frankly, but it seems entirely fucked up that we would be given this kid. Can't you see that? And for the kid to be so sick? I mean, come on. My wife still isn't right from the death of our son. How could I possibly ask her to care for a sick child?"

After a considerable time in silence, the priest took a deep breath and tried continuing.

"We cannot understand your grief. Neither Claudia nor I have had children. I am so sorry. We didn't know this is what you were dealing with, and if we had, we would have approached you both differently. That said, there is a reason you were given this child. You have to know, I think it is a blessing." Ruth admired the priest's perseverance. "Of course it is up to you on how to move forward. This child will likely die without someone to help care for her. But she will likely soar and survive if someone does decide to champion her case. We didn't pick you. The mother did."

"Christ."

"Perhaps. But I'm guessing it was just a scared, teenage girl. Come on, Ben. Let's have some tea and talk about options."

"No orphanages?" Ben asked, again.

"If only there was an actual orphanage system," Padre Pedro interrupted. "Extended families are asked to absorb children into their homes instead. I help parishioners every day with the adjustment of an unexpected child at the dinner table. In most ways, this is the very best outcome. Children are protected and watched."

Ben remained silent.

"I do have a small orphanage," Padre Pedro continued. "I have several dozen children I am responsible for, and most have either severe physical or mental disabilities. It's only me. I have no way of caring for another infant in addition to my others. Even being away in a moment like this is a difficult chore. I have to ask local friends to step in an keep an eye on the place so I can be in the community, give mass . . . You get the idea."

"Jesus."

"Well, yes and no." Padre Pedro laughed.

"I apologize. I didn't mean to curse, it's just so much to understand at once. You take care of all of those kids on your own?"

"The older kids have chores. They help take care of each other too."

"You don't have to take her. We can manage. I've managed with hundreds like her before." The doctor's words were sincere. They all felt ashamed for the pressure they had put on this man and for their assumptions about the young American couple.

Ben slumped in his seat.

"I didn't mean to push a sick child on you. It's just that this baby needs help." The doctor pushed bifocals on top of her head. "It is hard to ask every foreigner paraded through the hospital by administration for donations. Like my department is some sort of circus of maladies. If seeing that child, who most certainly would not have survived without the hand of God guiding her journey to your home, then what can I do? I'm tired of begging. Yes, you are the fool with the doorstep big enough for a basket. You are a fool if you don't take this chance to help her."

"Claudia, he just has questions." The priest stood.

Ben cleared his throat.

"I appreciate your passion. I'm not just some shitty foreigner who wants you to beg. Okay? I'm here in your country working to make it better, too." He crossed his arms and leaned back in the chair. "Give me a break. I didn't ask for this kid to be dropped off at my door. I didn't ask for my son to die. And it would be better if you didn't call me a fool while asking for help. Perhaps this is where your fundraising strategy has gone wrong."

Other than the machines working to monitor the baby, the room went silent.

"I am sorry for my temper, Mr. Duncan. I am not getting enough sleep and I have another 25 children in the next two rooms who need me. Please find what you need to within your heart to care for that child. She needs you. We all need you!"

Ben nodded. "We will pay for her care here. That much I can do. As for bringing her into our home, I need more time to consider this. And a lengthy conversation with my wife."

Padre Pedro grinned, victoriously. "Hey, that's a start. A big gracias to you, Ben."

The doctor put her hand out to shake Ben's hand. "You are most likely saving her life. Thank you, Mr. Duncan. I appreciate your generosity. I will also reconsider my fundraising pitch."

Ben, let out a laugh, clutching the note in his hand. Ruth glanced up to see Raleigh waiting in the doorway.

"Ah, Raleigh. Just in time. I need a beer, and to find my wife."

"I can certainly help you with the first. Probably until you forget the second." The Aussie laughed.

"Padre, care to join us?" Ben put out his hand.

"Rain check? I have to get home to those kids."

"A rain check it is."

Ruth wanted a beer, but knew better than to speak up. She carefully returned the baby girl to her bassinet and watched as the doctor's assistant wheeled her to the nursery.

Their baby bird would live to fly another day.

12. EK'EKO

Macy fiddled with her headphones and shifted in her seat. The Toyota truck was far from comfortable, although certainly reliable. Once she understood Sam's assignment, she began preparing for the overnight trip to Entre Rios.

The driver made everything so much easier; she couldn't have known how dangerous the roads truly were until she'd been on them herself. Imagining being on a crowded bus on these hairpin turns made her stomach sick. Damn if Ben wasn't right again.

She gave up trying to make conversation with the stoic and silent Fernando. Sitting through the fourth hour on the road, enjoying the changing landscape and mulling over the details she'd learned from Sam, she re-read his email for the tenth time:

> *A small silver mine in northern Argentina collapsed after an earthquake tremor hit the region last week. The mine, owned by a wealthy Argentinean cattleman, has been suspected in the past of poor labor standards. Of course the owner won't face charges; his son-in-law is the governor of the region. Some 30 of the workers inside were Bolivians, men who'd illegally crossed the nearby border seeking higher salaries. They're all dead. The majority of the men were from the small southern town of Entre Rios. All Saints*

Day on November 1 is one of the biggest festival days in the country. There is certain to be international attention as the Argentinean ambassador and Bolivian president will meet in the town square with the family members.

Get the story from several angles. Who were these men? What is life like in this small town? What do they eat?

Typical, Macy thought, of Sam to consider this aspect. The man was known for his diverse appetite.

And most importantly, capture the disgust on the Argentinean ambassador's face when he must shake Evo Morales' hand. And vice versa.
Post them to the site as soon as you are done processing. We've got room for these immediately and I want to scoop the Republic *and the* LA Times *with our 'squat community newspaper.' Little do they know our best stringer just went international. Be careful, doll. Much love, Sam.*

"Fernando, have you heard of the silver mine in Argentina?"

He grunted.

"Silver? Mine?" She made motions of digging with her hands and then pointed to a simple bangle she was wearing.

He looked away.

She waited without inspiring a response.

"If you don't want to talk, do you mind if I listen to some music? My Spanish is pathetic. I can keep rambling in English, but something tells me you don't care for that either. How I wish you could give me some sense of where we are, how much longer or what this town is known for. I have no idea what we are walking into. And, you aren't listening to a word I'm saying, are you?" She stared at him, smiling. He remained unfazed by the babbling. Macy put in the ear buds and cranked up James Taylor, feeling her nerves relax as she nodded to the familiar beat.

He seemed to relax when she stopped speaking.

James Taylor soon shifted to Simon and Garfunkel. Macy sang along quietly. After a few minutes, she noticed Fernando's thumbs were tapping on the steering wheel. Could it be? A slight smile hid at the corners of his mouth. She pulled out an ear bud and carefully put it into his brown ear. He nodded his approval.

"Never did I think 'Cecilia' would bring us together." Fernando simply smiled. Within a couple songs, Macy had done what her husband apparently hadn't been able to accomplish in several weeks: get the grumpy driver to laugh. Maybe they'd never be best friends, but the ice was beginning to thaw by the time they reached Entre Rios.

When they pulled into the small town, they'd traveled several hundred miles around mountains, over rivers, and into a pastoral village. The outlying hills were a quilt of crops. Cattle and goats grazed along the edges, wrangled by dusty children with large sticks. The exterior of the town was circled with a large, off-white wall, reminding Macy of a fairytale kingdom. Only rather than a castle in the central square, she saw a large Catholic church with aging green ropes streaming down from a tall bell tower. The square had a handful of native trees, shading a few benches. The surrounding buildings included several small hostels, restaurants, and an open-air market.

Macy was giddy to finally be out of the car. Rubbing her shin, she pulled off her lens cap, grabbed Fernando's hand and led the two toward something that smelled delicious.

"What are these?"

Fernando looked at the pumpkin empanadas and salteñas. Fishing for a few Bolivianos in his pocket, he purchased several of the pastries wrapped in newspaper and two bottles of warm Coca Cola. The pair strolled around the square, eating and stretching their legs. Fernando ate the pastry by carefully biting one corner and slurping the pumpkin and tomato-sauce filling through the hole, and then delicately enjoying what remained. Macy split hers in two to examine the contents. In the process, she fed much of the filling to the sidewalk. What didn't fall land on the ground ended up in the center of her light blue t-shirt.

"Great. Just great."

For the second salteña, she watched her driver carefully and mimicked his movements successfully. She'd noticed a group of Bolivian men in the square, sipping chicha. They watched her every move; she guessed by their volume they had been drinking the fermented corn beer for several hours, laughing loudly when she'd spilled. With dozens milling around, preparing for the next day's festival, she was the only foreigner to have arrived in the square. Although her features weren't fair by American standards, her height, clothing, and the expensive camera slung around her shoulder immediately gave her away.

"Feel free to let me know if I'm about to make an ass out of myself, Fernando." She nudged him and pointed at the group of men. "Otherwise I may be the afternoon entertainment for the entire town."

He grumbled something she didn't understand, scanning the square for more food.

"I am really glad you are here with me, and if I haven't said so already, thank you for driving. I know this wasn't your plan."

He nodded, tipping back the green Coca Cola bottle.

Macy sat on a bench in front of the church. A group of indigenous women rested, knitting nearby in the shade, rough balls of homespun wool at their feet, and raven-haired, sleepy babies wrapped tightly to their backs. Each woman wore a distinct fedora-like hat.

"Fernando, we need to find a cheap hotel, an Internet connection, and a place to camp out for this All Saint's festival. I want to be in front of the front row for the official greeting. Also, I want to meet some of the families who lost their men to the mines," she paused, humming and staring at him, waiting again for a response. Macy tapped her foot. "Mr. Fernando, I know you understand English and have served as my husband's translator more than once in the last few months. I need your help. I'll make sure you get half of whatever I'm paid for the shoot. Fair?"

She stood up, brushed her greasy hands off on her cargo pants and looked around. The sun was beginning to set. Men hung strands of lights from the trees to the corners of the square. A round woman with long gray braids sat peeling potatoes next to a dozen different shapes and sizes of other tubers for sale in her stall.

"Plus, if you don't help me, I'll tell Ruth and all the others you are a closeted folk music lover. And not just any folk music. Gringo folk music." She smiled and for once, he returned the expression readily.

He nodded. "Si, señora."

"Ha! We are getting somewhere, Don Fernando." With a big laugh, she headed back to the truck. Within an hour, he'd secured two tiny rooms at a hostel. The Internet café was two streets over, and while it was only a dial-up connection, it would work until she could get home to Tarija to upload the final shots.

She scouted the area, taking photos of the preparations, families at a cemetery a couple miles outside of the town gates, and convinced several older women in the church to allow her to take photos of them lighting candles. By the time night fell, the pair had walked more than five miles. It felt more like 50 after bouncing in the truck during their long journey.

Over bowls of chicken and boiled yucca soup, Macy reviewed her shots of the day on the back of her camera. She sipped a glass of red wine. Fernando drank coffee, his shoulders tense, with one eye always on the restaurant entrance.

"There are a few here that will work for the *Daily Sun,* but nothing I'm sending off to the *Times*." She shrugged. "It's a good start. Here's to hoping tomorrow's events will give me some flash. Something juicy. What do you think, Don Fernando? Are any of these tiny town festivals ever juicy?"

Predictably, he remained silent.

After a freezing night on the small, rope cot and an ice-cold rinse of only the most critical areas, she met Fernando downstairs the next morning. This time, she ate like a native, enjoying the hot sausage and pumpkin salteñas with several cups of tea. As the day's proceedings began, the camera came to life in her hands. Exposure, aperture, f-stop: she'd missed her trusty friend. So much of her life had been experienced from behind the crosshairs of her Canon. The rush of self-satisfaction made her eyes dance when she clicked a dozen shots she knew instantly would be ready for the wire.

The officials met. Evo was more than an hour late. While waiting, the Argentinean ambassador walked the square like a true gentleman, shaking hands and meeting with the widows of the miners. By the time the two shook hands, it seemed most of Entre Rios' residents were more likely to vote for the southern, charming foreign leader.

The festival that proceeded was a mélange of culture unlike anything Macy had ever witnessed. The Catholic priest and a line of catechism students led a procession with papier-mâché characters from the Bible, including Jesus and Mary. The younger children carried demons. Next in the parade came those paying their honor to Condormami—the spirit of the house. In Bolivia, she learned, keeping the spirit of the home happy was critical. Angry Condormami led to crop failures, animal theft, and babies born with clubfeet.

Macy photographed families carrying tiny altars from their own homes. Many participants also wore large wooden crosses or rosaries.

The combination of the ancient faiths was particularly noticeable to Macy when the Ek'eko dancers and flutists concluded the procession. Ek'eko was the Aymara god of fertility and good luck. Women carried babies of all ages, holding them to the skies and singing their thanks. Boys, wearing tiny hats full of red and orange feathers, danced around the women, playing their flutes. By the end, this mixture of people came together to light candles and stand before the church in the square. There were hundreds of people. Macy couldn't capture the event quickly enough. She replaced her battery twice, recognizing she was setting herself up for hours of processing. Yet, she couldn't stop searching through her viewfinder.

Seeing those proud mothers holding their gorgeous babies, cradling them with thanks, signaled the return of tears. Macy had no idea why it seemed every woman within a hundred yards had dressed up to thank the saints for their babies, but she wished she was celebrating among them, holding Jacob high to the heavens, rather than wondering if he was there, looking down upon her. Overwhelmed, she took a few remaining shots before asking Fernando to take her home.

Under a thick blanket of stars with the Southern Cross's glimmering, Fernando drove home across the gran chaco. Once wanting his conversation, Macy was now grateful for the driver's silence. She didn't have the energy to explain. A steady stream of tears came as she reviewed the photos on her camera. Mercifully, she soon fell into a deep slumber, face pressed against the passenger glass, the weight of the day falling away.

13. STUNG

What Macy hadn't noticed while shooting in Entre Rios was the young indigenous woman selling honey in the square who grew increasingly more alarmed as the afternoon passed. Without her own child to bless, the girl went unseen through the photographer's lens.

What is la señora doing here? Where is my wawa? Why is she crying?

The questions stung Luz's heart. She had hidden among the shadows in the estate neighborhood of Tarija, waiting to find a foreign couple who would care for her baby. Her daughter started losing weight, headed the wrong direction, and with her paternity certain to cause Luz far more trouble than it was worth, she had acted quickly. When she saw Macy and Ben walking hand in hand to dinner in the square, returning with arms entwined hours later, she knew. They loved each other. Plus, living in this neighborhood with high gates, pedicured gardens, servant quarters and four-wheel drive vehicles parked in long, circular drives—they would have the money to fix her. And if they couldn't, they would know someone who could.

This wawa would fly, just not from her native nest.

She'd nursed the baby one final time, swishing her hips in a long pollera skirt and rocking back and forth along the sidewalk. After buying the basket, she convinced a child coming out of the middle school to write a note for her in exchange for a few coins. She didn't want the note in her own, poor scribble; she'd been out of school for too long. Luz kissed her beautiful daughter, one last time.

"I will love you always."

With the note tucked beneath, she wrapped her sleeping babe tightly in the blanket knit by her mother and placed her only child gently in the basket. Tip-toeing to the doorstep with tears running off her chin, she placed the precious gift at the door and then ran away to the safety of the shadows across the street. Crouching on her thick heels in a doorway with a perfect view of the fragile delivery, she waited for someone to find the baby. For someone to save the one Luz loved most.

The hospital would have asked too many questions. Her family was resigned to letting the wawa pass. This was her only choice. She knew these wealthy gringos would know what to do.

Maybe they even knew Henry?

Before she could witness the discovery of her daughter, a police officer came along, his only job to jostle the indigenous folk out of the wealthy neighborhood with his bully club. By the time Luz returned to her spot, with a sore arm from an efficient swat, the basket was gone. From the gate, she could hear her wawa crying safely inside the home. Oddly, there were droplets of blood on the sidewalk leading to the door Luz hadn't noticed a half hour prior.

"Wawa," Luz cried, wrapping her arms around her shrinking waist. There would be no way to know if her child had been hurt today, or ever.

Now, seeing this photographer without her child in sight, Luz shivered.

Where is my baby bird? Is she alive? What is she doing here with that camera and indigeno? What have I done? The thoughts pounded in her head.

Under the same moon, the young beekeeper quietly planned her return to the big city. Luz told her family the baby died; she'd taken the wawa to the hills for a burial. This wasn't uncommon, and when she returned several days later, dirty, hungry and sincerely mourning, they took her story for truth.

With eyes swollen like they'd been pierced by angry bees, she kept repeating one sentence to herself, mumbling it in a whisper:

"What has she done with my baby?"

14. COCA

Why were these men sitting in her kitchen? Why did all Americans like the old food-prep table?

Ruth didn't bother trying to hide her exasperation at finding Señor Duncan and his Australian friend sitting in the kitchen, beer bottles scattered at their feet. Cookie crumbs clung to the corners of their mouths, with an empty sleeve of expensive Oreos sitting between them.

The cookies were one of many pricey American imports the Lebanese grocer stocked. If the beer had been milk, she'd have considered this a look into the future of her own boys. May God bless them with such luxuries!

"Señor, please sit at the dining room table," she cajoled in slow Spanish. The Aussie translated in turn, his words slurred from their afternoon happy hour.

"Please, señor. I must work in here. You shouldn't really sit here. I know it is your house, but sir—" She lowered her voice, pulling him gently to his feet. "It isn't proper."

"What is she saying? Why do I have to leave?" Ben swayed. His boot tipped one of the green Paceña bottles, sending shards of glass across the tile floor.

"Oh shit," he said, giggling.

"Bloke, let's move along to the other room." Raleigh steadied his friend, leading the two men to more comfortable chairs and a much larger table. The room was dark, with the shutters pulled tight.

Ruth shook her head as she swept the glass into the dustbin. Soon, the men had their muddy boots on the dining room table, another round of cold beer and plates of cold fried chicken, left over from the night before. They continued, sucking at their greasy fingers between slurps of beer.

"The problem with coca is that we can't give them anything more valuable to grow." Ben's voice carried.

Ruth stuck her hands in hot, soapy dishwater. Before she could think to turn on her radio program, their conversation caught her ear.

"I've been here for years, scratching my head at the same problem. And yet the Aussies and Yanks love the stuff, don't we?" It was harder for Ruth to understand this man; his accent was different than any other she'd ever heard.

"Don't look at me." Ruth heard Ben laugh.

"Yeah, well. Me either. Now. But at uni, I had a taste or two. And now I wonder, did it get to Sydney in someone's bum?"

"Do you think today's bust was Shining Light? I still don't understand why Peruvians would be heading south with their coca leaves before sending it north to the States as cocaine." Ruth leaned against the doorframe, just out of sight.

"Mate, there had to be a million dollars in leaves there today. I don't know if it was the Peruvians, or the Mexicans, but some cartel has their fingers in this community. When was the last time you heard of a Bolivian drug pin?"

"The Mexicans? Really?"

126

"Man, last year, we followed a shipment of Bolivian coca leaves from Santa Cruz by cargo ship across the Caribbean. It came to port in Cancun, unloaded in a matter of minutes before we lost it heading into the jungle. We can't compete with the Mexicans, mate. They cut people's heads off."

Ruth listened with wide eyes. Ben sighed heavily.

"I never thought studying agroforestry would mean avoiding being beheaded." His voice was shaky.

"Look. We aren't going to be beheaded. But these muppets aren't playing around. We do our jobs here? We get these Bolivians to plant other cash crops? We are going to have a lot of people angry with us, including that joke of a president. Evo may have to find another drug of choice."

"Nothing quite communicates his foreign policy as much as that stupid wad of leaves in his lip." Ben's words were slurred. Ruth strained to understand.

"You have to remember, it isn't illegal to grow the stuff, man. It's just not so nice when they involve the Latino foreigners. This drug trade is a giant political game. And we are pawns."

"God, this is a disaster. What happens to those girls now?"

"The ones from today? They likely have been arrested for this nonsense before. They may look like girls to you, but they work in the drug trade. They are probably on a prison transport to La Paz and then to a jail. Or, placed in buses outside in front of the press and then quietly freed once they get them out of Santa Cruz."

"Is Evo coming in for this?"

"No idea, mate. But I'd guess he's out of the country, or he'd be here by now. That administration has nothing on your mobsters, but they are still shady as fuck. There is no doubt someone in his cabinet knows about our bust today. More than likely, he also knows I once did blow and now have an addiction to the Bolivian misses instead."

"God. God! Those poor girls." Ruth brought her hands to her face. She felt her cheeks grow warm. Señor Duncan was a good man. Even in all of this nonsense, he was most concerned about the indigenas. The poor. The girls sent off to prison. She'd seen photos of women who did this type of work in the papers. They did always look like girls, not women. Likely talked into the dangerous work to feed their hungry babies. Ruth understood this source of motivation well.

"Don't be confused." Raleigh ran a hand through his hair. "Those women were on a cattle farm outside the city limits up to their asses in coke. They knew exactly what they were doing."

"But they aren't from Tarija, obviously."

"Why? Because they aren't Japs? Because they don't look German? Man, these are the people of Bolivia. They are hungry and they want their kids to go to school and they don't mind if that means doing something illegal. Their president certainly wouldn't be allowing this publicized 'internationally monitored' round up if he didn't have something else cooking politically."

"Yeah. I guess. But it still doesn't feel right. They were just kids."

"They were drug manufacturers. What's wrong with you, Yank? This is why we are here. Don't you remember what you applied for?"

"I guess I didn't realize this would be the job. Putting kids in jail. Some hole of a prison on the other side of the Andes. Afternoon happy hours and beheadings."

"If we do our jobs, we stop this bullshit. We've got to come up with something more productive for these people to grow, so our people can slow down snorting the shit."

"Making the demand and street value greater."

"You have another idea?"

"Just say no?"

They both chuckled.

"Did your colleague in Afghanistan ever get back to you?" Ruth watched as Raleigh rudely leaned back in his chair.

"I haven't heard from him."

"Well, mate. I don't mean to burst any patriotic bubble here, but I think you need a come-to-Christ with reality."

"I didn't know you were religious, Raleigh."

"I like to scream his name when one of those brown Betties is on top of me. Otherwise, you know how I feel about faith. It's shit. If your country can sink billions—wait. Is it at trillions now, this fun little war of yours?"

"Raleigh, for the last time, we didn't fly planes into our own buildings. It was a reaction to an attack."

"Fine. So, your little 'non-petrol focused war' that somehow dribbled over to Afghanistan has taken trillions—let's just say trillions for this conversation—from your Yankee wallets for what? The poppy harvest was bigger this year than ever before. I just got the Aussie report on international trade."

"Look, man. We can't do everything. And it wasn't like you guys didn't jump in to help us. How many times have I listened to you ramble about your hot shot SASR?"

"Exactly my point." The Aussie took a deep breath and shook his head with a know-it-all smile. Ruth was tired of this visitor. When would la señora return? Her moodiness was preferable to Raleigh's arrogance.

Ruth scoffed. Both men looked her way.

"Er. Excuse me. Uh." She squeezed her hands in front of her, nervously. She hadn't meant to make herself known. "Is there anything else I can bring you?"

"Ruth, were you listening?" Ben's eyes were glassy, and his bottle empty.

"I. Uh. Well. Is there anything else you need, Señor Duncan?" She spoke to him in Spanish, as always.

"Coffee, Ruth. We've got the world's problems to solve, and more beer isn't going to help."

"I'll take his, then. And more chicken. Andalé!" Raleigh said it without looking up.

"Is that the way you speak to your help?" Ben's voice hardened.

"I don't keep help, mate."

"Be kind to her, *mate*. She's the one washing your clothes these days and preparing your food."

"You're never going to find your place in this country."

"If finding my place means being a dick, I don't care to."

"Fine, bloke. Your house. Your rules." Raleigh laughed. "Excuse me, Ruth. Thanks for more beer. And chicken. Please."

"See? Not so hard." Ben slapped his friend on the back.

Ruth shuffled into the kitchen, a smug smile across her face. Had anyone ever spoken up for her? She couldn't remember.

This Señor Duncan. He was a good man.

15. SLOTH

"So you are a photographer?" The priest set a copy of the morning addition of *El Pais* on the café table.

"Oh, shit. They were published here?" Macy looked up from the newspaper to see the clerical collar. "Shit. Shoot. God." She sighed heavily. "The wrong words always seem to come out when I'm around clergy. Sorry."

He waved away her apology. "I had no idea you were so talented." Peter looked at her with wide eyes, pointing at the paper. "This says they were AP wire photos. When did you go to Entre Rios?"

Macy motioned for Peter to take a seat next to her. She'd been reading a photography book included in her mother's care package and sipping a now cold cup of Colombian coffee at a small outdoor café in one of Tarija's squares.

"Thank you. I wasn't sure if you were speaking to me after our ride to the hospital." He pulled out his chair and motioned to the server. "Café con leche y pan tostado, por favor."

"About that. I owe you an apology."

"Actually, let me. I didn't realize. Well, Macy. There is no polite way to say this. I didn't realize you'd recently given birth. I was insensitive."

"What?" Macy placed her cup down a bit too forcefully with a clatter. "Who told you that?"

"I couldn't help but notice when we arrived at the hospital . . . well, your shirt was wet when you handed the baby off to the nurse. I've hired a wet nurse or two. I don't mean to be vulgar, or to pry."

Macy sighed. Thankfully her milk was finally drying up. She remembered her doctor's email on the topic: "Everyone heals differently. Be kind to yourself." An email she deleted without responding as she'd desired: "Thanks for the cliché, asshole."

"I'm sorry I became ill. That . . .that it got on you." She felt her face burning. "Thank you for staying with me. I have been meaning to come to the church to say as much, but as you can see, I was called away on business."

Peter nodded. "Yes. I still haven't seen you or Ben in mass lately."

"Or ever," Macy said, with a big grin. "Well, that's not true. Ben's Catholic. You'll likely get him to service sooner or later."

"And you?"

"Oh my mother raised me in a variety of faiths, hoping I'd pick the one best for me. It was a very laid back, liberal childhood, Father. I ended up selecting atheism, much to my Episcopalian mother's disgust."

"Well. I didn't mean to make this about faith yet again, but as you can imagine, such conversations seem to follow me."

"Like a storm?"

"Ha!" He snorted. "I was thinking more like a shadow. Anyway, tell me about Entre Rios."

Macy examined the newspaper. They'd selected one of her best shots, a young mother holding her child high in the air, celebrating the gods and smiling with tears coming down her young face. Long brown braids trailed down her sides while her two dusty sandaled feet stomped in glee. A smaller photo of the president and ambassador ran inside, after the jump. *El Pais* editors didn't hide their bias for the indigenous Evo, who knew little of how to run a country other than what his communist friends in Cuba and Venezuela instructed him. The interior photo should have been front fold. Instead, an impoverished, happy teenage mother spread her arms beneath the headline: BOLIVIAN MOTHERS CELEBRATE.

"I was a photographer before we moved here."

"It appears you are a photographer today."

Macy smiled, accepting the compliment.

"My former boss called from Flagstaff and asked if I'd be willing to take a few shots for a wire assignment."

"I've been to Entre Rios. You made an otherwise unremarkable town look like a *National Geographic* feature."

"I've never shot for Nat G. But, thank you. This is. Well, photography is my thing. I'm at home behind my camera."

"What did you think of the town?"

"Quaint. More what I thought Bolivia would be like when Ben said we were moving. Tarija isn't a metropolis, but it feels like a big city."

A motorcycle putted by on cue, sending a cloud of thick black diesel over the café.

Peter laughed.

"Out of curiosity, do you know what those people are looking at?" She motioned to several couples, arms entwined, staring upward at the trees in the plaza square.

"Do I." He smiled at her mischievously. "Guess."

"I've been sitting here for two hours guessing. Birds?"

"Sloths."

"Sloth? Like the sin? You are kidding me."

"Sloth like the sin. And sloth, like the two-toed animal that moves an inch an hour and is native to those trees, and this part of the world. There's a local lore about those beasts. Want to go see if we can find one?"

Dropping a few Bolivianos on the table, the two made their way, where soon enough they discovered, through a blanket of leafy camouflage, a pair of the brown oddities moving ever so slowly.

"They are beautiful."

"Well, of course they are."

"I mean, truly beautiful. I wish I had my camera with me. I was uploading photos when I left, otherwise I'd have it with me. I wish I could get a closer look."

"It is a Bolivian lover's tradition to come to the square to see the sloths. The locals think it brings a relationship good luck."

"I should bring Ben."

"Yes, you should."

Macy cleared her throat. She wondered what the priest knew. She was aware the pair met at the hospital when she'd been away.

"I take it you've never been here with a woman before?"

"Oh, yes. Many times. Just not that way." He laughed, accepting her ribbing with grace. "This park is the best confessional. You wouldn't believe how many secrets I've heard here, with only those lovely animals above and the grove of trees to serve as witness."

"That must be so strange."

"How so?"

"I'm not certain which part strikes me as more bizarre. The idea of someone coming to you to divulge their sins with the hope of being forever forgiven, or the idea of you having to listen to all of their babbling."

"I like babble."

"And gossip?"

"Sometimes there is a bit of that too."

"Do you ever feel bothered? You must know everyone's deepest fears and secrets. It must be a burden."

"It's hard to understand, I realize. But I've always known this was the work I was meant to do. " He paused, facing her. "I am pretty good at chatting with Bolivians, but it has been many years since I've had regular conversations with Americans. I'm rusty and I'm just not great at reading sarcasm. So . . .are you sure you want to talk about this?"

"I guess we can't help it." Macy shrugged and smiled. "And you'll know when I'm being sarcastic. Trust me."

He smiled and took a deep breath, running his hands through his hair before beginning.

"Yes, does it bother me when I hear of sin repeated. When I hear about behavior I can't imagine happening. When I see a parishioner arrive with his wife covered in bruises only to have him later come into my confessional for some sort of forgiveness. It's hard. I want to protect her. And at the end of the day, I'm still an Irish Catholic kid from New York who may have ended up in the priesthood, but grew up boxing."

"Huh." Macy didn't know how to respond.

They stood a bit longer in silence, watching the couples in the park circle and the sloths above eat their leaves with patient determinism.

"Do you ever want to hit them back?"

"I'm human, Macy. Of course I want to punch the jerks and teach them a lesson. I've got to handle my own confessions from time to time too."

She smiled. "Even the holiest are a bit cracked."

"You want to see what really makes me angry?"

"Yes. Somehow, I do."

Making small talk, they walked from the square past the zoo, over the hill and to the small white church where Macy had originally found the boy ringing the bell. Macy could faintly feel an ache across her knee, but the stitches had been removed and her limp was gone.

"This has been my home for 30 years. I was placed here after things went wrong in Peru.

"So, are you finally going to tell me that story, or are you going to continue to just hint at it in that annoying way?" She smiled. "Wait. You fell in love with a woman? Some gorgeous Peruvian beauty queen, like those Miss Universe girls."

"No."

"Oh, holy shit. You fell in love with a man?"

The priest's wrung his hands, and she watched with regret as his face turned crimson.

"I'm sorry. I didn't mean to be smug. You can tell me. I didn't mean to be a jerk. I just can't imagine why they would ask a priest to leave?" She whispered the words, overcome with intrigue.

"I led protests against the government in the 80s when it was most certainly not popular by our government, or by the church, to do so."

"Protests?"

"The US was funding militia. And they were doing the worst things you can imagine to the women and children they would come upon. They flat out killed the men. But the women and children were held as sick collateral. I'd brought enough attention to what was happening by the time they could find *me,* I was thrown into a van and sent back to the US on the first flight out." He raised his bushy gray eyebrows at this before continuing. "Thankfully, a childhood friend helped me present a strong case on social justice. I was reinstated within a couple years, but warned I wouldn't be rescued next time. Time to work with kids. Not drug lords."

Macy stared at him, her mouth open. "Jesus."

He smiled, "Precisely. You and your husband have the same sense of humor."

Startled by his confession, Macy felt her pace slow. She nodded, wanting to know the priest better.

"No smart retort? Come on, Macy. I thought you were on your game."

"Uh, no father. I'm sorry I made the gay joke . . ."

"Just call me Pete. Please."

"Pete. Thank you."

"You're welcome, Macy. Now, want to see what pisses me off today?"

"Please." She smiled. This man was far more interesting than she'd given him credit for. Macy shook her head. She'd learned this lesson countless times, assuming people were simpletons, when this was the rare exception. He was a priest who talked to God, but he also swore. There was something good to be discovered here.

"Follow me."

He led her behind the small chapel and past the bell tower to a long narrow building with a half dozen doors. As he approached, a cry went up into the air immediately echoed by a torrent of other voices.

"Padre! Padre!"

The doors swung open and children of all ages poured out of the rooms. Macy watched with wonder as raven-haired children of all sizes and shapes swarmed to the priest like birds to St. Francis.

"Macy, these are my kids. Niños, la señora Macy. Digan 'hola,' por favor."

"HOLA SEÑORA."

Macy stood back, shaking her head. These were his children? Then something caught her eye: several of the children had similar features, ones she soon recognized as those of Downs syndrome. A handful of others had a missing limb, or a clubbed foot in a brace. Several bore the telltale facial scar of a cleft palate surgery. Macy feared there were more children whose scars weren't physically visible.

"Please tell them hello for me." She sat down, overwhelmed. Several of the younger girls crawled into her lap. One began to play with her hair. Macy felt sweat gather on her brow and her heart begin to pound.

"You can tell them. Even in rusty Spanish, your smile will do wonders. Repeat after me: 'Hola niños. Como estan?'"

Before she realized what was happening, Macy was parroting Spanish and looking at her only Bolivian friend with new eyes.

"You care for all of these kids? How?"

He just smiled and went back to playing with the little ones in his lap.

The sun grew heavy in the late afternoon sky before she decided to say her goodbyes and find the way home. One of the children raced to ring the bell on the hour and the pair walked back toward the street.

"I don't know what to say." She stuffed her hands into her pockets and rocked back and forth on her feet. "I haven't been around children, but those kids are lovely. I'm not sure I've ever met a group so kind."

"They are special."

"How did this happen?"

"One by one."

"And you care for them all?"

"I provide as much parenting as I can. Their food, clothing and limited healthcare comes from my extended family. It's become a thing to send Christmas gift money here instead." He shrugged.

"Why does this anger you? It is hard to see anything other than the love in this place."

"Their mothers wanted to keep them. None of these kids were left because they were undesired. Most of have twisted limbs, split palates, hearing loss or retardation because of no prenatal care." He clenched his hands into fists. "We're talking about pennies worth of preventive care. And that ape of a president has the gall to go before international communities and say he represents the people. Or the one before him, and the one before him. Did you see those kids?"

"Yes."

"Tell me what you didn't see when you climbed upward toward Entre Rios."

Macy searched her memory. She'd been more interested in getting Fernando to chat than she'd been in noticing obvious public health failures.

"No wells?"

"There is water. People can't live in the hills without water."

"Uh, bad latrines?"

"Yes, but that's not it either. Come on, fancy journalist." His voice rose a bit with the goading.

"The hills. Shit, it was the hills. They were yellow. No green crops."

"Bingo. Lack of access to fruits and vegetables. No folic acid, no healthy spine. Or brain."

Macy thought about the pills she'd taken during her pregnancy. She'd joked the vitamins were horse pills and made gagging noises to get them down in the morning with her sad cup of decaffeinated coffee.

"Why did you show me this?" she said, suddenly feeling very sheepish about undeserved privilege.

"I need your help."

"I don't know what I could do." She spoke barely above a whisper, feeling the weight of shame. "I could barely breathe this afternoon."

"Show the world. Get up in those mountains, show people back home the hills. Show them pregnant mothers. What they are eating. Where they are living. What the babies look like when they arrive. Show the good and the bad. You'll see it all. Then, come back here and show the world there is a community of children here who survive because their mothers wanted them too. They weren't among the discarded."

"Photos."

"Now, you're getting it."

"For foreign donors?"

He smiled. "You can't look at those kids and not care. I won't believe that. I just won't."

"I don't know if I can do that." She swung her hand out and

pointed toward the orphanage, overwhelmed. "It's a huge project. I don't even know how we'd get them published."

"You took a handful of photos last week that thanks to technology are now spread across the globe. Something tells me you'll figure it out. Just try to tell me no." Coyly, he smirked. She'd been set up.

"Damn it."

"And stop swearing. You're going to be around a lot of kids. You're too pretty for those ugly words anyway." This time, he felt his own shame rise as his words fell out without thought. He blushed.

"UGH!" She stomped her feet. "How is this happening? How am I becoming friends with a priest?" She smiled and smirked. "Worse! A priest who won't let me curse! It's a damn . . .darn good thing you drink, Father."

The bell began to toll again, just a few minutes after the hour. Francisco smiled wildly and waved between tugs, a happy teenage boy in love with the noise and clueless to the confusion the sound sent down upon the city at that time.

"Francisco!" The priest leapt back toward the church. Turning quickly he yelled back at Macy, "See you tomorrow, amiga!"

"Damn," she whispered, smiling.

16. SWEET LIKE HONEY

The twisting dirt road from the altiplano to Tarija was among the most deadly in the world, proof found no further than the rusting carcasses of unsuccessful journeys seen littering canyon floors beyond each turn.

Luz tried calming the tense knot in her stomach. She had slipped out in the middle of the night to find a city-bound bus.

Again.

The youngest daughter, the one who had always followed the rules, was quickly becoming La Doña's biggest headache. An unexplained pregnancy, followed by the birth of a child scarred by the sin itself. Her mother had consoled her; this was an unfair punishment for such a good girl, until the day that "good girl" disappeared without a word. One moment she'd been off to tend to her bees, the next she was gone.

La Doña was not pleased.

Luz barely escaped her mother's wrath when she'd returned days later—an anger fueled by the specific anxiety of a missing teenage daughter. Luz told a tall tale of burying her wawa, crying sincere tears of sorrow and loss. Little did her mother know this loss was one of abandonment, not death. In turn, Luz fell into her mother's arms, instead of over her knee.

Now, Luz stared forward, wisely unwilling to feed her nervous stomach the glimpses of bent and tattered vehicles below. She knew this trip would have serious consequences. In her bones, she could feel the weight of a decision to once again flee her village by night.

La Doña was no fool, and patience for her youngest daughter's wild behavior was quickly running dry. Luz still refused to name the father of her child. In turn, her mother castigated her to tending the llamas, keeping her in the hills until she had finally relented, recognizing perhaps some secrets were better kept quiet.

Luz hated to disappoint her mother, but ever since seeing la Americana, she could think of nothing else. More precisely, ever since seeing that woman without her wawa, Luz had become inconsolable. Consumed, her heart beat faster. Luz must find her daughter, even if it meant once again leaving her dear mother distraught.

Bouncing along in an old American school bus, resurrected in South America as public transportation, Luz knew this trip to Tarija would be impossible to explain with lies. She hoped to quickly return to her village with her baby, who she may have to name Lazarus.

She remembered some of the things Henry taught her. How funny it would be the day he did return, the day he came back to the altiplano to see his blue eyed daughter with a man's name.

Luz rested her head on the next seat. The man next to her wove rough yarn through his swollen fingers. Every few minutes, he'd stop his work and dig his hand into a bag of salty, fried yucca coins, licking away the grease before resuming his task. A woman in the next row, wearing a worn brown felt bolero, slept on top of dried bags of corn. A baby cried from the front of the bus, begging for his mother's breast.

The transport was full of hungry rural peasants, dreamers of a better life. Luz guessed that they thought life in the city was more plentiful, and that a much bigger world existed outside of their yellow hills. Listening dutifully to their radios, they would gather at night after simple meals of fava beans and grilled guinea pig to hear the world news, soccer updates and radio novelas. These radio programs captivated the masses, telling stories of romance and adventure far beyond their altiplano. This was what the people of her village did. Didn't everyone dream of life beyond the dusty paths their feet already knew?

Luz entertained herself by creating stories for each of the passengers. They would sell their wares to buy fresh vegetables, fruit and perhaps a mug of yerba buena before finding a bus for a return ticket up the mountain pass. They'd enjoy the sights and sounds of the busy city, ready to recount each detail they could remember to any village neighbor willing to listen. Most rural altiplano Bolivian peasants were lucky to afford the 5,000-foot descent into the city once a year, always hungry for their next turn. By contrast, Luz hoped this was the last time she'd have to see the big, noisy city.

"Miel?" She opened her cloth bag and pulled out several recycled glass jars full of the sweet, amber liquid. "Miel?"

One by one the vendors shook their heads no. They had a local honey supplier. Their glances communicated what would remain unsaid: they didn't need some indigenous girl's dark, dirty honey. She was a colla, after all. An altiplano indio.

Who knew what the bees even ate all the way up there?

The mestizo vendors would prefer the honey from their camba vendors. The camba, those of western Bolivia, were long considered worldly. Better educated. Wealthier. The colla were poor highland farmers. Their skin was darker. They were smaller because of a limited diet. They lived and died by the way of the llamas. A good year for breeding meant more milk and meat. A cold year meant more babies died, and the children who survived struggled to thrive.

These city vendors didn't need to say their thoughts aloud. The colla versus camba rivalry remained fierce, even here in a busy market, where the two ethnic groups combined to create the mélange of Bolivia. Highland people. Jungle people. Germans. Japanese. Spaniards. Quechan. Mennonites. Cubans. And those from other South American countries who'd crossed the border.

The market in Tarija was a microcosm of the continent; those of a dozen shades and sizes, some in traditional pollera skirts, others with a wad of coca leaves fat in their lips, all gathered to meet a universal need: hunger.

Maybe I can find a colla vendor. Someone here must need my honey. It's the best in the region. It's the best in Bolivia!

Luz pulled her shoulders back, unwilling to be restrained by ethnic discrimination.

It was the last stall in the central Tarija market and when she was ready to retreat defeated, she noticed the girl from Entre Rios. Martha was the baker's daughter, there with a trolley's worth of the regional bread. Perhaps it was Martha's long, black shiny hair or her ample chest, but the vendors who'd just turned away the indigena beekeeper were now happily stacking up bolas of the colla bread.

Luz pulled her hat down further over her eyes and quickly hid behind a stack of baskets. The bottles of honey in her bag rattled and her heart pulsed in her ears. What should she do? If Martha saw her, she'd surely send word to La Doña. Luz had arrived only that morning and had yet to sell anything, or come up with a plan to rescue her daughter. She wouldn't have long before her mother would send someone to the capital to look for her. She'd thought of a thousand possibilities: sneaking into the home at night, lighting the house on fire to create a distraction, begging the local mission nuns to help her recover from the biggest mistake of her life.

Prison wasn't an option. She was certain they sent arsonists, but Luz wondered if mothers who abandoned their children were criminals by the law. Certainly, these women were already castigated for life with the punishment of uncertainty.

She'd have to come up with another plan.

Luz followed a faith of coincidence: people came into her life for a reason. This was something Henry taught her, leaving behind several books on new-age theology. She'd picked that doorstep to leave her wawa for a reason. She'd later seen the photographer in Entre Rios for a reason. Martha must be here for some greater reason too.

Sucking her bottom lip and feeling droplets of sweat trickle down her arms under her blouse, Luz emerged from behind the baskets. She carried her bag of honey jars toward the baker's trolley.

"Hola Martha," she started, looking at her feet.

"Qué sopresa!" Martha grabbed the girl by the shoulders and gave her a big squeeze. They continued rattling along in Spanish, their sing-song voices in the tune of teenage girls.

"What are you doing here?" Martha grabbed Luz's bag and peered inside. "Oh, tell me this is from your bees, please? My father started making the most delicious icing from your honey. People everywhere are asking for it. We've been waiting for you to come back to Entre Rios to buy more."

Luz blushed. "Yes, this is mine. My bees are happy. They love this time of year."

"May I buy this? I want all of it. I am going to take it home to my father. He will be so pleased! Are you selling in Tarija now?"

"I. Well. I. Yes. I am selling in Tarija now. But if your father wants the honey, I can see about sending him more instead."

"Oh, would you? We have run out of his sweet salchichas and galletas every weekend. He would be so pleased to know I've run into you. I sent a word to your village, but didn't hear. What a blessing!" Martha smiled a happy, toothy grin. Her chest barely fit into her blouse, the buttons threatening to bust any moment. Staring at the gap between pulling buttons, Luz reaffirmed why the same vendors who shooed her colla honey away were happy to buy bread from Martha.

"You may have this honey. It is all I have with me." Luz stared hard at Martha, remembering how the girl had once bullied her for her lack of faith. Now, an unwed teenage mother to an abandoned child, Luz swallowed what remained of her pride, and tried to keep her voice even. "I'd be happy to sell it to you."

The two went back and forth briefly concerning payment, Martha providing considerably more than Luz could have expected, along with several loaves of small, fresh bread. Luz knew the offer included a long-overdue apology, one that didn't need to be spoken to be accepted.

"I heard of your baby, Luz." Martha didn't make eye contact. "We all know. I am sorry."

148

"Thank you." Luz would not let herself worry about Martha returning to the village with the news of their conversation. She had one mission: to find her daughter.

As the Bolivianos exchanged hands and they bid themselves goodbye, Luz came around a stall corner with a giant smile on her face only to once again be struck dumb by good fortune.

"Blessing, indeed," Luz said under her breath, jiggling the coins in her pocket.

Out of the corner of her eye, she saw the photographer's maid. That dark woman, round like an egg, held a large basket in one hand and a list in the other, just has she had the day Luz left her daughter on the step. She studied the housekeeper carefully, tucking the woven bag under one arm, guarding the bread.

Watching the indigena, Luz realized the burning-down-the-house plan wouldn't work. People could be hurt, and she couldn't let that happen. La Doña would never forgive her for burning down someone's house.

As the maid made her way through the market stall aisles, Luz's interest was piqued by the same quiet conversation Ruth kept trying to initiate. With the butcher, grinding organ meat. With the farmer, guarding tomatoes and oranges placed in precarious pyramids. With the spice vendor, weighing each bit of cinnamon and cumin on a rusty, ancient scale likely rigged in his favor.

"Necesito una niñera. Conoces alquien?"

One by one, the vendors shook their heads no.

"Trusted milkmaids are rare," whispered the woman selling oranges. Luz leaned near, trying to hear every word. "Camba women would never breastfeed a colla baby."

"Ay, that nonsense." Luz heard Ruth say the words with such indignation, she nearly spit. Moving on, the housekeeper stopped to ask a man selling coffee beans by the tin can full. There were burlap bags full of the aromatic beans, lined up by color from rusty red to the darkest of night.

Luz heard Ruth describe the child, feeling her stomach ache with each detail. "Blue eyes, black hair. She's beautiful. And she needs a nanny. She's probably half and half! You must know someone!"

Luz smiled, hesitating grabbing her own breasts in crude delight. It had been several painful weeks but she was certain she'd still be able to nurse a child.

Once Ruth made it past the last stall with her basket bountiful, her plan became obvious.

"Señora. Excuse me but I heard you asking the butcher if she knew a milkmaid?"

Luz felt the woman's eyes take her in from head to toe. Luz's feet were gritty, in sandals she'd borrowed from Carmen. She felt the dust between her toes. Her hands were calloused from hard work. Her teeth were straight, but needed a good brushing.

"Yes. But you will not do." Ruth hurried along, shifting the heavy basket from one hand to another.

Luz scoffed. "But why?"

"I do not have time to explain. More so to a girl who has forgotten her manners."

Luz's face burned. She was right. Speaking to an elder, especially this elder, shouldn't be rushed. She played to Ruth's need for formality and respect.

"Excuse me, señora. But, ma'am, please reconsider. Please. My milk is in, I am a hard worker and I can take on many jobs.

Any job you may need." Luz could hear the desperation in her voice. She held her breath hoping the woman didn't hear it too.

Ruth stopped, turned and looked the young woman in the eye.

"When was the last time you ate, child? And I don't need a wet nurse. This baby can't suckle."

"Yesterday. But I have this bread now. Would you like one?" She reached in her sack and produced two of Martha's bolas.

Ruth sighed. "Where is your child?"

"She. He. He died. Two weeks ago. I'm a beekeeper from a village outside of Entre Rios. I came into the city to sell my last honey."

"And were you successful?" Ruth split open the bread and dug her fingers into the airy center. She lifted the bread to her nose, breathing in the warm, comforting yeast. Crunching and savoring slowly, to Luz's delight, Ruth nodded toward a nearby park bench across the street from the market. Luz grabbed Ruth's basket from the ground, hauling the fruit, eggs and meat with a smile.

"Yes. I just sold the last of it. The bakers love my honey. They say my bees are happy, and happy bees make good honey."

"Child, you can't keep bees in the hills happy if you are looking after a child in the city."

"Oh." In her haste, she hadn't considered who would care for the hive. Then again, the quicker she could return to her village, the better. "My sister will take care of the bees . . ." Luz was thinking quickly. "And the money will be good for my family." Luz took a breath, hoping her next step was a wise one. "I want to go to school, and I won't be able to as a beekeeper.

My father is dead. I am the youngest child. Unless I find a way to pay my school fees, I will be in the hills forever with my hive."

"And do you have brothers?"

"Yes."

"And did they go to school?"

"Most of them, yes. My eldest brothers are stone masons."

"But there is no money for you?" Ruth's face reddened.

"La Doña, my mother, well . . . she doesn't believe in girls going to school. She and the nuns aren't friends. We are to learn to tend the animals and then tend the babies."

Ruth snorted. "And how are you village women to ever be better than your mothers? Do you want to tend animals and children?"

Luz didn't reply, instead looking at her dirty feet. She didn't need to live in a big city to feel important. She only needed her wawa, to feel the weight of that baby in her arms. Happiness had once been in her grasp and she'd foolishly given it away.

"And that baby? How did the baby die?"

Luz paused knowing she would have to commit this lie to memory and repeat it often. Best to keep it simple.

"He died in birth. The cord." Tears gathered in the corners of her eyes, thinking of her wawa. How happy she'd been to hear that first scream.

"Oh, child. I am sorry." Ruth's tone softened. She dug her hand into Luz's bag and pulled out another ball of bread. "These are my favorite, slightly salty and sweet," she paused. "Thank you."

Luz tried to ignore the hunger pains as she watched the last of her bread be eaten.

"I have four boys. They were all born hungry and they still are today. Your next child will be healthy. You'll see."

Luz nodded, letting the tears roll down her cheeks. They sat on the edge of the market, clouded in the diesel from trucks journeying down the adjoining street.

"If you get this job, you'll return to your village and use the money for schooling?" Ruth scowled, her face creasing between her eyes with scrutiny and concern.

Luz's head shot up. "Yes, I will. I promise!"

"Well. I cannot hire you, but I can bring you home and feed you a good meal before the Americans make their decision. Come on, then. Carry this basket for me. And child, what is your name?"

"Luz!" She hadn't had the time to consider an alias.

"Well, Luz, I appreciate your perseverance. Reminds me of a girl I used to know. My name is Doña Ruth Castro."

The two shook hands.

Looking down at the basket, Luz saw it was the same one in which she'd placed her baby daughter weeks prior.

17. 2 CORINTHIANS 5:17

"Well." Macy took a heavy breath.

"I think we needed that." His breath was warm in her ear.

"We did."

She rolled over to stare at her husband. A red flush covered his cheeks and ran along his chest. Macy closed her eyes, pulling the sheet taut over her warm skin. Heavy velvet curtains were haphazardly pulled together, a gap letting in a bit of moonlight across the rug.

"God, Mace." He smiled, out of breath with beads of sweat around his blond hairline.

There was so much to say, and yet no need. She'd come home from Peter's orphanage with a sense of purpose. Over a brief dinner of spicy albondigas soup, and a bottle of red wine, she'd rattled on about the children.

Their wounds. Their happiness. How confusing it was to have the new assignment from the priest. Macy swung her head gently, her long hair shaking behind her as she spoke.

Mid-sentence, Ben stood from the dining room table and took his wife's hand. He led them upstairs and didn't make a sound as he undressed her, and then himself.

For the first time in months, she didn't protest. Macy met

his kiss. In their connection, she felt nostalgia, calm, and a brief taste of the normalcy that could return to their lives. They made love slowly. She was thankful for how gentle and careful Ben was, treading, not diving, back into familiar waters.

Pulling at the sheet, she stared at the ceiling, letting his hand wander and come to rest over her navel. She was thankful there was no physical pain. It felt great to feel his skin against hers. He pulled her to him and the pair fell asleep together, naked. It was the first time they'd been together since Jacob's birth.

Macy couldn't help but smile as she was lulled to sleep by the familiar sound of Ben's deep, baritone snoring.

She awoke to the sound of a lone rooster somewhere in the neighborhood, greeting the sun with all his might at least an hour too soon, Macy guessed. Even in the early hour, the house smelled richly of coffee and something warm, baking with cinnamon. Macy crept out of bed, throwing on a robe and went to the kitchen.

Ruth was nowhere to be found. Macy filled two mugs with coffee and grabbed a plate of cinnamon rolls before anyone saw her half-dressed. Breakfast in bed with Ben. She smiled.

Macy turned on the small lamp next to her side of the bed and read for more than an hour before Ben awoke. She scratched his back as he arched like a cat.

"Remarkable. You really are remarkable." He cracked a smile, pulling her on top of him.

"I made you some breakfast." She motioned toward the side table.

"Uh huh. You aren't that remarkable . . ." They both laughed. "But I'll take it all the same." They sat together picking at the sticky rolls and drinking the warm coffee. She slid out of her robe as he told her details of his work. She talked about the photos hitting the wire and her burgeoning friendship with of all people, a priest. Soon enough, they were once again sighing with relief, holding each other in an embrace.

"What did you decide about the baby?" He'd asked, gently.

She propped herself up, staring at her husband, the passion and relaxation fading as the sunlight grew.

"Now?"

"Well?" he said, running his hand up her side. She could hear the playfulness still in his voice.

"The baby." She sighed, pushing his hand into hers, holding it tight.

"Yes." Ben propped himself up on one arm, turning toward his wife. He studied her face.

"I'm not ready to try again, Ben. I don't even know if we . . . if I can. It hasn't worked once."

Ben took a deep breath.

"I mean the baby girl. The one abandoned. We need to talk about this." His voice was firm but kind. He was not trying to pick a fight. "I don't feel comfortable making decisions by myself on this. And, she's sick, Mace. I spoke with the pediatrician. She made it through the first surgery, but there will be many more." His voice trailed.

"Oh." Her voice softened with relief. "I misunderstood."

"The pediatrician says she'll do better recovering outside of the hospital. Something about crowding and staph infections. And she is a baby. She needs someone to care for her. There was something mentioned about orphans and detachment disorders, but I didn't get it all. They want to know if we would consider being her advocate. Of having her here. I know this is happening fast." He was rattling all of this information off like he'd had too much espresso, even though his coffee cup was still half-full. Had he been thinking of this during sex?

She crossed her arms over her chest. "I don't think you should do that."

"Just like that?" He scoffed.

"Ben. Please. You asked. I do not think you should be that baby's advocate."

"Hear me out, Macy Duncan." He flashed a smile at her—one that had worked countless times before to change her mind. "I've spoken with Ruth. We can hire a local girl to come in and nanny. You won't even have to see her if you don't want to."

"A nanny?"

"Yes. Ruth found her at the market. A local girl who just lost a baby."

"Oh." Macy let out a heavy sigh. He'd said it softly, but it brought tears to her eyes. Women lose babies everyday. She knew that, but wrapped so tightly in her own grief, she'd forgotten she wasn't alone in this sisterhood. Macy considered the weight of a young woman, in her home, who had also recently lost a child.

"The nanny—this girl. She is just a girl. Well, she's here. She is staying downstairs in the maids' quarters for the week. Ruth and I agreed it would be best to let her stay until I spoke with you."

"Ruth and you agreed? Why are you having these conversations without me?" Macy heard her voice turn shrill.

"Mace, come on." He took a deep breath. "I've tried talking to you. I am trying now."

"So, I'm the last one to know. There is a girl living in my house and I don't even know about it?"

Ben jumped out of bed and zipped into pants.

"Wait, Ben. That came out wrong. Wait. Come back here."

He pulled back the drapes, letting harsh morning light flood the room. Running his hands through his hair, he plopped on the edge of the bed.

"It's just . . .I am starting to feel better Ben. I am taking photos. I am going outside. I'm walking. My leg is better. We had sex . . ." She blushed. "I've missed you. Hell, I've missed me."

"I've missed you too."

"So, I can't be tethered to this house to care for a sick child."

"Have I ever tethered you? Are you even capable of being tethered?" He cracked a half smile.

"I am doing what you asked. I haven't even taken a bath in more than a week!" She tried to keep her voice light.

"I can't get the vision of that sick little girl out of my head." He sighed. "Or the others in that hospital." He continued, meekly. "I couldn't do anything to save Jacob, but I can do something with this one. We can do something."

"We don't have to, Ben. Not now." Macy heard the selfishness in her voice. She wanted time for them. She wanted more time for herself. "Please. I feel like I'm just starting to turn this corner. Happy, even."

"I love you Macy." He paused. "But I will not be able to live with myself if I don't do something about that baby. We have to help."

She heard an urgency in his voice.

"I've spent the last 24 hours thinking this over," Ben continued, "weighing how I would ask you to let this happen. And then I remembered I don't always have to ask."

"Like moving us to Bolivia." She tightened her arms across her chest. He'd made that change for their family unilaterally.

"You like it here more than you are willing to admit."

"You're going to leave again. You are going to be out of town, chasing farmers, and leave me with this kid. Kids? And the help! Aren't you?"

"I have to work."

"Yes, but we don't have to have a baby in this house!" she screamed.

Ben scowled at Macy and she knew in that glance this wasn't a battle she was going to win. If time under the sheets wasn't going to put a smile on his face, there was nothing she would be able to say to do so.

"Don't call Ruth the 'help.' It is rude. Why do people keep saying that?" he continued, his tone flat. "That 'help' went with me to the hospital to see the baby the first time. She feeds you. She buys the groceries. And she took care of that baby when you ran off. Ruth has been amazing, Macy." His voice turned grave. "Have you heard her complain?"

"That isn't fair." Her arms remained tightly clutched around herself.

"Life isn't fair."

She grimaced as his voice rose.

"Not for you," he continued, "not for me. Not for the scared woman who left her kid at our door. Not for the kids I have to arrest every day because they are knee deep in coca for some drug lord. And not for our dead son."

Macy put her face into her hands.

"Don't!" She mumbled into her hands, feeling her anger and sadness pulse. "You're not going to fix this, Ben. I'm not going to be bullied into caring for an orphan."

"Too late." He grabbed his shirt.

"What? What do you mean?"

"I've already hired her. The baby arrives tomorrow. I will not turn away a child in need, Macy. Or a young woman who needs a job, for that matter. We don't do that. We aren't those people."

He took a deep breath, giving her a chance to respond. Macy remained silent, with her mouth open.

"I've held her, Mace. She was given to us. I am so stupid that I thought we could actually talk about this. That you'd stop being so fucking selfish for just a second. If you had seen those children yesterday. If you could see them. If you really had looked at her—this would all be different."

"But, Ben!" Macy let out a sob.

"I've done this—coddling, pampering, whatever you want to call it— long enough. I've looked the other way when you rejected me. I've even poured you another bath." She watched as he buttoned up his shirt too quickly, missing a hole. "I can't fix this. I can't fix you, or us. You won't consider help. Go be a photographer. Look at people, connect with others, from a distance. Do what makes you happy."

"Ben. Wait!"

"I'm helping that baby."

As she scrambled to find her robe and chase after him, the heavy front door slammed.

"Ben!"

18. TRINITY

Luz paced in the small room. It was strange to be awake at this hour without the hungry grunts of llamas, and the wind rushing over the hills of the gran chaco. She hadn't packed fresh clothing. Her breasts were no longer producing milk, but a sour smell lingered. Kneading her chest for a moment, she wondered, what if her milk didn't return? Would her wawa recognize her? Would she recognize her baby after the surgery?

Most urgently—could they escape today?

Luz sat on her tidied bed in the maids' quarters. Her hands fluttered, loosening braids and running fingers through her dark hair. Slowly, she combed out the waves. Just as gently, she replaced the plaits, tying them in bundles behind her.

If there was ever a time to pray, this was it. She didn't know how to start the conversation. Looking upward at the off-white ceiling, she folded her hands in her lap as she'd seen the old women at church do. Clenching her eyes tight, one image immediately flooded her vision, the same sight that haunted her sleep the night before. There was her mother, La Doña, waiving her hands at the golden hills, pacing with anger and worry.

Luz's eyes shot open and she felt her chest tighten.

It was time to find her wawa. No need for prayer now. She couldn't let herself think of her mama, or the bees or Henry for that matter.

Slowly, she pulled the bedroom door open. By the faint light entering the room's small cracked window, she guessed daybreak was near.

La Señora Ruth would be arriving soon. Luz would help prepare breakfast. She could use the time to meet the Americanos. Plus, La Señora Ruth told her the baby would be arriving today from the hospital.

Her baby.

They'd paid for surgery! She'd made a funny squeak at the news, trying to contain a teenager's joy. This drew a peculiar look from her new boss, Ruth. The basket baby plan worked!

Her wawa was alive!

As quietly as she could, Luz crept into the kitchen. She'd prepare tea and her one specialty: honey and yucca empanadas. These would make anyone's mouth sing. Entering the dark room, she jumped with fright to hear a man cough and clear his voice. Equally surprised, a man stumbled for the light, flooding the room with electricity.

"Perdon, Señor. No no sabía que usted estaba aquí."

"You. You must be the village girl." He coughed. His voice was rough, like she'd caught him half asleep. "Oh, God. Where are my manners? I don't remember your name. I'm so sorry." A pot of coffee and the morning newspaper were scattered across the small kitchen prep table. The remainder of yesterday's cinnamon rolls sat in a circular pan on the stovetop. Telltale circles joined deep lines around his eyes. His clothing was rumpled and she could smell the beer on his breath from the other side of the room.

"Yo soy Luz." She looked down at her sandals as she moved toward the table, placing one palm on the coffee pot. Lifting the container, Luz looked at the bedraggled man, who was now standing, scratching the back of his head. "Quiere más?"

"Uh. Sí?" He cleared his throat. She realized he couldn't understand much of what she was saying. Luz pantomimed as much as she could, smiling and nodding.

Shuffling, she moved around the kitchen, quickly memorizing the location of utensils and pots as she swung open cabinets. Finally, he pointed toward a door, where Luz discovered a larder of food, more than she could have ever imagined.

She gasped upon entering the pantry.

Large sacks of rice, beans, dried corn, and sugar rested on the floor, each with their own measuring cup balanced on top. Dozens of cans of varied vegetables, fruit, and jam, wrapped in colorful labels in a language she couldn't read, sat stacked on shelves. Jars of oil, some light green like the first weeds of spring. Others dark, autumnal golden. Rows of glass spice jars, most in hues of orange and brown. A bag of pebbly salt.

Finally, Luz's fingers found the metal bin of coffee beans, next to a large glass canister of tea bags. She smiled at the jar of honey. Holding it near the light bulb, she couldn't see a bit of comb. It was too bad she'd sold all of her own honey the day before; it was the best in Bolivia. It would have been nice to leave a jar as a note of thanks for their caring for her wawa.

What was happening to her bees? La Doña would surely take over, using the yucca smoke to slowly put the bees into a daze and extracting the honey and comb. Luz remembered the countless lessons her mother had shown her before one day, simply walking away, handing off the critical aspect of their family farm to her youngest.

Luz shook her head, still tucked in the pantry and out of sight. She had to stay focused! She must win their trust. Once in charge of caring for her own child, she could plan an escape.

Feeling her palms sweaty against the coffee tin, Luz returned to the kitchen, ready to find the mortar and pestle and place the kettle on the fire.

Where was the cooking fire? Was there a garden? And why were the lights in this kitchen so bright?

"Ay, que bueno que estás ayudando. Gracias, Luz." La Señora Ruth took off her sweater, hanging it on a peg on one wall of the kitchen.

"Luz! That's right. I'm sorry I didn't remember. Luz, welcome to our house . . .I don't know what to say. I hope you are doing better." He didn't meet her eye. Luz could feel his sadness.

"Señor Ben, afuera de la cocina, por favor!" Ruth kicked the back of the chair gently, emphasizing her point.

Luz watched with wonder as the owner of the house did as his maid requested, gathering his newspaper and transferring to the next room. He cracked a half smile at the housekeeper as he moped into the next room. They both heard him plop heavily into a chair.

"He's been drinking," Ruth said, refilling the kettle and lighting a match. Luz again watched, amazed, as the pilot light caught, flickering blue. Ruth set the kettle over the flame and grabbed the bean grinder, throwing a handful into the small machine before Luz jumped at the new noise.

Did La Doña know of such magical machinery?

Soon, the kettle was singing, eggs were popping in fat in a heavy cast iron skillet, and a small radio above the sink puttered the morning news, mixed with the occasional Tarija traffic report.

"How did you sleep?" Luz felt the woman's eyes examine her from head to toe. "Did you find the bucket?"

"No, Señora Ruth."

"You need a bath. And those clothes need both a good washing and mending. If not burning. Do you have others?"

"No, Señora." Luz stared at her feet, face burning. She didn't have many other clothes in the village anyway. That sour smell must not have been as faint as she'd hoped. Luz had gone through Carmen's things before leaving, taking the nicest pollera skirt, trimmed with navy blue handmade crochet lace, and a rainforest green button down. She'd never had new clothing, just new hand-me-downs from the many sisters and sisters-in-law who came before her.

"Dios mio. Well, the baby is returning today from the hospital. She'll be fragile after surgery. That poor thing needs our very best care until the gringos figure out what they will do." Ruth stepped back and took a deep breath to convey her annoyance. "You'll need a bath. I'll see about something for you to wear."

"Sí, Señora."

"Oh, stop that. I'm Ruth. There is a señora of the house, and it isn't me. Just call me Ruth. Or Doña."

"Doña." Wisely, she played to Ruth's desire for respect, recalling yesterday's interaction.

"That's better. Also, do not speak in front of the gringos unless you are asked. You are to work, to take care of this child and to stay out of the way. Is that understood?"

"Sí, Señora Ruth. Er. Doña."

Ruth shook her head, hands deep in sudsy water. She motioned toward a towel, handing clean items to Luz.

"Now, let's just see if we can sneak you into La Señora's tub for a good wash. There is only a shower drain in the maids' quarters, without warm water."

Luz watched as her superior, with a plate of eggs, bacon and toasted bread in one hand and a pot of fresh coffee in the other, motioned toward another prepared plate.

"Sit there. Eat." Ruth pointed with her nose at the small table and chairs. "I'll be back, and I have some questions."

Luz barely tasted the eggs, she was so hungry. She added a dash of salt and was wiping her plate with a slice of toast to enjoy all of the fatty yolks when Ruth returned.

"Is your name really Luz?"

"Sí" Luz stayed seated at the woman's gesture as she returned to the sink to wash what remained. Luz sipped a cup of black coffee, feeling the acid and warm meal fight for place in her stomach. She hadn't thought to change her name. No one would know her in this neighborhood.

"And, are you really from the mountains? A colla?"

"Yes, Ruth."

"Why were you in the market yesterday?"

"I was selling my family's honey. We need the money."

"No one buys colla honey in that market. Why were you there?"

"I promise, Doña. My mother asked me to come. We have extra this year and it is the very best. Wet spring. We get more for it in the city." Luz wondered if she added too many details, or if her lies were believable. Thankfully, the housekeeper nodded, wiping her own hands before joining her at the small table with her own cup of coffee.

"And were you successful?"

"Yes, Doña Ruth."

"And won't your mother expect you to return with that money? Does she know you are staying?"

"My mother. Uh." Luz struggled for something clever. Keep the lies simple and believable. They would be easier to memorize. "My mother wasn't happy I had a baby. I told her I would look for work in the city."

"You are not married?" Ruth stared hard. Luz felt her stomach flop. She couldn't create a husband in addition to all of the other lies.

Keep it simple. Keep it simple!

"No. I am not married."

"Ah." Ruth took a long sip of her coffee. "Do you love him?" She raised one eyebrow.

"Oh." Luz stopped to think. Yes, she did love Henry, but he'd left her. Real love didn't abandon. "Yes, I think I did. But he did not love me."

Ruth patted Luz's hand. Her tone softened, if only for a moment. "He probably loves you more than you know."

Luz hadn't let herself spend any time daydreaming of Henry. Once he didn't return from England as promised, she realized her folly. Luz was just another village girl who became pregnant by a charming foreigner.

"How old are you, child?"

"Fifteen, Doña."

"Fifteen," Ruth said, shaking her head. "Fifteen."

"It is better the child died." Luz gulped. It didn't take much to bring up tears discussing the death of a child. Until yesterday, she hadn't known if her wawa was alive! "I will return to my village and be able to go to school now." Tears rolled down her cheeks.

"Oh, Luz. Let's never wish death. It was God's will, not ours."

Both women abruptly turned toward the kitchen door.

Their conversation was interrupted by heavy feet descending the staircase.

"Dios. She's up early." Ruth stood.

"And where are you going?" Ben's voice boomed from the next room, even though his words slurred.

The two women scurried to see what was happening, but they were barely to the door before Macy pushed her way into the kitchen, ignoring her husband at the dining room table.

"Ruth," she said, pulling a thermos out of the cabinet, "I need some coffee and some of that toast. Please." She forced a smile. "I will be with Padre Pedro today if you need me."

Luz watched as the woman she recognized as the village photographer pointed at different items in the kitchen. She was mesmerized by the foreigner, how Macy used her hands in large, sweeping movements to show what she meant. How the American's face was so swollen, she could barely open her eyes. She was also wearing men's clothing—jeans that were too big, a sweatshirt and a backpack with boots. Other than her long, wavy brown hair, the American looked like she was ready to work in one of Potosí's silver mines.

"You. Are you . . . Ruth, is this the new nanny?"

"Señora Macy, ella es Luz."

Luz was shocked silly when the woman suddenly threw her arms around her, hugging her tightly.

"I know we don't know each other. But I am so sorry for your loss." She stopped to sniffle. "You aren't understanding a thing I'm saying, are you?"

Macy leaned back, staring at Luz. Luz could now see the woman had been crying for many hours.

Was everyone in this house sad?

Luz nodded, unsure of anything the woman was saying, hoping Ruth would help translate later.

"I don't want you in my home anymore than I want that baby in my house. But my husband has made it clear he needs to be the hero. So, thank you for being here, Luz." Macy hugged the girl tightly again until Luz let out an unintentional squeak.

"Ruth, have a good day." Macy paused, as though considering her words. Looking through tired, puffy eyes she continued. "And, thank you for being such a help to my husband."

"Now you are thankful? I guess better than never." Ben stood in the doorway. "They don't understand what you are saying. Did you bother to open that Spanish/English dictionary I gave you? And where are you going dressed like that?"

"To work. I'm leaving to work. Sound familiar?"

"Well, you'd better run away again quickly. The baby is arriving soon."

"Do they leave babies with drunks?"

"Hey, at least I will be here!" He stormed back into the dining room.

Luz watched with disgust as the pair screamed at each other. After yet another series of barbs she didn't need to have translated—anger was anger in any tongue—the front door slammed and they heard Ben's work boots thud up the stairs, slamming the bedroom door with equal force.

"Is it always like this?" Luz paced in the kitchen.

"No." Ruth shook her head. "I've been worried the señora was sick. And I've never heard Señor Ben raise his voice. Oh, Lord. There is a darkness in this home. They know your sorrow. Mercy, me." Ruth crossed herself.

Luz wondered what sorrow she was describing. Had they lost a child? She didn't dare ask any questions, or speak unless necessary.

They remained in the kitchen, saying nothing for a few minutes, letting the house settle and anger in the room dissipate. The music started again after the morning radio news, breaking their trance.

"Child, let's get you in the tub. God knows when she plans on returning, and that baby is going to show up any moment. I'll go through the extra closet downstairs and find you some new things to wear. Oh, and I need to get those bottles sterilized." Ruth placed a hand on her head. Luz got the feeling the woman's work was never finished.

"Bottles?"

"The baby had surgery on her mouth," Ruth explained, not knowing the teenager knew the child's injuries better than anyone. "You may have to spoon or bottle feed her."

"Oh." Luz had been deeply disappointed to hear the day before that she wouldn't be able to breastfeed. But her daughter would live!

"Don't look too blue. You're still responsible for keeping that child alive. You'll just be using these." Ruth placed glass baby bottles in a pot of water, lighting the flame before tiptoeing the two carefully upstairs.

Pouring the hot bath, Luz watched in awe as the water steamed. She hadn't had to carry firewood, haul well water or beg for time alone. Within minutes, she was submerged with a new bar of soap, her very own! Before Ruth retreated, Luz caught the housekeeper looking over shoulder, smiling.

"Thank heavens some darkness is easier to wash away."

Luz sighed happily, sinking into the sudsy water,

imagining holding her wawa. As the brown water drained away, she scrubbed her head with the towel before combing her long hair into new, shiny braids. She examined her figure in the mirror, having never seen herself fully naked before. She could have stood there for hours, mesmerized by the sight until she heard a bell ring downstairs.

"Luz, the baby is here!" Ruth called.

The girl couldn't dress fast enough in the borrowed clothing: a long skirt, t-shirt and lightweight hand-knit yellow sweater.

She arrived downstairs after drying off the floor and tub. A visiting nurse transferred the precious bundle into Ruth's arms. A basket of medical supplies and medicine rested at the housekeeper's feet.

"Here, child. Your charge has arrived." Ruth cradled the infant and stepped toward the teen.

Luz couldn't fight the tears, ones she hoped the others mistook for grief. She carefully wrapped her joyous hands around the baby. The wawa took one look at her mother through those long, dark eyelashes and let out a coo.

"She likes you already," the nurse said.

Ignoring the fresh scar, and the baby's dangerously fragile frame—she'd lost considerable weight—Luz's tears fell on her daughter.

"She's perfect."

"Welcome back, little one," Ruth said, as the baby wrapped her fingers around the maid's pinky.

19. VITAMIN B

"Did you find any leads?" Padre Pedro bounced a bubbly toddler on his knee, keeping an eye on a handful of other children in the yard. A single soccer ball and two homemade goal posts kept the older ones entertained. Macy looked, but there was no sign of the bell-tolling Francisco, or "Quasimodo," as she'd secretly nicknamed him.

"No leads yet, but I am sure my friend Sam will help." Macy ran a soft cloth over a lens. She'd filled the backpack with camera equipment, nestled between several soft, cotton t-shirts. Ben's NAU sweatshirt was smuggled out of the house at the bottom of the bag.

"What's the plan?" He smiled. "We could always start with a prayer and blessing of the project?"

"Uh." Macy squirmed.

"I'm kidding, Macy." He poked her gently. "Take these photos and we'll let God do the rest. I don't need to badger you into prayer. Plus, your work speaks for itself. How did the photos of Entre Rios go over in the States?"

"I haven't heard much, but the paycheck hit my account a couple days ago. I suppose they are on the wire. You just never know who is going to see them on that kind of assignment."

"That's what we need with these photos. 'The wire.'" He made air quotes with one hand, still holding the baby with the other. "Front page. *New York Times*!"

"Good grief." Macy laughed. "Wouldn't that be nice? I'd love to just drop photos off and say, 'Send these to the *Times*!'" She knew she'd have to call in a favor with Sam just to get the shots published at her former community newspaper.

"Think big." He smiled, hopping up. "Let's get the kids lined up. Want to start here?"

"Jesus. I mean. Stop! Just wait a second Father. I'd prefer to not line anyone up quite yet." She took a deep breath and gathered herself. Macy appreciated his enthusiasm, but working with children took time. Otherwise, she'd end up with memory cards full of photos of kids looking right at her, posing, and sticking out their tongues. Some behaviors were inherent, regardless of culture. Macy would have to build their trust and hang around long enough for the orphans to forget she was there.

The school was a simple collection of small rooms, linked by a central corridor. The floors were stained cement, cracked here and there, but painted with bright yellow lines delineating a lane for children in wheelchairs. A lone bulletin board in the hallway had an annual calendar with each child's birthdate. There were a few photographs of the kids, and one of Padre Pedro wading into a river with a boy dressed in white.

"I'd like to spend a day just watching," Macy said. "For the best shots, to really get the story, I need the kids to be willing to ignore me."

"Ignore you? And you said you weren't faithful!"

"What? You lost me."

"It will take nothing short of a miracle to have an

orphanage full of mentally and physically handicapped children ignore an exotic stranger with a backpack full of even more interesting objects."

"You'd better start praying then." She raised one eyebrow, smiling. "You're the one who wants this story, remember?"

Padre Pedro raised his free hand, shaking his head and laughing from his belly. "Fair point. You're the boss. And you know if these only end up framed on my desk and sent out with next year's Christmas cards, we are still better off. Gracias, Macy."

"My pleasure. I need a project right now anyway, according to my husband."

He raised an eyebrow. "Everything okay at home?"

"No, but I don't see how it can be any worse than what we've already survived." She said it under her breath, but he nodded, an expert at hearing what people wanted to admit, but didn't want to discuss. "I'm going to wander."

"Enjoy yourself! You know where I'll be if you need anything!" He winked at her, and she laughed as he flushed red and winced.

"Sorry."

"Awkward." She giggled. "You forget I'm here too."

"I'll do my best. Thanks for being patient."

It was her turn to nod encouragement. Macy watched the priest wander over to the group of boys playing soccer, their physical disabilities not impeding their joy for the game. Soon enough, he had the soccer ball under one arm, still carrying the toddler under the other. The boys filed into the building. Francisco ran off to toll the bell on the hour, as instructed. Macy noticed he did so with precision: 10 rings.

She stood in the shadow of the building, watching one of

the older girls with Down's carrying handfuls of toddlers into another room. Carefully, trying to blend in as much as she could, Macy followed the stream of children. Several of the kids who were of elementary-school age used crutches, dragging a limb.

Inside the long series of rooms on the south side of the small chapel and bell tower, Macy found dormitories and a clump of playrooms. She nodded to a worker, a woman with a broom sweeping out the bedrooms and tidying sheets. Macy passed a nursery with a huddle of bubbly toddlers and two infants rocking in archaic timer swings. One of the infants had splints on his tiny feet from a club foot surgery. The other child's eyes were crossed, although Macy noticed she giggled from the swinging, unaware. From the next room, she could hear Pedro's voice, booming.

"Buenos días clase! Hoy vamos aprender nuestra alfabeto."

"Otra vez?" A small boy with a deformed arm leaned forward in his seat. Again? Again we must learn the alphabet?

"Mida, Rogelio, vas a la escuela pronto. Tienes que esperar hasta la siguiente operación. Después vas a la escuela propio. Está bien, querido?"

"Está bien, Padre." The little boy sighed. Macy had no idea what was said, but the child's disappointment was palpable.

She slid into the back of the room, trying not to disrupt the flow. The priest stood at a scarred blackboard with a long piece of chalk in his hand. The alphabet and numbers one through ten were drawn on the board. Even though she was quiet, the presence of a foreigner in their classroom was like dangling catnip before a box of kittens.

Chatter and giggles arose in a cloud of curious childhood happiness.

"Basta, por favor!" Padre Pedro rapped his knuckles on the desk. Macy listened to his quick Spanish; she imagined he explained who she was—certain only of hearing her name sandwiched between several sentences. Finally, other than a few peeps of excitement, the room quieted.

"So much for blending with the shadows, huh?"

"I'm sorry," she whispered. The children let out a few more giggles.

"No need to whisper," he loudly whispered in return. "They can all see and hear you."

She laughed. The children let out a cry in return.

"Just sit in the back and interrupt me when you have questions. We are reviewing the basics again. I want all of my children to leave literate, and with a handful of life skills. We do the same lessons many, many times."

Macy nodded, slinking into a small chair. She listened to the lesson continue. Patiently, he pointed to each letter and asked the group for the sound. Rogelio, in the front row, was the loudest. She watched keenly as he propped his head with the stump of his deformed arm, and tapped a pencil on his desk with the other.

"Ahhh! Beeeeh! Seeeeeh! Deeeeh!"

He was quite obviously bored and tired of the repetition. This kid knew his alphabet, at least phonetically. Macy wondered if sitting in the rudimentary classroom would help her pathetic Spanish skills. She should have brought a notebook. Looking around, she realized, she should have brought notebooks for all of them. Some of the children held pencils, few had paper or other supplies.

Most of the children continued to stare at her, unable to focus on the lesson.

"Father. I have an idea," she interrupted. "Offer them a prize to pretend I'm not here."

"A prize?"

"What would work? What do they love?"

The priest stopped for a moment before a large smile took over his face.

"Ice cream, if you are serious. They only get that expensive treat every couple years when my siblings come to visit."

"Tell them I will bring the entire class an ice cream party tomorrow if they can pretend I am not here. If they pay attention to you, not me. Will this work?"

"Ice cream always works."

"Let's do it!"

He laughed and made a scooping movement with his hands as he relayed her offer in Spanish. There was a quick outburst of laugher and cheer before promptly the class looked forward, some snapping their bodies to attention. The priest continued his lesson, now with complete command of his audience.

Macy took a deep breath, unzipping her backpack. She knew the bribe would last only so long. She needed to work, and do so quickly. She placed the camera body in her lap, gently unrolling one of the lenses from a t-shirt. Snapping the lens into place, removing the cap, and staring through the crosshairs—she examined each child from head to toe.

Macy rose from her seat, walking the room's perimeter.

There were 11 students. Three had Down syndrome, including Francisco, aka: Quasimodo. Five children were either missing a limb or had notable disfigurement. Several others had the telltale scar of cleft palate repair. One little girl wore an eye patch.

She clicked the shutter, again and again. The kids continued to stare forward, as she pushed a bit closer. By the end of the lesson, she'd taken portraits of each child from different angles. She knew this was insufficient. Anyone could take a headshot. She had to continue the story and capture photos that would tell why this school was important.

Different.

Transcendent.

It wasn't until later that evening, sitting alone with a glass of wine at her dining room table, that she noticed what each of the students had in common. While their ages, height, and skin tones varied considerably, she had at least one photo of each child smiling. If she hadn't captured these images, her cynicism would have kept her from believing what they showed: these were happy kids.

Macy put down her camera, wiping the viewfinder, and poured herself another glass. The freezer was full of ice cream from the Lebanese grocer. She'd even found Hershey's syrup and sprinkles for tomorrow's celebration.

Tomorrow.

It felt good to have something to look forward to. She'd come home to a quiet house. Ben and Raleigh were gone again to Santa Cruz, per a sticky note on the bathroom mirror. In turn, she drank the bottle of Malbec she'd bought as a peace offering. Swirling, watching the telltale veins of a good red wine slide down the edges of the glass to pool at the bottom, she wondered if her husband was still angry.

Ben had angered so quickly, his words still rattled around in her head.

"Life isn't fair."

In the midst of such a busy day, Macy hadn't stopped to

think of Jacob. It was the first time she could recall in more than a year that her entire day hadn't been consumed by the thoughts of their son. The first eight months, in preparation for his arrival, the last few in mourning. The realization struck as she sat staring at the wine glass, twirling the base between her fingers.

Is this what it felt like to move on? The pain was there, bubbling on the back burner if she wanted access. But after today, it was a little further away, and as hesitant as she was to admit it, there was relief in the distance.

It felt good to be a photographer again, not the woman crying in the tub. Holding her camera, admiring each of those children, she remembered who she was.

Macy waited for the stream of tears, but tonight they would not come.

Neither Ruth nor Luz bothered her as she reviewed photos for hours on both her camera and laptop at the dining room table. When Macy walked through the door hours earlier, Ruth had a pot of soup ready on the stove, which she served with a plate of empanadas, like those Macy savored in Entre Rios. Macy noticed these were sweeter, with a honey glaze.

Macy opened her browser, searching for birth defect information in Bolivia. What were the causes? Was there a way to prevent these illnesses? What was the social situation that left so many kids abandoned at a church?

Or at her doorstep.

She looked away for a moment. Where was that baby? Were Ruth and that young girl taking care of her? She hadn't heard a single cry since arriving home.

That baby. That basket baby had one of these deformities too.

The photos on the first few sites made her nauseous. Children with gaping holes just above their tailbones from extreme Spina Bifida. Infants with one eye. Premature infants born with their intestines exposed. Hundreds of photos of cleft palates in varying degrees of severity.

She slammed the laptop closed.

At least Jacob had been born whole. In one piece. It could have been worse.

Macy gulped what remained of her glass of wine.

Tomorrow.

Tomorrow she would learn each of their names. These were the stories Macy was meant to tell.

20. AGONY

Luz cradled her wawa on her chest, as she'd done the weeks prior to arriving in Tarija. Carefully, she moved around the kitchen with the broom, sweeping and rocking. She was more concerned with the movement than her productivity. If she swayed just so, her daughter would stop fussing and fall back to sleep. Plus, Ruth's meticulous housekeeping rarely left a crumb out of place in the tidy kitchen. Dinner simmered from pots and pans on the old stove.

Luz couldn't bear to hear her daughter's raspy, gurgling cry. The noise whistled through sutures closing the infant's upper lip. The taught stitches also ran along one side of the baby's right nostril. Anyone near the child could hear her discomfort with the wheezing of each breath. It wasn't just the after effects of surgery, for which her wawa was receiving regular doses of pain medication, but the arm restraints that kept her from touching the wounds.

The baby still flailed, days later, with an optimism seen only in children—ever hopeful one of her arms would come free.

For Luz, watching this constant struggling was worse than any pain she ever experienced. Worse than the time she was kicked in the face by a llama, which she had foolishly startled. Worse than when her cousin mischievously struck the side of her hive, leaving Luz with welts and fat fingers for days, having retrieved one angry bee at a time from her long braids. Listening to her daughter in agony was even worse than the blinding pain she'd endured months earlier, when giving birth on her mother's clay kitchen floor.

Bang! Bang! Bang!

Luz jumped, startled from her daydream by the heavy iron knocker striking the front door. Her daughter whimpered from the tussle. Luz heard Ruth greeting visitors, inviting them into the house.

"Luz, come please. Bring the baby!" Ruth commanded from the front room.

With hesitation, she made her way from the kitchen to find the group.

Who could be waiting for her?

A pair stood as she entered the room. Ruth introduced them quickly before motioning for Luz to unwrap the baby from her chest and hand her to the woman, a physician. The man, introduced as a local priest, nodded, watching the child intently. Luz saw a kind smile in his eyes at first sight of her baby.

"The wounds look clean, and there are no signs of infection. It seems you've found the right nanny for the child." Doctora Claudia held the baby under the light of the dining room table, carefully examining the sutures. "It isn't easy to care for a child in such pain. Is she eating well?"

"Yes, ma'am." Luz looked at her feet.

Women could be doctors? The only women to ever come to her village clinic arrived with bags of immunizations and pamphlets about nutrition and maternal health. The health promotoras were mocked loudly; few villagers were capable of reading the handouts, much less willing to take birth control advice from city women.

"You know you aren't to breast feed her," the doctor raised an eyebrow. "I understand you recently lost a baby."

Luz's face flushed. Her ears burned with the strange realization strangers knew, and believed, her lies. "Yes. I was told," she muttered.

Even though Luz wasn't certain she could produce more milk, there was a special intimacy in the action she missed dearly. She often dreamed of holding her wawa this way, singing lullabies and stroking her black mop of hair as the child suckled.

"Child, look at me. I am not scolding you. You've done an excellent job of helping soothe this poor babe for the last few days. And I am sorry for your loss."

"Thank you." She met the woman's eyes, noticing the doctor's short salt and pepper hair. She didn't wear any makeup or jewelry. Her clothing was simple and modest.

Maybe you had to be like a man in a man's job?

"You must give her formula and medicine by spoon," the doctor reviewed, as if Luz hadn't been doing as much for the last few days. It was a tedious, lengthy process to place each spoonful of formula into the babe's mouth without grazing the wound. "The stitches on the roof of her mouth are tender. Fragile, even. You must be very, very careful."

"I promise." Luz tried to keep her voice flat, hiding her annoyance. Instead, she examined the priest standing next to the doctora. She wondered if the foreigner understood their rapid Spanish, and was pleasantly surprised when he entered the conversation.

"She will have to come back to the hospital at the end of the week to have these sutures removed, and we'll see how she progresses over the next several months. She will need more surgeries as she grows. Some children need them every few years," the doctor tapped her foot. "But this first one is the most important. It will hopefully keep her alive."

The American men Luz had met in the last few days were different from Henry. Both the priest and Señor Ben dressed shabbily, even by village standards. And they didn't seem to wash as often as they should. Luz studied the priest's face, taking in the heavy bags below his eyes, the hair growing out of the mole, the graying temples.

"Alive?" Luz asked, barely over a whisper. "What could happen?"

"Well," the physician cleared her throat and forced a smile, "she may not be able to speak properly, if the palate doesn't repair correctly. She will likely have chronic ear infections. We may consider tubes in the future if the Duncans, or the next guardians, are willing to also see her through this. And we want to reduce the visibility of the scar as much as possible, simply as a courtesy. She is beautiful now, and she will be beautiful always." The doctor gently ran a gloved finger over the baby's lips, listening as she whimpered.

"The next guardians?" Luz asked as timidly, stepping next to the doctor, grabbing her daughter's hand. Luz panicked. Hadn't this family agreed to care for the baby? What was the agreement?

Maybe she could have her daughter back after all, even if she had no idea why an ear would need a tube, much less how she would manage to provide such a thing.

"You aren't out of a job quite yet. Just make sure to stay on top of the pain medication. Unlike our older patients, she won't be able to tell you when she is suffering, other than this raspy whine. If she develops a fever, or you are concerned about her health at all, immediately bring her back to the hospital and have me called." The doctor pulled out a small instrument Luz didn't recognize and peered into the baby's ears. "We are lucky the Duncans agreed to keep her here. She'll do better, and her chances of infection are much lower within this setting."

"I wish the kids at my house had such great care." The priest put a hand on Ruth's shoulder, interrupting the doctor. "Are the restraints bothering her?" He looked to Luz.

"No, Father."

Of course they were bothering her! She was an infant with her arms being held at her sides most hours of the day. *My poor wawa.* Luz desperately wanted to cry. She bit hard on the inside of her mouth.

"Are you taking them off one at a time and allowing her arms to move for a few minutes every other hour?" Claudia spoke as though she was rattling off a checklist.

"Yes, señora. Señora Doctora." Ruth, Claudia and Pedro laughed at her kind deference.

"You really are doing this child a favor. You both are." The priest smiled with a wide, toothy grin.

"Ay, Padre. We are just doing what we should do. Who leaves a sick child? I don't understand this city." Ruth shook off the praise, scowling. She let the baby wrap her tiny fingers around one of her own. "It is shameful." Luz was stung by the housekeeper's judgment, wincing at the words.

"Thank goodness the mother left the child here. She did this baby a favor, Ruth." The priest's voice rose as he spoke.

"Yes, well. How is this country supposed to improve when women can just leave babies on doorsteps? I don't care if we have an indigeno for President. This isn't right. It is a disgrace. And it has been happening since my mother was a little girl." Ruth shook her head. "I can't imagine leaving one of my sons."

"It has been happening since Moses," the priest reminded gently. Everyone laughed politely.

"This child's mother thought she was doing best by her daughter to leave her, just like the women who leave their children with me at the orphanage," he continued. "These aren't easy decisions. But like the mothers that came before Solomon, sometimes you must sacrifice your own happiness to save the life of your child. That is what this mother has done."

"You are married?" The doctor asked Ruth, examining the baby and notably changing the topic.

Luz watched with curiosity and a tiny smirk, as it became Ruth's turn to have telltale crimson cheeks.

The older woman stammered. "I. Well." She sighed. "No, I am not married."

"Oh, pardon me. I just assumed because you said you have boys. Excuse me."

"We never married, but I have four boys. Now, if you'll excuse me, I have dinner on the stove. Will you be staying?"

"No need, Ruth. We have other children to check on at the orphanage." The priest reached again for the housekeeper's shoulder, giving it a reassuring squeeze. Luz watched, wondering what he knew. "And you are right. We do need to stop the basket babies. The good news is" he smiled, the corners of his bright eyes gathering in crinkles "I have a feeling Señora Macy may help."

"Ha!" Ruth made the noise aloud unintentionally,

immediately covering her mouth with shocked shame. "I. Well, we saw some of the photos, Padre." Luz watched the housekeeper shift her weight from one foot to the other, nervously.

"Did she show you? They are quite good." The priest overlooked the housekeeper's careless remark.

Luz also squirmed, ready for the doctor to return her child. She had continued to clutch the baby's hand during the examinations, a gesture she hoped would be perceived as protective, not possessive.

"Well, she didn't actually show us. I noticed them when serving dinner the other night. On her computer."

"She's with the children now. We will just see what she can do. I have a good feeling about her, Ruth. Remember, we all need a bit of grace." The priest winked as Ruth looked at her feet.

"What about Señor Ben?" The priest looked upward, craning his head. Luz guessed he was trying to hear if anyone was upstairs.

"Señor Duncan is in Santa Cruz with Señor Raleigh," Ruth said. "Something about the coca leaf. I'm not sure. If you'll excuse me, Luz can finish here. I'm afraid the picante de pollo might be burning!" Ruth smiled as she left, but Luz noticed the housekeeper was still flushed from the conversation.

Even a poor country girl knew better than to speak out of turn about her employers. Such comments were not tolerated, and Luz guessed Ruth couldn't afford to lose her position, with four mouths at home to feed by herself.

Life was always more complicated than it seemed at first blush.

The doctor carefully returned her wawa. Luz didn't

hesitate. She tucked the infant into the sling over her shoulders, making sure her daughter's hands were still secured.

"How much longer with these restraints?"

"We can talk about that when you bring her in to have the sutures removed. We should be able to ease them then, but I still can't let her touch her face. It is so much more difficult with surgeries on children at this age. Older children you can convince to leave their wounds alone. Babies. I've always said the restraints are harder on the mothers than the patients!"

The doctor and priest laughed. Luz tried not to cry.

She had no idea.

No one could help ease her burden.

"Thank you, doctora, for the surgery." Luz whispered. Claudia nodded, her face unchanged.

"You are welcome. We are lucky the Americans agreed to pay for her care. Who knows where this young one will land next, but at least she will be in better shape." The doctor patted the baby's bottom through the sling and headed toward the door. The priest followed in turn. She saw them off, with plans for another check up in a few days.

Quietly, Luz returned to the kitchen. Ruth stood at the stove, stirring a pot of caldo, humming to herself. Luz noticed a long line of colorful laundry blowing on the line outside. Music sang from the small kitchen radio over the sink.

Luz looked down, into the eyes of her daughter. The infant squirmed left and right trying to once again get as comfortable as possible in the sling, with her arms wrapped to her small body.

Stepping away into her room, Luz whispered her promises to the baby once more.

"Just until you are well, my love. Just until you are well.

Then we will return to La Doña and . . . Your mama is clever, love. I found a way to save you! I will find a way to explain. We will find a way to be happy. You will have better. You will be better."

She stroked the baby's head, singing the words again and again until they took the melody of a folk lullaby. "My sweet wawa."

21. COMMUNITY

"Macy, they were good, but don't you think if I could pull strings at National Geographic, I'd be working for National Geographic?"

She twirled the long phone cord with one hand and bit at the cuticle of her thumb on the other.

"It's just. Sam, you have to see these kids. I can't explain it. I can't tell you how important this is." She grimaced, hearing her own whine. They had been on the phone for 20 minutes. It had taken her two days to get him to finally return her call; he had been covering a forest fire, and he fell all over himself with apologies once they finally connected.

"Your last assignment did well on the wire, Mace. Is this about money? I can send you money."

"Sam, have you heard a single thing I've said? No, this isn't about money. I mean, if you want to send some—I'll give it to my friend Pedro, who will put it to good use."

"How much do you need?"

"Sam."

"Macy, are you okay? Your mom says she hasn't heard from you in a month."

"She's being dramatic. We emailed last week."

"You should call her."

"Sam! Come on!" Macy sighed, throwing one hand in the air, still clutching the phone between her chin and shoulder. Was it last week? Or maybe the week before? She remembered the questions better than the timeline: When are you having another baby? How is Ben? When can I come to visit?

Sam's laugh was punctuated with a small snort. During their handful of years of working together in the newsroom, her mother had shown up regularly to check on her only child. Macy suspected there was more to the visits—that maybe the two sworn singletons had a thing for each other. If anything ever had happened, mercifully they kept it quiet.

"Listen, this isn't about money. Sam, there are kids in this country dying from stupid diseases. I mean, really stupid diseases. Things we stopped a hundred years ago in the States. And no one knows. From what I hear, some of these villages are so remote, antibiotics are a rarity. Antibiotics." She repeated the word gruffly, the exasperation heard in each syllable.

Again, Sam laughed. They'd covered antibiotic resistance cases that kept popping up at the local hospital in Flagstaff; one college student had lost her arm from rare flesh-eating bacteria after coming in for stitches. The accident had been routine; she'd taken a tumble on the ice and needed fewer than a dozen stitches on her wrist. A week later, the arm was amputated at the elbow, leaving the hospital administration scrambling.

Before the family signed a non-disclosure, Macy's series of photos, of the student and a few hospital workers willing to blow the whistle on poor sterile practices, went national—her first. Reluctantly, it was even picked up by their rival newspaper in Phoenix. She'd won an award from Associated Press for the work, and scorn from many. These nurses and paramedics were their neighbors, after all. A few weeks after accepting the award, she delivered Jacob in the same regional hospital. If he hadn't been born dead, she would have been forever suspicious.

"Good grief. Not antibiotics again." She heard his deep, raspy laugh.

"No, no. Not exactly." Macy had a whine to her voice when she wanted something from Sam. He was her surrogate father. She'd gone as far as leaving Father's Day cards on his desk after her internship. He never acknowledged them, but they would go up on display in the windowsill for a few weeks.

"Bolivians are poor and have shitty life expectancies. Sadly, this isn't news, darling," he continued. "Especially to the good folks over at National Geographic."

"Sam, you have to see these kids." She rocked from foot to foot, once again wearing running shoes. She hadn't bothered asking Ruth to wash them after her fall. The blood gave character. She was always looking for these sorts of oddities when photographing. Her shoes were a clue to a bigger story. No one wore spotless tennis shoes in Tarija anyway.

"Send me the photos," he said. She could tell by his voice he was frowning. "I just can't promise you anything. Photos of kids in an orphanage aren't special. Even your photos."

This was his "asshole tone"—the voice Sam took when his staff misbehaved. Macy rarely had it levied her direction.

"You will feel differently when you see these shots. When you get to know these kids."

His disdain clattered across the newsroom floor, thousands of miles away.

"You do not get involved! Isn't that the first rule? You do not care about the subjects, Mace." His voice rose.

"I still don't have any bumper stickers!" She responded with a nervous laugh.

"That's because you don't have a bumper. You leave my newsroom at the top of your career and find an orphanage full of causes you've gotten involved with? Did I teach you nothing?"

"Sam, I didn't mean to. But . . ." Macy hesitated. He was right. "I know. I'm pathetic. I have gotten involved with the subjects. But you know what I haven't done? I haven't thrown myself in front of a bus. Or slit my wrists."

"What? Why would you say that? Why even joke? Is it that bad? Really? Mace. God almighty! What is going on down there?"

She took a deep breath. "Now I'm being the dramatic one. It's just—well, Sam. It's been a dark period."

"Where is Ben? Are you alone?"

"He's working. Look, I'm fine. I'm just . . . Being at the orphanage means I am out of the house. I'm working. I have my camera in my hand every day and I'm staying up late editing and . . ." Her arms were shaking with the admission. She'd considered ending it all more than once. The black gloom that clung to her every thought was so thick after Jacob's death, it had a taste. A stale, acidic bile that sat in the back of her throat, constantly making her ache.

"I just remember what it feels like. To be a photographer. To be me. It is a gulp of fresh air." Biting too hard, pulling skin from the cuticle, Macy drew blood. Smarting, she shook her head, knowing better. She continued, in a lower voice. "Sam?"

"I'm here. I'm listening." He whispered, the anger gone.

She wondered if he was holding off tears. She hadn't meant to scare him.

"I don't sit around thinking about him all day. Jacob. You know what they say—you help yourself by helping others? Well, that trite nonsense is apparently true."

"What about Ben? What does he say about all of this?"

"Oh, Ben isn't saying much to me these days." She said it without considering her words. Throwing a hand over her mouth a moment too late, she knew immediately the line, among others, would be repeated to her mother, and the storm of concern it would brew.

There was silence on the other end of the line.

"We will be okay, Sam. I love him, and God knows that man loves me. He's off working in Santa Cruz. There have been riots over the coca crop and he's been very busy. We'll find each other." There was some deep, superstitious canyon in her psyche that spoke up on occasion; the moment her husband stopped loving her, she would know. There would be a flood of anxiety.

She would feel it. Life itself would feel different. Broken. Unanchored.

Like it did when her father left.

When Jacob died.

"Do it sooner than later, Mace. That man does love you."

"I know."

It was her turn to let the silence linger until they both heard the rattle of the long-distance static on the line.

"I need a different angle if I'm going to do anything with these other than run them in the Sunday travel section," Sam continued, clearing his throat. "Why would people in Flagstaff care about a house full of sick kids in Bolivia?

Fundamentally, why should they give a shit? Theoretically, sure they care. These folks go to church and all. They run charity 5k races. They care superficially. Make them care emotionally and I'll find a way to run these elsewhere. I could call someone down south too. Maybe the Vapid Valley would want to see Bolivia . . ."

"A different angle. Hmm . . ." She sucked at her thumb, tasting copper pennies in the back of her mouth. She could hear Ruth in the kitchen, putting on another pot of coffee. "I can do this. Do I have a deadline?"

"A deadline? I didn't ask you for this work! I am not some National Geographic pimp. I wish I was, but you think too highly of my abilities. Don't get your hopes up, even for Phoenix coverage." He chuckled.

"It feels good to hope, Sam."

"Shit. I know. I'm sorry. I want you to have hope, doll." He let out something that sounded like a frustrated howl. "But, for Pete's sake, just be careful. Okay? You were my best photographer not just because of your eye, but because you didn't get attached."

"I'm still your best photographer." She smiled. The words felt good rolling off her tongue. Her confidence was returning, one shot at a time. "It is different now. You'll understand when you see them."

She heard him sigh, and the distinct metallic tapping of a pencil against the old rusty desk in the newsroom. She imagined him sitting halfway on the edge, swinging one leg.

"I'm worried about you, Macy. Call me more often. Collect, even. Okay?"

"Thank you, Sam. You know I adore you. Tell my mama hi for me?"

"One favor at a time, darling. You can call your mother!" He hung up the phone.

She listened as the dial tone hummed. Sam was not fond of saying goodbye.

She knew her request was a struggle for the newsman. He loved her like a daughter. The loss of Jacob shook them all. But she also suspected her first and only mentor would be more than willing to "play the asshole" as long as it took to remind her of the pledge of indifference any great journalist must take.

You can be committed to a cause by covering it, but you cannot take a side.

A different angle. If anyone could help her sell the emotion, and a call to action, it would be that persuasive priest. How had he spurred her to get involved? The last thing she'd wanted just a few weeks ago was to speak of children. Today, more than a dozen called her by name, and an infant was recuperating in her own home from a surgery she unwittingly helped finance.

Not that she believed in God, but if there was one, he'd given Padre Pedro magical charm. He had been so good at talking her into a task she didn't want to do, she wondered why his pews weren't brimming each Sunday.

Gathering her backpack full of gear, and pulling on a sweatshirt to face the brisk spring morning, Macy bid Ruth goodbye for the day. The maid had become accustomed to the early outings, which often left Macy gone until dark. Ruth handed her a small sack lunch and a thermos of café con leche, heavy on the milk, just as she preferred.

The coffee helped settle her stomach, which had been bothering her for weeks. She suspected it was the water.

"Gracias, Root. Que tenga un buen día!"

"Ay! Que gusto!" Ruth smiled widely, her short dark bob of hair bouncing a bit with appreciation. Macy added 10 Spanish vocabulary words to a spiral notebook daily, with scribbles about context, how she had heard them used during the day. She reviewed them before falling asleep each night. It was an exercise in memorization that helped her forget who was missing from the other side of the bed.

Ben would come home. He'd return to her. She wrote him letters, and left long voicemails. He knew she was sorry. It was only a matter of time until he came back, and they could talk it out. This time, she told herself, she would apologize.

She would explain.

Or she'd hit him.

How could she love someone so much, and also be so willing to push him away? She missed him dearly. And yet she was still angry about their last conversation.

"Go be a photographer. Do what makes you happy."

Macy fought tears, thinking of Ben. The smell of his neck. How he pleaded for weeks outside of that bathroom. How he cried for Jacob in his sleep.

It had only been a few weeks since he'd left for Santa Cruz; he would come home. She could make this better. They just needed a bit of a break. Every relationship went through periods like this, or so she hoped. She had no example in her parents; her father left at the first chance.

"Hasta luego!" Macy cried, pulling the heavy iron gate behind her. The walk to the orphanage had become routine; she was certain she could do it with her eyes closed. Every broken piece of sidewalk, each cobblestone, the seven flamboyant trees along the walk, had become friendly landmarks on her daily commute.

"Señora Maceeeeeee!" Francisco was the first to see her, like most mornings. He stood at the bell tower waiting for her arrival. He began to pull the bell, literally sounding her arrival, regardless of the time. She'd explained time and time again that he could greet her with a hug instead. Instead, each morning he reminded her how much he enjoyed the bells. And how much he loved her.

"Buenos días Francisco." She smiled, holding open her arms. The teenage boy blushed, but always accepted the embrace. Macy nodded at Señor Campos, the baker across the street from the church, who resembled a Muppet, with his tuft of gray hair and notorious scowl.

"Y buenos días Don Campos!" Macy called across the street, still hugging the boy. Shaking his head at the mistimed chiming, the baker and his broom returned inside to the yeast and ovens. They had done one version or another of this same dance every morning for the last few weeks. Eventually, Señor Campos would come out of the bakery with a smile. And perhaps she could persuade Francisco to end his love affair with the bell tower. She hoped.

"Good morning, Macy. How are things today?"

"I spoke with my editor this morning, Padre Pedro. I have an idea."

"Has he seen the photos? Did he agree to run them?

"I haven't sent anything yet. I was wondering . . ." She watched as Francisco ran over to the younger children, helping line those on the soccer field to file in for morning classes. "Do you know any of the mothers?"

"The mothers?"

"You must have met some of the women who left their children with you. Do you know their stories?"

"Yes." He raised one eyebrow. She noticed he was once again wearing his faded Yankees cap. Graying hair poked out, unwilling to be wrangled. He needed a haircut. Hell, he needed a vacation.

"Well . . . how about it?" She smiled, tapping one foot.

"How about what?" His eyes were wide, but the bags underneath revealed his work was never-ending.

"I need names. Addresses. I think if I could get to know these women, I could understand why they left their children. If I can learn their stories, I can figure out how to prevent this from happening again." Macy spoke too quickly, feeling shaky from too much morning coffee.

"Prevent what?"

"You know. The birth defects. The problems."

He winced as though her words had smacked him in the face. Stammering, Macy tried to recover.

"Not that the children are the problems. Of course not. It's the lack of care. The high birth rates. It's. Oh shit." She shook her head. "Shoot! Well, maybe if the women could have prevented the illnesses . . ."

"You want me to give you names and addresses so you can go speak with women who have left me their children?" He crossed his arms, squinting. "I can't do that Macy. You must know that." He forced a smile. "You are welcome to come inside and spend more time with the children. They have been asking about you."

"They don't have addresses? Okay. How about just their villages?"

He shook his head. "Those women gave me their children. They gave them to me—their most precious belonging in the entire world. And asked me, a priest, to protect their kids."

"Which you are doing . . ." She searched for understanding in his eyes, but saw only exhaustion. He'd likely been up all night with one of the infants. It was the "season for colic," he always said. She suspected the season was never-ending.

"Part of protecting their kids is also protecting those mothers, many of whom are children in my eyes. I am a priest, Macy. You know what that means. Would you like to come in with us? School is beginning. You are welcome in the classroom. And I am thankful you are here." His arms were still crossed tightly. She noticed a muscle tick shake beneath his right eye.

"Is this some sort of confessional rule? I don't get it. Don't you want to help them? Didn't you ask me to do this project in the first place?" She could be persuasive too. She'd talked countless subjects into letting her take their photos, some during the worst moments of turmoil they'd ever experience. "Look. I want to know the whys. The reasons. These children were abandoned and sadly photos of their deformities aren't enough. We are talking about international coverage. It has to be more than medical textbook photo stock."

"Yeah. Some sort of confessional rule." He turned to go in the orphanage. For the first time, she could hear the sarcasm in his voice. "I've got to start class."

She felt her annoyance growing. Why was he being so difficult?

"I'm not talking abortion. I'm not going to urge these women to make other choices. I want to understand why this," she motioned toward the line of children waiting patiently outside for their priest-teacher, "continues to happen. Isn't that why you asked me to help?"

"No, Macy. I asked you to help these kids specifically. And

please do not mutter the word, 'abortion,' of all your profanities, here." He spoke quietly, but she heard the anger bubbling to the surface. "Those mothers trusted me with their stories and their babies. I will not give you their information. Final. End." He stomped off toward the school, calling the children inside and closing the door behind him.

"What just happened?" Macy said this to an empty courtyard after the last child entered the old building. She stood, blinking away hot tears.

A heartbroken romance song blared from a radio in a market nearby.

The tears came quickly. They were hot and angry and gathered on the neck of her sweatshirt. Tasting the salt in her mouth, she wiped her nose on the edge of the sweatshirt, frustrated. He was her only real friend in Tarija. Ruth was her employee. Although she didn't have a formal job description, "caring" would have been line item number one.

Padre Pedro cared because he wanted to.

Damn him. She'd have to find a way to start the conversation again.

Macy looked at the school and orphanage, considering her options. Rather than immediately apologizing, she trudged across the street, swung open the bakery door, and plopped on a lone bench to gather her thoughts.

"Ah, la Americana finalmente viene a mi panaderia. Qué quiere, guapa?"

Macy stared at him, understanding one or two words.

"Señor Campos, I don't know what the hell you just said, but I need some more coffee. And maybe some Pepto. How do you all live here? Do you always have the runs?"

"Runs?" He raised both eyebrows. "What do you mean by 'runs?'"

"How? What? Uh. No. No runs . . ." Macy brought a hand over her downturned eyes.

"What? We Bolivians can't speak English? You don't own the language, gringa." He smiled, warmly. His eyes revealed a kindness that surprised her. Was this the same man who stood across the street, banging his broom on the cobblestone at each mistimed chime of the church bells?

Macy coughed, raising a hand to cover her eyes. "Oh God. Excuse me. I didn't realize you spoke English. I didn't mean to be impolite." She stammered, again. "May I have some coffee please? And, uh, maybe one of those sweet rolls." She pointed at the counter behind him, trying to muffle an embarrassed laugh.

He went into the back, returning with a heavy, handmade ceramic mug full of coffee and a small bottle of the pink medicine. He winked at her, setting both on the table. Returning to the counter, he pulled out several sweet rolls, placing them in the oven to warm as she guzzled the Pepto, hoping it would also cure her social disgrace.

"How well do you know Padre Pedro?" She motioned toward the church, taking a big gulp of the dark coffee.

"I know him."

"Perhaps you could join me?" She pointed toward the other seat.

"Not today, guapa. But I will tell you this—Padre Pedro cares for those kids. He never takes a day off. Even his vacations are with other priests. Can you imagine a vacation with a priest?" He laughed, his generous stomach shaking in the process. "He has to be the hardest working Boliviano or gringo in the world. You should take some pastries to him." He winked again. "And do something good with those photos of yours."

Macy smiled. Word had gotten out around the neighborhood once her photos from Entre Rios ran in the local newspaper. Several of the market vendors had started calling her, "Señora Camera."

Señor Campos held his broom and looked over her. She sipped, but the black coffee made her stomach cramp from the acidity. She eyed the Pepto. The cinnamon and cloves in the sweet roll made her tongue dance by contrast. Macy stuffed her mouth full too quickly, surprised at her appetite.

"What is it with you Bolivian men? Are you all so charming?" She licked her fingers.

"Ah, that is the magic of South America, querida. So, you want a dozen? Or two? You know he has a lot of kids over there . . ." His mustache reached up toward his ears as he smiled.

"Two dozen would be great. And Señor Campos, next time the bell rings? Come talk to Francisco."

"Talk to Francisco? I talk to that boy everyday! He works here in the shops after evening mass, sweeping. How do you think I don't talk to the boy?" His cheeks grew red. She knew immediately she'd misread the situation. Again.

She scratched the back of her head.

"You employ Francisco?"

"Of course I do! I am his father!"

"Wait. What?" She stood. He carefully filled two boxes of pastries behind the counter. "You are Francisco's dad?"

"He didn't come from me." The baker pointed to his groin, and then to his heart. "I chose him."

208

"You've lost me, Señor Campos."

"What do you talk about with that priest friend of yours? How is it that he does not speak of our program?" He laughed. "When I come outside to shake my broom it is because that silly boy isn't wearing the watch I gave him. He rings the bell to get me to spend more time with him. And it works! I should know better, but all of my neighbors complain I haven't yet taught him to tell time!"

"You watch over him?" Macy shook her head and sat back down in the small bakery, placing the boxes on her lap. "What the hell?"

"When he is 18, I will help him get a job." Señor Campos wiped down his countertop as he spoke. "If he cannot get one, he will come live here and help me with the bakery. We must make room for additional children at the orphanage."

He said this as though it was a simple formula for a healthy community. Children in plus children adopted equaled more room for other children. Rinse. Repeat.

"How long has this been going on?" Sam was right. She had become too attached and was blind to the rest of the story. What else had she overlooked?

"Forever."

"Forever?"

"Since Padre Pedro took over that small church. Years ago. My tío owned the bakery then. Before I had my own niñas. Before I studied in California. Before I lost my beloved Lupita, may God bless her soul." He genuflected.

Macy raised an eyebrow.

"I still like those California ladies." He smiled, bashfully. "But, I married a colla, like me. Four daughters. No sons. When Lupita died of the cancer, I took Francisco as my son."

"I see." Although she didn't. Macy's head swam with the possibilities. If Pedro had set up a foster-mentoring program, she could photograph the pairs. Perhaps there were children who were working and successful in the community.

"He cares for those children. We provide the daily bread, so to speak." He paused. "You didn't know?"

"How many of them are there? Like you? Community parents?"

"A dozen or so. Padre saw my grief and he knew I needed something greater. When he selected Francisco as my son, he gave me hope, although I couldn't see it then. I had to get up and face the day, see my daughters were fed, and get that damn bell to stop ringing across the street at all hours. If I got him to stop ringing the bell, the customers would return at normal times, unmolested. I did, and they did."

"So all teenagers there will have a place."

"Yes, Señora Camera." He grinned. The baker was a gossip. "And then we persuade our friends to take one too. It is a beautiful thing, this adopting of the children from Padre Pedro."

"Yes, Señor Campos, I'd guess it is. Would you let me photograph you and Francisco?"

Resting his broom against a wall, he ran his hands on either side of his long, gray mustache and straightened his apron to cover his generous stomach.

"Sí! Ahora?"

"No, no," Macy said, laughing. "Not now. Let me speak with Padre Pedro to arrange something. Thank you for these. And for your time."

"Ah, finalmente famoso!" she heard him whispering, as she left the shop. He danced around the small space with his broom. She'd left a handful of Bolivianos on the countertop.

Macy looked up at the cloudless bright blue sky, gathering her courage before entering the orphanage. The pastries were to be delivered with an apology.

22. PECADILLOS

"The ambassador wants his cuffs starched too," Anna said, handing over the basket of laundry. Ruth nodded, standing on the back porch.

"Not a problem. Thank you again, Anna."

"Ruth, you're doing me a favor. That house is never clean enough. Their children are hellions."

"I have four too. I know what that feels like."

"Yes, but I doubt you are hosting five-course dinners for senators," Anna said, raising an eyebrow.

The two laughed. "Really, Anna. This is making a difference for our family. I bought the boys new backpacks last week and you would have thought I had given them the moon."

"Well, amiga, most of us have been there. And then again, most of us stop before we get to four when he won't marry us."

Ruth blushed. She'd shared pieces of her story, as the two had become friends during these laundry swaps.

"Well, what can you do? I love him."

"Condoms." Anna's voice was flat.

Ruth shook her head and studied her feet. She didn't care to go into her family planning decisions. The church was clear on birth control. A sin! And at this point, there wasn't worry about pregnancy. She suspected she was going through the change. Her eldest was in his teens and she hadn't had a regular cycle in months. She hadn't seen Andres for longer, so there was no risk of yet another arriving.

"So, starched cuffs. Anything else?"

"You are doing a great job, amiga." Anna brazenly slapped her friend on the butt before disappearing past the clotheslines, through the back gate into the Spanish ambassador's backyard.

Ruth stared at the mound of soiled clothing. Washing strangers' underwear was torturous. Then again, there weren't many other opportunities she could come up with to make this tidy extra sum each week.

What wouldn't she do for her children?

Ruth headed back into the kitchen to prepare the buckets of hot water. She would scrub the linens first—it was tricky to get rid of the wine stains, but she had her magical ways. Then the little boys' soccer uniforms would have to soak. She washed the señora's lingerie last, always tempted to raise it to her nose before pushing it under the blanket of bubbles in a freshly poured bucket of water.

What would it be like to have a life where you had a bureau full of such soft, lacy things?

Ruth's daydreams were interrupted by the cry of the baby —who still had not been named. Looking up from the laundry, she watched through the window as Luz nuzzled the infant, whispering in her ear and stroking her head.

She'd made a smart choice by hiring the teenager. It filled the housekeeper with pride to think of the day when she could put her back on a bus to her village, with a pocket full of school fees and hope for the future.

Ruth hurried inside, tucking the remaining buckets and laundry in the shadows of the house. She wiped her wet hands on her soiled apron.

"Luz, I need to go to the market this afternoon for groceries. Would you like to come and get out of the house?"

"No, doña. Thank you. I don't think that is wise."

"You are probably right, mija. You are so good with her," Ruth said, watching as the baby curled her fingers around one of the housekeeper's. The baby was growing quickly now that her palate was healing. She watched the girl blush, accepting the praise.

"I haven't told you that enough. This isn't an easy job you've been given and you are doing a great job with it. I'm sure it is hard not to think of your son while holding her."

"Yes, doña."

"Speak child! Why are you so quiet today?" Ruth examined the girl. She too was growing, it seemed. Like any malnourished altiplano girl who arrives in the big city, Luz seemed healthier after a bit of attention. The Duncans provided clothing for the girl, which Ruth had bartered for in the markets—hemming and mending as necessary. And the teenager's skin and hair were responding to regular meals and bathing. She looked brighter than when she'd arrived at the home just a few weeks prior.

"It is very hard, doña," the girl said, choking on her tears. "To be a mother only for a moment."

"Ah. You will be a mother again." Ruth pushed the girl's braids behind her shoulders, patting her on the back. "You must finish school first. Do what I didn't do. And what your mother didn't do."

"Yes, doña."

"Luz, if someone had given me a chance to save money to pay for my school fees, I wouldn't be an unmarried mother of four. God bless those children, but it isn't an easy life. I want to read. I want to have a handful of Bolivianos end up in my pocket and not be confused by the differences in values. I'm always convinced I'm being tricked," she admitted. "I want to pick up a copy of the evening newspaper and understand the headlines. To sing along with the hymns at church!" Ruth had gotten carried away.

"I want this too, doña." The girl looked at her with wide eyes, obviously startled by the housekeeper's frank confession.

"We will make it happen for you." Ruth was resolute. "This child goes in for tubes next week in her ears, and another check up on her mouth. Soon enough los Americanos will have to decide what to do about custody. Either way, we will be able to send you home. I am certain your mother must be worried."

The pair looked at the baby, who began to fuss.

"Excuse us, doña. She needs a clean diaper."

Ruth watched as the girl hurried to her quarters, where the baby spent most of her days too.

That poor girl's mother. What must she think? She sent her to the city to sell honey and now she hasn't returned in weeks. Ruth made a mental note, they should see about sending word on the next bus to Entre Rios: Luz would be home soon. Ruth considered this while gathering her things for the market, including a perfectly written list of necessary items.

Ruth Leona Castro was many things, but illiterate wasn't one of them. Manipulative? Perhaps. Clever? Certainly.

She smiled, thinking about being sneaky, as she walked through the market stalls. Sometimes children needed coaxing in ways that burdened them with the guilt of their predecessors. If Luz thought she was going to school to learn for all the women of her village, and those who loved her elsewhere, she was destined not to waste that tuition money on something foolish. It was just a small fib.

Jesus would understand. He wanted the best for Luz too, didn't He?

She made another mental note to add this pecado to her list for confessional before Saturday mass.

Ruth's basket was heavy with whole chickens, carrots, avocados, and a few bananas when a clash across the market got everyone's attention. A barefoot indigenous woman was being pushed outside, shoved by two older men.

"We told you! We don't know anything. Unless you are shopping, you are trespassing!"

"Someone must know something! She was here! We know she was here!"

Ruth watched with other shoppers as the woman dug her heels in the ground, clinging to the men and flailing. "Please! She is my baby sister! I must find her!"

"Out! We will call the police, you dirty colla! Out of this market now! Don't let us see your ugly face here again!" The men pushed her out one of the stalls on to the street, where she landed in a clump. Ruth, and everyone else on this side of the market, could hear her cries from the street. Pedestrians walked around the grieving woman, all too polite to get involved, yet too rude to help.

"What was that about?" Ruth questioned the fruit vendor.

"Ugh. More altiplano trash pestering shoppers." The vendor didn't look up, or she would have realized Ruth too was a colla, she just didn't wear a felt bolero hat.

"Ah," Ruth said. "I can see how her asking questions must really bother your critical work. Selling of fruit. What really would we do without you?" She dropped a few Bolivianos in the woman's hand, grabbing her oranges and clicking her tongue. The vendor clucked her tongue in return, throwing her braids behind her shoulders a bit too forcefully, indignant.

These were the same vendors, regardless of indigenous group or class, who would come together to call themselves "Chapacos." Everyone living in Tarija—Tarijeñans—called themselves this name of false pride. Tarija was different, they would tell visitors. Cultures blended in social harmony; they even had their own city-wide song, sung brashly at parades and celebrations: Chapeco Soy!

Ruth knew otherwise. As did any poor indio woman in this city, whose genetics forever cast them as outsiders.

The housekeeper stomped outside of the market, pulling the girl up by the arm. She was certain the orange vendor wasn't the only one watching.

"Child, you've created quite the scene. Get yourself together. You aren't going to find whomever you are looking for here, crying."

The woman looked up at the housekeeper, taking her lead. Ruth took her to a nearby bench, in front of a church. Reaching into her basket, she handed her a bola of bread and several bananas. This would be easy enough to spare.

"Thank you, señora. Why did they have to be so mean? It's just like the village women say, 'Every city hen thinks she's a rooster.'" Tears streaked her face.

"This will help. It is all I can offer you. I have to get back to the market before my bosses miss me and their groceries," Ruth stuck her hand out, offering a warm roll. "Better luck to you, child. And you can tell those village gossips, us city women are just like them, too often both cock and hen by necessity. The work goes on."

"Thank you again," the woman whimpered, stuffing the roll of bread into her mouth. Ruth tried to walk away without further involving herself, but couldn't. The woman's dirty fingerprints smudged the bread. Ruth watched with astonishment as every last crumb disappeared.

"Fine," she said, plopping down on the bench next to her. "I don't know what it is about picking up strays at this market lately, but I'll give you five minutes. This tired hen could use a sit. Who are you looking for?"

"My baby sister," she continued to whimper. "She went missing a month ago."

"Many women leave from Tarija for La Paz. The work is better. Or maybe she went to Potosi to work in one of the mining camp kitchens?"

"She doesn't know how to do anything other than work on our family farm."

"Never underestimate what a woman will do to get away from a family farm," Ruth said, raising an eyebrow. "How old is she?"

"Fifteen."

"Fifteen! She is just a child. Why wasn't she in school? Where have you looked?"

"Everywhere." Ruth watched as the woman sobbed into her hands. "Everywhere. My mother is going to be so angry with me."

"Breathe," Ruth counseled, pulling out tissues from her pocket and patting the woman on the shoulder. She remembered the night she'd packed up her boys and headed for Tarija. No one came to look for her, as much as she'd wished her mother or sisters had.

"A family friend saw her here, in this market, several weeks ago." The woman muttered into her tissue. "My sister sold her honey. My sister, she is a beekeeper."

"A what?" The woman had Ruth's full attention.

"A beekeeper." Ruth could barely hear over her own heartbeat as the woman continued. "It is my fault. I hadn't protected her. And when the baby was born, La Doña had to fight off the elders from drowning the baby"

"What happened to this baby?" Ruth felt beads of sweat gathering on her brow.

"My sister kept her alive for weeks, but the wawa did die. My sister buried her in the hills. We never knew where. If I had only protected her." The woman continued crying, now into a long, lace hand-knit scarf tied around her neck.

"The baby died?" Ruth tried to ask, as casually as she could muster.

"You cannot bury grief with a child, no matter how deep you dig."

"How was she wounded?" Ruth asked, measuring her voice against the anxiety building in her gut.

"Harelip. Cut from here to here." The woman gestured, running her finger from lip to the side of her nose. "When she left this time, we thought she'd gone up to the hills to mourn. But then she didn't return within a week—my mother wouldn't sit down, she was so upset. Pacing and pacing, back and forth. I'd never seen her like that. And then the baker's daughter told us she saw Luz here. This very market."

Luz. Daughter. Harelip. La Doña.

Ruth thought quickly to the last time she'd seen the girl

with the baby. Luz was nuzzling her in the kitchen. Off to change her diapers. Whispering in the child's ear.

Alone.

23. PURPLE POTATOES

"Madame Duncan, he cannot speak to you. There are riots. These are tense times for our country."

"Riots? What do you mean, 'riots'? Linda, what does this have to do with Ben? What is he doing?"

"I cannot say any more, madame. Please excuse me. I should not have said this, but it is in the papers. You can read as much."

The papers? Riots?

Macy's heart jumped at the admission from her husband's assistant. In the third week of calling Ben's office, she was finally starting to put pieces of the puzzle together.

"Where is Ben, Linda? I demand to know! I am his wife!"

"He is in the capital. He cannot speak with you. He is on assignment." Her voice no longer held emotion. Macy might as well have been speaking with an automated answering machine.

"Where is Raleigh?"

"He and Señor Ben are together, madame."

"Is there anything else you can tell me Linda? What if this was your husband?"

"I do not have a husband, madame."

"Humor me. Pretend! I haven't heard from him in three weeks. Doesn't that seem odd to you?"

"Madame, USAID would contact you if he wasn't safe. He is on assignment. This is all I can say."

Macy grunted, shaking a fist. "Look *Señorita,* I know you are just doing your job. But if for whatever reason something happened to Ben and I don't know about it, I am going to be beyond angry. Do you understand me?"

"Yes, madame."

"And stop calling me that! I am Macy Duncan."

"Yes, Meeses Duncan."

"UGH!" Macy slammed down the receiver.

Was there training for spouses she had missed when they arrived? What did Ben really do for USAID? She thought back on the few conversations they'd had about his work since arriving. Should she call a senator? The ambassador? Her mother?

Macy dialed the orphanage, but the priest did not answer. Considering her options, she called the only other friend she thought could calm her down.

"Sam, what the hell do I do?"

"I am sure he is fine. You really haven't heard from him in three weeks?"

"No." She felt tears gather. "I just kept calling, thinking he didn't want to speak to me. This morning, packing, it hit me. What if he can't speak to me? What if something has gone wrong?"

"Macy, take a deep breath. I am sure things are fine. Ben is a good man, and he's scrappy. He wouldn't want you worried about him."

"Sam, did you read the news?"

"I keep up with Bolivia, doll." He sounded sleepy. "But listen, there are riots in your new country every week. Coffee growers in this region on strike. And Japanese farmers in this region on strike. This indigenous group hates that indigenous group . . ." His voice trailed off. "It isn't all that different than American news, if you just replace x with y. 'Corn Farmers Fight Monsanto.' 'Bus drivers strike in San Francisco.' 'Crip and Blood violence resurges as Central American gangs strengthen in southern California.'"

Macy wondered if he was reading actual headlines from the wire. "So, I don't need to call my senator?"

"Ha! No. When your senator starts calling you, then we may have an issue. He's a federal employee working in an isolated area. This sort of stuff has to happen. Remember life before cell phones? You do remember life before cell phones, don't you?"

"Sort of."

"Mace, you don't sound like yourself. What else is going on? Are you okay?"

"No."

"Talk to me." She could hear Sam shifting into reporter mode.

"I am not sure. I just . . . miss him. It has been too long. And now I feel stupid for not worrying about him sooner, and foolish for calling you panicked. Our marriage is off balance, Sam. I'm not sure how to set it right."

"Shit. I'm not the best for that kind of advice."

"Neither is my mother."

The two remained silent until the long distance static crackled.

"Well," he finally stammered, "I have good news." Macy felt like she could hear him smiling on the other end.

"Yeah?"

"Smith from the AP Wire called. He used to be the Kandahar stringer for their service before landing in DC."

"Okay . . ." Macy felt her heartbeat calming.

"His poppy feature was just published in *NatGeo*."

"What?"

"You heard me."

"Sam! Can he get my photos published?"

"It is as good of a chance as we've got. I like the ones you've sent so far, Mace. They are good. They are great, really. Better than I was willing to give even you credit for. But you still need your angle."

"I may have it."

"Tell me."

Macy thumbed through the Lonely Planet guide. She'd ordered a stack of books on Bolivia, and several on maternal and child health from an online bookstore. She also printed several articles from medical journals, after sweet talking Sam into the password for the newspaper's research service. With a backpack stuffed full of the references, and a small duffle with clothing, she left Tarija, but not before writing Ruth a quick note explaining her departure. The housekeeper was nowhere to be found.

Nor was the girl or the baby.

Macy had given herself a few hours to read, pack and plan before once again phoning Ben's office. The line picked up, and Linda's voice repeated the same government script greeting on cue.

Meester Duncan was still out in the field.

"He cannot speak with you this week. He is on assignment in the capital."

"Yes, Linda. We just discussed this. Remember? Put Fernando on."

"Fernando cannot tell you anything other than I already have, Madame."

"Put Fernando on the phone, Linda!"

"Yes, Meeses Duncan," the young woman relented.

Fernando drove, stoic and silent. It hadn't taken much to convince him to take her again toward Entre Rios. The drive wound them across the barren desert, where little more than century plants grew. The landscape seemed otherworldly, with an occasional spiny plant sprouting miraculously from the rust colored earth.

Secured in Fernando's dented Toyota pickup truck, she thumbed through the travel guide's pages, dog-earing sights she wanted to photograph, spices to smell, oddly shaped gourd instruments to hear. There was so much to this country, the only landlocked in South America. Such simple facts felt like a pebble in her shoe.

How had she lived here for so many weeks without bothering to read a single word about Bolivian history? How had she gone so long without asking Ben the details of his work? How could she know so little of Padre Pedro's work?

When they reached the edge of the desert, the colors faded: an ombrè of dust to life. The mountains, while still arid, had spots of green here and there where underground springs kept roots watered. They began the climb from the desert floor toward the high plains. The view oddly reminded Macy of the stretch highway between Phoenix and San Diego, where tumbleweeds gather on barbed wire, wind turbines soldier on in the distant desert, yet RV parks full of life sprout from the barren land.

The engine whined, shifting from gear to gear, ascending toward a cloudless cerulean sky. Fernando took each serpentine turn slowly, letting a sigh escape as they safely made it around one bend after the next. Macy's ears popped. She was thankful for Fernando's silence. Linda was right; the driver wouldn't tell her any details of her husband's assignment, nor why he wasn't the driver on call with Ben and Raleigh in the capitol, protecting them from the riots.

There was little Macy could do, as Sam advised, other than hope for the best and remember how resourceful her husband was. He was an Eagle Scout, after all. He'd reminded her of this credential many times, usually after he'd completed some handy task around the house.

Macy returned her focus to the *JAMA* articles in front of her, as the scenery outside shifted into the golden highlands of eastern Bolivia.

IODINE SUPPLEMENTATION DURING PREGNANCY

CLEFT PALATES: STUDY FINDS MATERNAL NUTRITION OUTWEIGHS GENETIC INFLUENCES

ISOLATED MICROTIA AS A MARKER FOR UNSUSPECTED HEMIFACIAL MICROSOMIA

There were too many moving parts to consider. *National Geographic.* Even with declining readership, it was held as the ultimate accomplishment for photographers. Macy dreamed of having her shots published in the magazine since receiving her first marigold-bound copy as a child. Her bedroom was wallpapered in the insert maps and other centerfold diagrams she'd carefully unstapled and ironed flat over the years.

She offered Fernando half of her pay, plus a bonus for the drive. This time, he had to make two trips, returning to retrieve her in several weeks. Plus, the journey was longer. They would travel past Entre Rios, further toward the eastern Brazilian border. She'd never considered the bus; again Ben had been right. The roads were perilous.

Macy had also negotiated a deal with Señor Campos. In return for his arranging her stay with his family in an altiplano village between Entre Rios and Villamontes, she would pay for pastries to be delivered to the orphanage every day for a month. Francisco would be responsible for coming to the bakery each morning to pick up the boxes of sweet breads, promptly at 6:45 am. This gave him enough time to return with breakfast for the children before ringing the first bell at 7.

It also would force the boy to use his watch.

She hoped the priest would consider the regular pastry delivery as her penance for however she'd offended him. They hadn't spoken in a week. Pedro uncharacteristically waved her away when she'd returned with the first box of Señor Campos's pastries; he had been busy teaching the children. Pedro didn't make time for Macy when she'd returned the next day with the ice cream either; Quasimodo had taken the brown paper bags from the Lebanese grocer inside, smiling and hooting. She lingered outside near the basketball hoop until she heard the cries of joy as the chocolate sprinkles and gallons of vanilla ice cream arrived to the destined recipients.

Señor Campos' second cousin agreed to host the American photographer. She would have her own sleeping area, but share the latrine. Macy could come and go as she'd like, but would be expected to help with chores. They were subsistence farmers and herders adding a stomach to their already cramped table.

The family sent their requests in turn: tomatoes, any fruit, peanut butter, a bolt of canvas, a cone of yarn (any color), dish soap, and as much toilet paper as they could haul from the city.

The third hour on the dusty road faded into the fourth. Macy highlighted the journal articles, reviewing the common causes of birth defects in the region. There were also lists of well-known preventives, including education, she noted. There was research to show the better educated the mother, the more likely she would have access to prenatal care. One statistic stuck out: two-thirds of the women of the world, not just Bolivians, are illiterate. A baby has twice the chance of survival to age five if the mother can read.

There were newspaper vendors and the occasional paperback stand in Tarija, but she hadn't seen a single public library.

Could Ruth read? Didn't she have four boys? Macy's mind wandered. She'd met illiterate women in northern Arizona on photography assignments; it always shocked her how socially smart they were to cover for their inability to read. The "soup of the day" diners. One Hopi woman taught Macy a memorization system for money; it worked beautifully, until a new coin or bill design was introduced. Then she would have to start again, learning a few tricks to keep herself from being constantly taken advantage of.

Macy returned to her readings, and the southern hemisphere. An hour later, she scoffed, getting Fernando's attention.

"'Alas,' concluded one Scottish immunologist, 'female

matriculation is not the top priority of the rural South American village.' What the hell does this guy know, Don Fernando? Does he think women want to be dumb? I hate this sort of thing," she said. The driver's full attention returned to the road, accustomed to her odd diatribes.

"I mean, really. What the hell can a guy from Scotland know about the educational desires of a group of Bolivian women? I bet he's wrong."

She looked at the camera at her feet.

What the hell did an American woman know about Bolivia? An American woman who didn't even know where her own husband was.

As they neared Entre Rios, she looked to the back of the truck. The groceries and her bags were tied under a black plastic tarp, now dusty from the long drive. Feeling her stomach tighten with uncertainty as they pulled into the town, she could only hope she had made the right decision.

Without Ben, Pedro or even Ruth's counsel, Macy decided to entrench herself in rural life. She knew exactly what she wanted to photograph: the story responsible for the story. The crops. The work. The women. The village—for what it was and what she suspected it wasn't.

She was a 27-year-old American woman working as a poorly paid stringer photographer. Her story was forming. Schools. Pupils. Young Mothers. Death.

Could she do this?

Fernando left her in front of the small brown and gray mud house after shaking hands with those who had emerged. The cluster of homes was made of varied materials.

"Be wise, gringa," Fernando whispered, pulling her close before returning to his pickup truck. "These are good people, but poor. Watch." He pointed to his eyes for emphasis. Macy leaned back, staring at him..

"English? Fernando, after all this time?"

"We all have our secrets." He smiled, one eyebrow raised.

Macy smiled, grateful for the brevity. "Thank you, Fernando."

"See you in two weeks, guera. Try to learn." He winked, returning to the truck.

Macy watched the trail of dust the truck left long after it was gone. "Here goes nothing," she said aloud to no one in particular. Turning toward the compound, a dozen curious faces watched her every move.

Macy noticed the main house had both a chimney and a metal roof. Another nearby building had a tile roof. Otherwise, the buildings here and there spotting the pale yellow hillside were covered in dusty thatch, reminding her of illustrations in childhood books of fairy tales.

Hansel and Gretel.

Had she left enough breadcrumbs?

Macy felt the altitude immediately; the thin, cool air rattled inside her. The light was brighter here, with the blue sky clear of any cloud. She smiled as a handful of children with dusty feet and colorful woven clothing appeared to each carry what they could into the main house. Macy followed, greeting everyone with both a "Hola" and "Imaynalla" as she thought appropriate. She'd made a brief phonetic vocabulary list of Spanish and the native language, Quechua, to help her get through the awkward beginnings. She also sent up a quiet wish for someone who spoke English to magically appear.

A woman built like a teapot approached, and waved toward a rope cot in a dark corner of the main room.

"Gracias, señora." Macy found her duffels had been placed on the small bed, covered with a heavy wool blanket, striped in shades of indigo. The other supplies were being joyfully divided among adults in the nearby kitchen. Macy hoped a few rolls of toilet paper would be mercifully saved on her behalf.

Her hostess remained quiet, watching the exotic guest. Macy sat on the edge of the cot, out of breath. At this altitude, she read it would take a few days and plenty of liquids to adjust to a normal energy level. Macy hadn't been feeling great before leaving Tarija. She jiggled the bottle of migraine tablets in her jacket pocket.

"Water?" Macy asked, bringing an imaginary cup to her mouth.

The hostess nodded, waving Macy toward the kitchen. She stood, still feeling dizzy, and pulled her down coat tight against her body. The wind rattled the metal roof overhead. Macy followed, trying to ignore the specks of light that clouded the edges of her vision.

The woman showed her a covered bucket with a small opening at the top, and a plastic cup tethered to the side with a piece of rope. The water was clear. Macy thoughtlessly filled the cup and brought it to her lips. The water was cool and smelled faintly of a swimming pool.

Macy jumped. Just as the cool water reached her lips, her hostess grabbed her hand, rattling in alarmed Spanish. Macy didn't follow. Gestures quickly explained the bucket cup wasn't for drinking out of, but for filling your own cup. The bucket and cup would now have to be sanitized again. Macy watched as the woman carefully filled a cap full of what smelled like bleach and added it to the water, rinsing the cup afterward. She also handed her American guest a yellow plastic tumbler. Macy filled it, drank quickly, and returned to her cot with ears burning, only thankful she hadn't also poured a cup to wash her dusty face.

Although the late spring sun still hung high in the horizon, Macy felt like she could sleep for days. It had been a long day and journey. From her corner perch, she took a preventive migraine pill and curled up on the scratchy wool blanket, too tired to change out of her jeans and jacket into something more comfortable.

She watched as villagers came and went, meeting her hostess, who stood stirring a cauldron over a raised wood fire. Macy noticed the neighbors traded items for shares of the supplies she and Fernando had hauled from the city. One woman brought a basket of eggs, leaving with some of the yarn. A small boy placed what she guessed were two jars of honey on the kitchen table, leaving with a smaller jar of bright blue liquid dish soap.

Her hostess was a shrewd businesswoman. Macy smiled through her headache, drifting in and out of sleep, feeling the medication take hold. She wasn't sure if she dreamed the other transactions involving an unhappy goat on a fraying rope leash, a newspaper unrolled to uncover a pile of pale green leaves, and a hand-knit crimson red scarf.

Macy stirred hours later to her hostess shaking her gently. She jumped, startled out of deep sleep. The woman's wind-chapped pink face smiled, pushing forward a tin plate of steaming food. Small purple potatoes, pale green fava beans, a fried chicken foot, a hard boiled egg, and a cup of rice filled the plate.

"Oh, thank you," Macy said, feeling her stomach jump at the smell of the savory food. "This looks wonderful. She placed the plate on her lap and took the woman's hands into hers. "Gracias. Gracias."

The woman's eyes danced. She pointed at her chest. "Gloria."

"Mucho gusto, Gloria." Macy dragged out her dusty Spanish. "Soy Macy."

"Macy?"

"Sí."

"Buen provecho." The woman made a motion to eat and stepped across the room back to the small kitchen.

Macy sat up to find her yellow tumbler refilled. She savored every bite of the salty food, even the crunchy chicken foot. Before she finished, a small boy appeared through the front door and crept toward her cot. He sat at her feet, smirking. Gloria hadn't noticed. She remained with her back to the pair, working in the kitchen.

He smiled, revealing missing front teeth. Wasting no time, he reached up and plucked a bean off her plate. Macy laughed. Before she knew it, he'd taken the egg and eventually she relented and gave him all that remained before Gloria came screaming at him with a broom, shooing the boy back outside into the night.

Macy again found herself laughing. With her stomach full and the pending doom of a migraine gone, she was as at ease in a stranger's home as she could be. Her hostess handed her a mug of what she guessed was herbal tea. Macy followed the boy's route, wandering out the front door, made of nothing more than a wool blanket attached to a wood beam with a row of rusted nails.

Homes scattered on the hillsides were lit with cooking fires glowing from within, like pumpkins on Halloween. Silver smoke danced up leaning chimneys. An indigo sky displayed the southern hemisphere's finest view of the heavens.

Macy felt like if she stood on her tiptoes, she might be able to touch the stars—a band of thick diamonds and glittering planets. She dug deep for breath, sucking in the earthy scents of rural life. Llamas in a nearby pen made an unfamiliar grunt. The chicken coop remained silent, all the wise ladies already deep at sleep. A few random dogs, with skin pulled tight across underfed ribs, wandered near the road.

Tomorrow, in the first sunlight, she would explore. She would learn this place.

Quietly returning to her cot, Macy pulled the wool blanket over herself, shivering from the night wind. Her lips were chapped, her eyes were itchy for more sleep, and scalp was sore where an elastic band held her hair back in a messy bun for more than 16 hours.

Macy thought of Ben, wishing more than anything he was there with her. She rolled over, curling her back to the wind whipping across the high plains. Tears rolled down her cheeks until she soon surrendered to deep, restorative sleep.

24. PACE

Ruth paced in the kitchen. She'd already pulled everything out of the pantry, wiped it down, restocked, and reorganized. She'd cleaned the floors by hand. She'd completed the neighbors' wash and ironing, which sat neatly in a basket by the kitchen's back door. She'd changed the linens on the beds upstairs, even though they hadn't been slept in since she'd changed them last. She'd done everything short of replace the flowers from the beds in the entryway courtyard.

Her hands shook.

The Duncan's house was sparkling.

And empty.

She had returned from the market to find the home eerily silent. No crying baby. No teenage girl making a racket, stirring together another batch of pumpkin empanadas with her metal whisk. No Americans pouring baths or glasses of spicy red wine.

The quiet she longed for most afternoons brought the housekeeper's anxieties to a boil.

Ruth raced to the girl's quarters to find the room scattered with nothing more than a few baby items. A bottle. A rattle. A stack of cloth diapers and pins.

Maybe they had just gone for a walk, Ruth reassured herself. Maybe Luz wasn't really the baby's mother. Maybe she had jumped to conclusions. She was tired and God knows she was overworked. Maybe she just had crammed the pieces of the puzzle together haphazardly.

"She doesn't know how to do anything other than work on the family farm."

Carmen's words rang in her ears. That, and care for her own sick child, Ruth thought.

Ruth walked back and forth, back and forth. Finally, the old phone in the kitchen rang. The housekeeper jumped in fright.

"House of the Duncans, how may I help you?" She tried unsuccessfully to keep her voice level.

"Ruth, this is Ernesto Campos, the baker. Are you okay?"

"Sí, Don Campos. Why do you ask?" Ruth had been into his bakery over the years, but never paid the man much attention. She was surprised to hear his voice.

"I am here at the orphanage. My daughters tell me you stopped in? And have since left many messages? The priest is gone for two weeks at the annual church meeting in La Paz. He is with his fellow priests and the sisters. We were tasked with watching over the children this year."

"Oh, that's right." Ruth dug her toe into the ground. How had she forgotten? Padre had mentioned the retreat several times. He looked forward to the annual conference for both a spiritual and physical renewal. A few days without children were "good for one's soul," he would whisper when no little ears were near.

"Is there something I can help you with?"

"No. This is . . ." Should she tell him the story? It would be comforting to have someone else know her suspicions. To reassure her the girl and baby would be home soon. That there was nothing to worry about.

Ruth gulped. She wasn't sure she could tell of the day's discoveries without becoming hysterical.

"Don Campos, it is of a personal nature. I forgot Padre was traveling. Forgive the insistency in my messages. I will speak with the priest when he returns. Thank you."

"Aren't you the housekeeper these days for the Americans?"

"Yes. For several months now." Ruth rolled her eyes. Why had she taken this job?

"Ah, I like the photographer. She buys sweet buns for the orphans. She's my best customer at the moment! She can be a bit rude, but Señora Camera seems kind enough. Do you like working for her?"

Silence filled the line. She knew he was waiting for her to gossip in response. Ruth pinched the bridge of her nose.

What if she had hired the mother of the abandoned child? Had she hired a kidnapper? How would she explain herself? What if she lost this job? How would she feed her own boys sweet buns? She'd never get another job as a housekeeper in Tarija if she didn't find that baby!

"Don Campos, I cannot talk just now. Thank you for the call. I will find Padre Pedro when he returns." Ruth's temples pulsed.

"Buena suerte Doña Ruth. Please let me know if there is anything I can do to help you. Stop by the bakery sometime. You know, I do have the best sweet buns in all of Tarija."

"Thank you, Don Campos. I will."

"Adiós."

"Adiós."

Could there be another explanation? Ruth had tucked Carmen away in an inexpensive hostel for the night, using her extra laundry money from the neighbors to do so. Ruth needed time to think, and to speak with someone — anyone who could give her advice without causing more panic.

Where was that girl? And the infant! She was still healing from the surgery. Even if they had gone for a walk, she shouldn't be outside gallivanting with all those germs. How long should Ruth wait before going to the police?

Didn't Luz know better?

Ruth had promised Carmen she would return in the morning; together they would walk the city, looking for her lost sister. Carmen had hugged the woman fiercely in return. Ruth knew she had done the right thing, although her kindness came at personal expense. She couldn't leave the woman to sleep on the street if Carmen was Luz's sister, nor could she bring Carmen home.

Mayra had mercifully agreed to watch over the boys if Ruth didn't make it home by nightfall.

Ruth continued walking laps in the kitchen. She'd found Macy's note taped to the refrigerator explaining some trip to the altiplano to take photographs. The note was addressed to Señor Duncan but left in the open. She assumed this was so she too would know why, once again, the Americans weren't home.

> *Ben,*
>
> *Left for the highlands on a photo assignment. Sam can explain if you want details. Fernando knows where I am. I will be back in a couple weeks.*

You need a new assistant. And we need to talk.
I miss you.

With love,
M

This woman! Why couldn't she help clean up the messes in her own house?

They were never home. And they were never together. Ruth shook her head. One problem at a time; the Americans' marriage was not a priority. She had a baby to find, and with Padre Pedro and la señora away . . .

Doctora Claudia! The doctora would know what to do, if anyone did.

Ruth hurried across town again, hoping she'd still find the doctor at the central hospital in the late afternoon. A handful of Tarija shop owners were unlocking gates and turning on lights after the mid-day siesta. Others remained closed, as families prepared for Friday-night mass.

The housekeeper made it to the hospital in time; Claudia was available, the receptionist on the pediatric floor informed her. Ruth found herself gripping her still shaking hands, now pacing the hospital linoleum.

"Señora Ruth, it is so nice to see you. Thank you for coming so quickly. Did the floor nurse call the house?"

"Doctora?" She leaned in to peck the woman on the cheek, as was the customary greeting.

"Come this way. You can see the child. We are lucky the nanny brought her in when she did. The fever was the first sign."

"The baby is here?"

"Yes." The doctor raised one eyebrow. "You didn't know?"

"Oh, praise the heavens. Praise God!" Ruth's legs nearly gave way, a flood of immediate relief. She reached for the wall, steadying herself. "Thank you, God!"

The doctor stopped, crossing her arms. "What is going on? Ruth?"

"I came home from the market and they were gone." Ruth giggled, her happiness overwhelming her, bubbling to the surface in inappropriate laughter.

She wouldn't lose her job! She hadn't lost the baby!

"I didn't know where they could be and I've waited for hours. Padre Pedro is away in La Paz. I just . . . I didn't know what to do. I came here to see you for help. Thank goodness the child is here." She shook her head, laughing. She'd let her imagination get away from her. A kidnapper? Luz? Ha! "Will the baby be okay? Did you say something about a fever?"

"Be reassured, the baby will be fine with a course of antibiotics. The nanny is sleeping in her room next to her. Come with me. I will show you."

As the doctor had described, the baby girl slept, swaddled in a light green cotton blanket. A tube of off-white liquid fed through her nose, delivering necessary medication. Luz snored gently from a chair, one hand resting on the baby's bassinet.

"She arrived mid-morning. She said the girl was vomiting and a fever came on quickly. She was worried perhaps the 'wawa' had influenza." Claudia whispered, leading Ruth into the hallway by the elbow. A dozen other infants were also in the room, which was alive with the beeping of machines and swishing of nurses, who walked between the rows of tiny, fragile patients. Luz and the baby slept through it all.

"Is it influenza?"

"Not likely. She has green discharge in her ear, likely has

the first of many ear infections, which are not uncommon in cleft palate children. We will be able to get it under control with the antibiotics. I put her on the drip just to be safe, and to increase her nutrition for a few days. The nanny is doing a good job, but this child is still underweight. The supplementation will help."

"I need to sit down."

They found a chair. Ruth considered the day's events.

Had she imagined the day's events? Could Luz be the child's mother?

"Any idea what the Americans plan to do with the child? Have they come up with a name?"

Ruth stalled. She wasn't certain her bosses had even thought of the child, much less named her.

"The señor hasn't been home for several weeks. He is busy working in the capital. And the señora has just left for the countryside to take photographs."

"Ah, yes. I saw her photos of Entre Rios in the newspaper. One of these days I suspect I'll see her. She does exist?" The doctor smiled, playfully.

Ruth laughed. "Yes. She does." Unexpectedly, Ruth felt protective of the Americans. "I should get home to my boys. It has been a long day. Thank you, Doctora. I am so glad to hear they are here. Please let Luz know I came by. I will help arrange transportation when they are ready to come home."

"I will do so. For an orphan, that little one certainly is lucky to have so many who are concerned about her well-being. Thank you, Ruth. The receptionist will see you out."

"Doctora Claudia, one more thing."

"Yes?"

"Is there any way you can tell who the mother is? Maybe by blood?"

The doctor squinted at the housekeeper, considering the questions.

"There are complicated tests we could send to Buenos Aires, but they would cost far too much money. Even if the Duncans wanted to fund such extravagance, I'd talk them into letting us use the money otherwise. I need vaccines. Another night nurse. Training for our pediatric surgeon in repairing burns. I don't need to know who the mother of that orphan is."

Ruth nodded. "I understand."

"Wait?" The doctor's eyes grew wide. "Do you think you know who the mother is?"

"I, uh. No. I just . . .I was just wondering if there was a simple test. Something that could tell us what region she came from, perhaps?"

The doctor had no ability to hide emotion. Ruth could tell she was waiting for more explanation, one Ruth was not prepared to give. Thankfully, as the mother of four, the housekeeper was quite versed in telling a convincing white lie.

"There are just too many children abandoned," Ruth continued. "I wish there was some sort of test. Perhaps then the women would be less likely to leave their little ones like this."

"Ah, yes. Testing as a form of public shame . . . Hmm." The doctor put her hands in her lap, as though considering the social implications of such a program. "No, no. It would never work. Women need access to condoms. Education too, but we should start with the condoms. If I could just get our priest friend on our side of this conversation."

"Our side?"

"Well, yes. You have four children and no husband." The doctor's blunt and miscalculated judgment struck Ruth.

"I wanted my children. And they have the same father!" Ruth's face burned, shocked with the woman's matter of fact observation. Ruth put her hands on her hips. "Not that this is your business. I will be on my way."

"I have offended you. I just assumed . . ."

"Because I am a poor maid and have no husband that . . . that . . ." Ruth huffed. "That I would agree with sin? You are incorrect! I do not agree. I love my boys as much as you would love your children if you had any!"

Ruth immediately regretted both her tone and lack of respect. Her mouth puckered with bitterness. Her boys were not planned, but this would never make Ruth Leona Castro sorry for being their mother.

The doctor didn't flinch.

"Very well. My mistake. Good day."

Ruth watched in disbelief as the doctor turned on her heel, returning to her office, through the doors of the nursery.

25. SOROCHE

Macy awoke to the symphony of rural life. Chickens clucked in the doorway, pecking at the dust. A lone donkey brayed somewhere in the distance. A log, almost spent, flickered orange from the kitchen oven.

What she couldn't hear was also noticeable. No romance music or news updates from Ruth's kitchen radio. No running water. No cars and their noisy tail pipes. No baby crying. No song birds.

Was the altitude too high for songbirds? But what about the chickens?

Macy ran fingers through her matted head of hair. The migraine was gone, but her stomach ached like it could return any moment. She needed a hot mug of caffeine—any form would do. And a latrine.

"Here goes nothing," she whispered aloud to the empty home, as she bundled up in an additional sweater. She could barely zip the puffy down ski coat; white feathers tried to escape from worn seams. Her hair whipped in the easterly winds, sending strands against her face and upward, toward another cloudless blue sky. Pulling her sunglasses into place, she scanned the hillside, spotting a black object moving in the distance. After a moment or two, Macy realized this was neither a llama nor other unknown highland animal. It was her hostess. The matriarch of the family, Gloria, was a speck on the horizon. She moved slowly, keeping an eye on the small group of animals.

Llamas? Alpacas? What was the difference again?

After a bit of poking around outside the mud home, Macy found a pit latrine hidden behind a gap-tooth fence. One of the rolls of toilet paper she'd brought along was hanging from a rusty nail hook. A split bar of green soap rested on one edge of the wood frame, near a bucket of murky water. Macy guessed by the color of the suds, the entire village had risen and used the facilities before her.

She locked herself in the latrine, using the hook and eye latch, and as quickly as possible got her pants down and back up, listening with unintentional curiosity at the depth of the latrine. The cool Andean air whirled around her, sending goose bumps from head to toe.

Grateful all the same for the scrap of soap and water, she emerged, ready to throw her hair back into a secured braid, hike the hill, and ask about a cup of tea.

A few minutes later, after crunching what seemed a cross between tundra and tumbleweed with each labored step of her hiking boots, Macy mustered a "Buenos dias" between blue lips. She stuck her head between her legs once reaching Gloria and the herd. Sucking as deeply as she could, she felt the thin air barely register. It had taken just 500 yards for Macy's chest to ache like she'd finished running a marathon. When her eyesight refocused, she stood to see a smirking, bemused Gloria.

The woman was at least eight inches shorter than Macy.

She'd read that Bolivians living at such altitudes were typically shorter, their bodies adapted to limited oxygen. Deep creases lined Gloria's eyes and forehead, but when she smiled, her entire face rose in a cheery glow.

"Buenos dias, Señora Camera," Gloria responded. She was missing several of her bottom teeth, which did nothing to take away from her obvious joy at the situation. Macy smiled in return, careful not to waste words until her heartbeat calmed.

She walked next to Gloria slowly, admiring the llamas and the little shrubbery available for their grazing. Several of the animals had colorful satin ribbons on their ears, like Mexican piñatas that had come to life. Macy made a mental note to ask why once she could figure out how to word the odd comparison in Spanish. With any luck, it wouldn't require repetition or too much gesturing.

Would this woman know what a Mexican piñata was? Macy looked at the horizon, empty of telephone poles or antenna on the few roofs below. There were no trees either.

No trees. No songbirds.

"Señora," Macy started, carefully, seeing telling black specks on the edge of her vision. She had pushed herself too far.

How could such a short walk be so far?

She looked back at the house where she slept. How would she ever be able to navigate these hills to find the right photos for Sam and *National Geographic*?

As she brought an imaginary cup of hot tea to her lips, gesturing with a smile for some caffeine, Gloria smiled, understanding.

This was the last thing she remembered before waking nearly a day later, with a warm cloth on her head, and a rustically sewn canvas pouch of herbs on her stomach. Macy tried sitting up from the cot, again under the indigo striped blanket, listening to chickens clucking just outside the door.

How long had she been here? What happened?

Like the alcoholic flashbacks of a debaucherous night, Macy's mind flickered images from the previous 24 hours— none of which helped extinguish her burning embarrassment. She had been sick in a bucket, and had a flash of recognition of two men holding her under her arms as she used a latrine in the dark of night, with only a swirl of starry sky overhead. Those tending to her had whispered the same word again and again: soroche.

"What in the world? Ouch. My God." Macy's hand went to the side of her pounding head. The other searched the pocket of her jeans. Miraculously she found another migraine pill. Gloria, who had been resting with her chin on her chest while perched on a tiny stool near the edge of the bed, hopped to her feet. Macy hadn't been drinking enough. All the guides had warned of severe altitude sickness. Soroche, the word used in this region of South America, referred to both the illness and the altitude. The guidebook said the soroche plant, with its bright pink flowers, thrived at great height. The local cure was mate de coca, a tea made of the same leaves used in cocaine production.

"Toma, por favor. Toma!" Gloria slid the mug into her hands.

"Gracias," she muttered through chapped lips. She stared at the mug, certain it wasn't something her husband or the DEA would approve of. Then again, they didn't have this headache.

The liquid tasted of winter grass and pine needles, but Macy didn't care. Tea water was boiled and safe; she motioned for another cup, weakly whispering "Por favor." Her lips split from dehydration, and she could taste blood as she gulped down the pill.

Gloria removed the sachet of herbs and placed a hand on Macy's head, feeling her temperature. Macy watched Gloria motion to several children including the village boy who had eaten off of her plate, to do something.

"Mana llamkasanichu samanaykipaq punchawnintin!"

They scattered outside, returning with buckets of well water that swished and slopped, leaving dark brown drops on the hard swept mud floor. Gloria led Macy into the kitchen, shooing the children outside, and pointed toward a lone plastic stool. She looked Macy in the eye and patiently nodded, pointing to the water.

"Okay," Macy said. Her bones ached like she had the flu. She had no energy to argue.

Macy felt the woman's rough hands work, gently unzipping the layers of her jackets and removing her sweater. Gloria slid the clothing down just enough to wrap a worn towel around Macy's neck. Carefully, she bent Macy forward in the seat and let her braid loose. Gloria ran her hand from the top of her head to her neck, shaking the hair free. She did so briskly, almost too hard. Macy grimaced, hoping whatever her Bolivian hostess was doing would ultimately bring comfort.

Before she could protest, the first cup of cold well water dripped down her neck, over her head and through her nest of hair into the bucket at her feet. Macy jumped from the temperature, but Gloria's hands were there, rubbing her back and pushing her back toward the bucket.

Her hostess miraculously produced a small bottle of hotel shampoo from the pocket of her apron. The pleasantly sharp and sweet smell of chemicals—those she had been tricked into thinking smelled like wildflowers until wandering the first field of paintbrush and asters—reached Macy's nose. The aroma of warm chocolate chip cookies couldn't have provided more comfort. Macy realized what Gloria was doing. In a ritual that crossed cultures, the woman was washing her hair to provide a bit of comfort.

Little by little, Macy felt her migraine fog and fever lift as the pill, caffeine and touch took effect. One cup of water. Another. A shift of buckets.

Gloria worked tenderly, washing and finger-combing the mass of hair before carefully pulling Macy upward into a seated position. She produced a plastic wide-tooth comb and patiently untangled every last knot, wringing her hair of water upon completion. With a gentle pat on the crown of her head, Macy felt her shoulders relax. Turning, she took Gloria's hands into her own.

"Thank you. That was the nicest thing anyone has done for me in a long time. You are so kind." Tears gathered at her eyes.

"Utkayta rimaptiyki, mana hapiyta yachanichu," Gloria responded. If you speak too quickly, I will not be able to understand.

Macy hadn't the energy to write out the phrase. The locked eyes for a moment, still holding hands. Gloria understood.

"Sulpayki anchata." Gloria nodded. Then repeating herself, raising her palms, "Sulpayki anchata."

"Thank you!" It dawned on Macy.

"Thank you." Gloria managed.

"Sulpaykee orgata." Gloria and Macy laughed together at her poor pronunciation.

Macy redressed and sat on the edge of the bed, her hair wrapped tight in a towel, her cheeks red from the cold water. Gloria returned with a mug of steaming hot broth, which Macy sipped until falling asleep, yet again.

The first week in the village took all of Macy's strength. Her legs remained weak from severe altitude sickness, but her mind was clear as the migraines mercifully ceased. Her dream of finding a bilingual teenager to help communicate was a fantasy. Instead, the tips of her fingers ached from flipping back and forth through the small bilingual dictionary Ben had given her. The binding of the paperback soon cracked.

She would write out sentences beforehand, practicing sounding them out with the phonetic guide. Slowly, Macy would work up the nerve to try her conjugation with Gloria, or the three boys who could regularly be found harassing the dogs in the family compound. Gloria, and the boys, spoke Quecha first, and Spanish second. Their everyday slang was a patois of the two.

Days later, the only Quechan phrase Macy repeated again and again to her hostess was, "Sulpayki anchata." Thank you.

Gloria would stop whatever chore she'd been in the middle of to listen to the painful pronunciations. Macy threw together sentences, often missing an object or correct pronoun. She would continue to look up various words in the dictionary until Gloria nodded, sorting out the linguistic puzzle of the moment.

On the sixth day, Gloria took the bilingual dictionary from Macy and placed it in her apron pocket. Leading the American outside with one hand, and holding a mesh bag in the other, she motioned.

"Mira. Sol." Gloria pointed to the sun. Macy nodded. "Y tierra." Earth. "Agua."

"I knew 'agua.'" Macy laughed.

"Llamkasani yachanaykipaq runasimita." Gloria raised one eyebrow. I am working to teach you Quecha, too.

"Uh, Quechua. One language hard enough Señora Gloria!" Macy continued to chuckle. "Espanol, por favor! How Ruth would laugh to hear me now!"

"Kusikuni kaypi kasanki." I am glad you are here. Gloria laughed in return. "Está bien. Español. Pero un día, hablarás la idioma de este tierra. Nuestra lengua."

Macy noticed how Gloria spoke in a near whisper, but her giggle was high, loud and carefree. The arch of her nose was like that of a raven's beak—pronounced. If Macy didn't know better, and the woman before her wasn't wearing a traditional Bolivian pollera skirt, she'd think she was on the mesas of northern Arizona, among the Hopi and Navajo. Macy had spent countless assignment hours on the reservations, photographing lightning storms, elections, and once a federal food drop when snow left both tribes further isolated from their neighbors in Gallup and Holbrook.

Gloria's skin was the color of burnt sienna—sun worn, rust and golden brown, with cherry red wind-chapped cheeks, and a pile of graying black hair she kept under a felt bolero, tied in a series of braids that dripped down her back.

The two continued this way, repeating back and forth in Spanish until Macy could remember the vocabulary words on her own. By sunset, she had learned how to gather eggs, spot a brooding hen, chop firewood, haul well water, herd llamas back into a corral, and pull up the right potatoes for the meal without disturbing the mounds of baby potatoes near by.

This would have been a feat of accomplishment any day for a city girl, but the fact she could point to each of these activities and now make basic one to two word conversation about them in Spanish felt like a miracle.

They ate what they worked on all day, a simple dish of roasted potatoes, soft boiled eggs and more of Gloria's delicious tea. Macy collapsed after doing dinner dishes. She had never been more tired.

The next day, Macy stood outside with the blanket door whipping open and closed. She washed her face with a cup of cool water, rubbing hard at her neck and behind her ears. It was too cold to bathe, and hauling and heating the water would have taken an army. Instead, she kept her hair pulled back and her face and teeth clean. It would have to be enough until she returned to Tarija.

As she brushed her teeth, admiring the llamas in their pen, two of the neighborhood boys took off in worn uniforms down a dirt path. Macy had yet to wander beyond Gloria's homestead, within the neighborhood compound of homes. She watched as they swung fraying backpacks over their bony shoulders, chatting with each other, likely relieved to be free of the day's farm work. They skipped past an older girl—Macy guessed was a neighbors' daughter—who threw seed from a bucket, feeding and entertaining a group of feisty, perpetually hungry chickens. The compound's younger girls entered the coop for the morning's harvest, emerging with aprons full of spotted blue, brown, and creamy white eggs.

"Wait!" she called out, as the boys disappeared over a hill. "Wait!" They continued, a trail of dust rising behind them.

She spat out her toothpaste and ran back inside, rushing to pull together her camera and pack. Grabbing her jacket and tying her running shoe laces tight, Macy soon joined the boys on the road. They were lollygagging, in no hurry to get to school.

"Comó se llaman?" Macy mustered, panting.

"Chucho."

"Chucho?"

"Sí, señora." The bashful boy looked at his feet. One toe pushed through a hole in his canvas sneaker.

"Mucho gusto."

"Y yo soy Huevos" said the older one, with a bit too much sass.

"Huevos, eh?" Macy knew this one. Eggs. But there was a double entendre, and hearing the foreigner repeat their joke made the boys blush and giggle. She guessed they were still in elementary school—too young to have worked up any real nerve with girls, but feisty enough to want to play off their insecurities as charm.

She hadn't been out of high school that long. Boys were boys.

"Huevos. Chucho." She tipped a hat she wasn't wearing. "Yo soy Macy. Dónde va?"

"Dónde vamos?" They squealed with laughter.

"Si, donde vamos?" She tried again, still uncertain.

"La escuela, Señora Camera! Adios!" The pair ran off, laughing. She watched as they entered a small brick building. Outside, an old metal bell tolled, pulled by another boy in a similar uniform. She peeked in the classroom. Three dozen boys of varied ages and two girls sat at long desks that reminded Macy of park picnic tables. The teacher hadn't yet arrived. A lone chalkboard on one wall had the remainder of yesterday's lessons: from the alphabet to algebra. Macy scanned the room. The children were silent, watching her. Their ages varied from elementary school to mid-teens.

The one-room schoolhouse wasn't terribly different from Padre Pedro's operation in the city, but it was vastly different from her childhood experience.

Who could possibly teach so many children of such varied ages and have any success?

"Buenas," a man with gray hair and tiny spectacles said, brushing past her into the room. His messenger bag was overflowing with papers and he quickly produced a chalk eraser, deleting the prior lesson.

"Buenos días."

"Entras hoy? Quieres aprender? Ya empezamos!" He was too stern for Macy, and his quick Spanish confused her. She smiled and waved goodbye to Chucho and Huevos. "Adios niños!"

The classroom erupted in laughter and the teacher rapped the board with his knuckles, trying to restore calm. At least she didn't say, "Goodbye Chucho and Balls!"

As Macy approached the line, the white cross painted on the front of the clinic's door came into view.

"Buenos dias," she said quietly as she snaked along the queue, curious as to who was inside. A short, Bolivian woman in a pressed white doctor's coat spoke loudly with her hands, demonstrating to a young mother how to swaddle the newborn in question. Macy followed along, although understanding only one or two words in the conversation. Quickly enough, the fussy baby with a cap of jet-black hair was tucked with arms tight into a yellow receiving blanket and returned to his mother's basket. She nodded, thanking the doctor before the next woman in line scooted forward.

This mother had twins in her baskets, both swaddled, and several months older. They were awaiting vaccinations, which the doctor did with such speed that the infants barely registered the pain before their mother had them wrapped once again. With wide, squat feet, she hustled out the clinic door with her heavy cargo.

Macy thought of the basket she'd found at her doorstep. She stared at her feet, feeling a wave of guilt for leaving the child in the care of the housekeeper.

"How may I help you?"

Macy's head snapped up. "Oh, you speak English! This is great." Macy grinned. "It is so nice to hear something familiar. A relief really . . . I've been here for nearly a week. . . ."

The doctor interrupted. "Ma'am, quickly. There is a line. Can I help you?" Macy's smile faded. "Oh. Right. I'm sorry. I, well, I am a photographer," she mumbled. "I'd like to take some photos today of the clinic and the women and learn more about their stories."

"Why?"

"Why?"

"Ma'am—I have a line of 50 women today. Each of these babies needs to be seen. And as you can see, I am alone. My assistant has the flu and I've been on my feet for six hours already."

"Why. Well. I am a photographer and am trying to learn about this area. I hope to publish the photos in the US."

The doctor glared. She had a small surgical incision on her neck, and unhappiness clung to her like a miasma. "You have to ask them. And you must stay out of my way." She stuffed needles into a red medical waste tub. "You have my permission if you are respectful." The doctor motioned the next woman forward, who held a child with a deformed foot. "Remember. Respectful! And do not interrupt!"

"Of course." Macy stepped back, examining the line. She was right. Several dozen women stood patiently waiting for attention. Their children were remarkably well behaved. A few breastfed infants while standing in line. Others threw a ball of string in a rudimentary game of fetch with a gaggle of toddlers. Macy walked the line again, now examining the highland residents more closely. Most of the children appeared healthy. There were several, however, with obvious deformities.

"Excuse me," Macy interrupted. "I am very sorry to interrupt. I know." She raised both palms as a sign of peace. "Would you please ask them permission for me to shoot and I won't bother you again?"

"You may not slow me down!" The doctor stomped her foot. Macy bit her lip to prevent laughing out loud. She hadn't encountered such a fiery personality in a very long time. The doctor seemed like a caricature, with her huffs and stomps and gruff demeanor. "Fine. I'll just ask them all." In Spanish, the woman quickly explained there was a photographer here and if the women had objections they were to raise their hands.

Macy waited, watching the line after the translation was snarled in her direction.

No hands were raised. The women, it seemed to Macy, were as curious about her as she was about them.

"Carry on," the doctor shouted. Macy jumped, finally letting out her laughter and getting out of the woman's way.

"Thank you. No more interruptions. I promise."

"Silence!" The doctor slammed her hand down. Macy slinked away.

Soon, she heard the women gossiping in the line about

Señora Camera. Her reputation preceded her, but she wondered, what could they know?

The women nodded one by one, presenting their children. Macy swapped lenses and batteries as necessary, moving through the room, searching for the areas with the best daylight. Macy examined each face through crosshairs and shot hundreds of photos once her subjects relaxed, returning to their discussions as though she wasn't there, a voyeur. Deep into the afternoon, fatigued, Macy started to pack. The school bell had chimed hours ago. Chucho and Huevo were likely already at home. Gloria would wonder where she was.

"If you leave now, you'll miss the most interesting patient of the day. Our penguin boy." The doctor's tone had softened with the day's light, miraculously.

Macy raised an eyebrow, timid and unsure of the woman's sudden change. "The penguin boy?" Feathers? Discoloration?

"Yes. Horrible case. You will understand when you see him."

The last woman who walked into the clinic was followed by a young boy, whose arms were under his jacket, by his sides. The mother made small talk with the doctor, between fits of coughs. Eventually, she lifted the child to the rudimentary exam table and began to remove his clothing. Again, Macy bit her lip, but this time to hold back a gasp. She was thankful to watch this scene with her camera hiding the horror she was sure was displayed across her face.

The child had been burned from chin to his toes. His skin, she could see once the clothing was removed, had healed in rough, painful crests and valleys across his body. His arms, as a result of the injury, were fused to the sides of his body.

The penguin boy.

The doctor carefully applied a salve to his skin. The boy didn't wince; his skin long since healed. The visit was a checkup, likely of the mother's mental well-being as much as the child's. The mother asked a handful of questions Macy didn't understand, although her tone was clear. She could imagine the pleadings.

This child needed a surgeon, a team of specialists, and a clean environment.

The doctor continued to surprise Macy with her calm, patient tone. Together, the mother and physician redressed the boy and soon, the pair of villagers were gone, headed to their home on the next hillside.

"Doctor," Macy didn't know what to say. "How? I mean. What happened? Would you tell me?"

"The child fell into a cooking fire. You will see these injuries all over rural Bolivia," she moved one arm across the room, signaling the villages dotted across the yellow hills in the distance. "I hear from colleagues this happens in other areas where ground level cooking fires are commonplace. He was bandaged incorrectly. The previous nurse tried to save his life from infection, and rightly so—mind you, by wrapping the boy in gauze. Unfortunately, his arms were wrapped to his body. Before they could correct the error, the fusing had begun."

Macy rocked on her heels, listening but scanning the digital screen of her camera, reviewing the photos of the boy and his mother. This was her story.

"To correct the fusing, he would have been at risk of additional infection. The family chose to leave his arms as they were. Sadly, he isn't alone. Penguins are all over Bolivia."

"A cooking fire?"

"How do you cook at night here, while staying in our village?"

"A wood-fed stove."

"Ah, it figures. Well, that is because the fancy baker cousin of hers paid for a stove. Most of us have a ring of stones on the earth in the kitchen. We fill it with sticks and logs until we get a good fire going and we cook over this. Our homes are always full of smoke, which locals believe provides a blanket of good health."

Macy remained silent. The doctor raised an eyebrow, challenging an interruption.

"How many children does Gloria have?"

"You know I am staying with Gloria?"

"Of course I do. Everyone in this village knows of our intrepid American." Her tone was dismissive and she shook her head like Macy's visit had been announced nationally.

"Uh, I am not sure how many kids Gloria has." Macy was taken back. "There are always kids running around the house, but I can't figure out who are hers, and who belong to the neighbors."

"She has eight, most are old enough to live on their own."

"Eight? Eight children."

"She gave birth to 11. I delivered seven of those babies, including several of the dead ones."

"I . . . I . . .God." Macy sighed. Her loss felt further away each day, and yet Jacob was always with her.

"You have two hands and eight children. One is likely to fall in or near the fire at some point. Most of us here have a burn or two." She raised a corner of one pant leg to show her deformed shin, marred with similar burn to the boy's. "Some of us are luckier than others. But we are all raised in these homes, under the blankets of smoke. Burns are part of this life."

"Can it be corrected?"

"Yes. Ovens."

"Well, yes. But I meant his arms. Can his arms be corrected? Healed? Surely a plastic surgeon could fix this?"

"Yes." She laughed. Macy didn't like the sound of it. "And, what do you call them? Uh . . ." she tapped the side of her head searching for the right word. "The horse? With the horn?"

"A unicorn?"

"Yes. The boy could also use a unicorn with this fancy surgery. Maybe it could fly him to the hospital and back? Ah! Make it two unicorns. One for the mother too."

Macy moaned.

The doctor snickered. She shoved medical supplies into boxes, which she stacked on a pull cart.

"If we can't build ovens, how can we fly children for fancy procedures? Tell me this, how many buses or cars have you seen since you arrived?"

Macy considered the question. It was true. She'd seen only one bus go down the road that brought her to Gloria's house. It was so full of passengers, and traveling at such a slow pace, neighbors rushed from their homes to sell hard-boiled eggs and llama jerky to travelers through the open windows.

"One."

"And where was it headed?"

"I would guess Tarija or maybe La Paz."

"Correct. One bus per week, more or less. And there are thousands of us up here. This is why I went to Cuba to study medicine and English, and why I returned. We cannot solve our village problems with fancy answers. We need ovens first. Surgery is a luxury we cannot afford."

The doctor pushed forward, faster down the path, further

from Gloria's. Macy needed to turn around, but she didn't want to end the conversation. She also didn't want to find her way back in the oncoming darkness.

"When will you return? Can I take more photos? You are really good with these women."

She snorted. "Of course I am good with them. I am them. I grew up in this village."

"We got off on the wrong foot. My name is Macy Duncan. I didn't get your name."

"Yes. We know. Four hillsides have spent most nights of the last week wondering what you are doing here. While I do not care, it would be fun to deliver this gem of knowledge to my sisters, whom I live with. They, sadly, very much still care about village gossip."

"Oh. I. Well."

"Do you stammer often? It might be an impediment." The doctor stopped walking for a moment to turn and grimace at Macy. "Very well then. No explanation? I'll just make something up. Good day to you."

Macy watched in bewilderment as the doctor pulled a knit cap over her head and continued at a quick pace, pulling along her supplies and medical records. She wondered if the doctor was bipolar.

"At least tell me where the boy lives. Perhaps I can get more information and can help get him the surgery he needs?" Macy followed after her, pleading. "I can get him help. I know I can."

"And the others?"

"I am sure we can do something."

"There are Americans here every few months. They bring used medical equipment and pat us on the heads and take photos with us like we are some exotic *National Geographic* moment. No, thank you."

"I. Uh." Macy's face burned.

"Dear, really. You should have that looked at."

"I don't have a stammer!" Macy now stomped her foot. The sun was dropping behind the horizon and the valley was full of golden light. Llamas grazed in the distance and the school bell rang when gusts of wind came racing through. "Where does that boy live? What hillside? Please. Please! This is important to me! And, well, my husband will be very interested in this too. He works for USAID and he knows plenty of people who could help. I'm sure he knows someone who could build the ovens."

The doctor stopped in her hurried tracks.

"USAID?"

"Yes. That is why we are here." Macy was working hard to breathe.

Macy watched in horror as the woman drew in a deep mouth of mucus and spit on the ground in disgust. It landed just beyond the tip of her shoe.

"You will never return to my clinic. Never! Traitor American! NEVER!" Shouting, the doctor continued on her way, waving a fist at the sinking sun.

Stunned, Macy felt goose bumps and the hair on the back of her neck rise.

26. STING

La Doctora Claudia spoke to Luz candidly and too quickly. Luz struggled to remember the details, muttered by the physician. If the doctor knew Luz was the wawa's mother, Claudia would have likely taken more care when describing the possible hearing loss, infections, wound care, and malnutrition.

Luz felt dizzy.

Would her baby live? How could she return home again without her child? Never mind everyone already thought the baby was buried.

Luz shook her head. Her child was still alive. Today, she had to keep fighting for them both.

"We know cleft palate children have more ear infections. There is the possibility of tubes, but she is still too young. And the Americans would have to agree to pay for another surgery."

"Should I try to keep her ears clean?" Luz looked at her daughter, wondering if she should have given the infant more baths in the kitchen sink. Did she wash her ears? Luz's heart pounded.

"Cleanliness never hurts, but no. There is little you can do. Village babies with these types of deformities rarely live as long as she has. You are from the village, aren't you?" The doctor raised an eyebrow.

"Yes, Doctora." Luz tried to keep her voice steady.

"And? What do they do with children who have problems at birth?"

"I don't want to say."

The doctor guffawed. "I have heard many stories. They drop them in old wells. They take them out into the farthest field and say goodbye. They send an uncle to drown them in the river. 'The Gods' will take care of them, won't they?"

Luz started to cry, angered by the woman's careless tone. Her ruthless assessment of rural living was cruel in its accuracy.

She hiccupped, holding the side of her wawa's bassinet for strength.

"Oh. I have upset you." The doctor stared at her blankly.

Luz wiped her nose with the back of her hand.

"Just follow the rules I gave you. Remember?" The doctor began shuffling papers. Luz could tell her tears had caused discomfort. This lady doctor really was like a man. Luz knew that if Ruth were there, she'd be hugged and given something warm to eat in this moment. There would be a steady hand, rubbing her back. Instead, the salt-and-peppered doctor stood before her, tapping a foot.

"Repeat them for me."

"Repeat?"

"Repeat the rules. You need to memorize them before I'm letting you leave the hospital with this child. She is still healing."

"No smoking. Get her shots. And feed her like this." Luz motioned holding an infant upright.

"Yes. Precisely! Good work, young woman."

Luz's mouth was dry and her hands shook.

"Any other questions?"

"How long will she need these medications? Forever?"

The doctor laughed. "No, not forever. But antibiotics will fight away infections when she is between surgeries. She'll need them as ear infections like this one emerge during the next few years as well." Claudia continued filing papers, staring at the task at hand. Her lack of eye contact made Luz nervous. She wanted the doctor to sit down for a moment and calmly explain everything to her one more time, lest she forget.

The doctor continued, "Antibiotics are inexpensive and easy enough to come by. We rarely have shortages at the hospitals these days. If she spikes a fever, you bring her to me. Do you understand?"

Luz nodded. Her own heartbeat pounded in her ears, giving her anxiety a sound.

Swoosh. Swoosh. Swoosh.

Maybe she should have listened to La Doña. Maybe her wawa was better off in the next life, as a star shining from the heavens on to this one.

The French nuns who ran the clinic in Entre Rios had antibiotics too. "Antibiotiques" they would whisper with a gentle smile and nudge, pressing the wax paper packets of yellow pills into the hands of mothers with feverish babes. But would they know how to care for her daughter?

Luz couldn't think of a single child in Entre Rios with a fixed lip who'd grown to adulthood. The thought sent shivers down her neck. The hare-lipped babies of Entre Rios who did survive were ghosts. Apparitions here one day and gone the next. Their survival came by the gracious hand of visiting medical teams or a rare donor who got the baby to a city surgeon. They never returned to village life afterward.

Luz would have to talk La Doña into paying for the surgeries. She wrapped her arms around her waist and rocked from side to side. Luz looked at the sleeping child, watching her chest rise and fall with the wonder and grace of life struggling to survive.

This miracle, she thought. My miracle! I have abandoned her once. I cannot leave her again.

The doctor stared hard, now with both hands on her hip. Her foot tapped twice on the linoleum floor.

"Will she be able to hear?" Luz's words slurred together, rushed and nervous.

"Most children with cleft palate have fine hearing. Time will tell. If we can keep these early ear infections to a minimum, she will do better. You should read to her. Hearing many words will help her vocabulary too."

If I could read to you, my love, I would. You will go to school and read and maybe go to college one day. Your village mama will be so proud of you, my love. One day, you can teach me.

"You were smart to bring her to the hospital when you did." The doctor's tone softened.

The teen wondered why hospital staff kept praising her for the obvious. Her infant had spiked a burning fever and begun vomiting. When she saw the green pus also in her daughter's hair, near her ears, a pain in her own stomach signaled an emergency. The walk to the hospital had felt like she was being stung in the gut by a hive of wasps. She raced through the streets cradling her daughter, not remembering how long it had taken to arrive, or the route she'd taken to get there.

Her wawa, breathing through her mouth with a feeding tube threaded down one nostril, now hummed sweetly through the incision. They'd given her a bath and clothed her in a new pink onesie. Luz's own stomachache had subsided the moment a nurse told her it was a simple ear infection and would soon be under control.

"When can I take her home?"

"Her fever is down and she has responded well to treatment. We'll finish this feeding and you may go. Oh! The maid came by earlier." The doctor wore an odd smile.

"The maid?"

"Yes. You know. The short one with the kids."

"Doña Ruth?"

"Yes. She said to call her when you want a ride home. She was worried when she couldn't find you. I noticed she came over to peek on you both before returning home, but you were both sleeping soundly."

Luz forced her mouth closed. She considered how quickly Ruth had been able to trace her steps. They'd been out of the home for less than a day. The housekeeper was on her trail.

"Thank you. How do I call her?"

The doctor laughed again. Luz stared at her, wondering if there was something wrong with the woman.

"I have never used a phone before." Luz refused to be embarrassed by this; the doctor must have known a village girl in worn clothing had little experience with city life.

"Follow me." The doctor shook her head.

As the nurses removed the feeding tube and prepared the child to leave, Luz watched as the doctor used a pencil to dial a rotary telephone, scrunching her face in dismay when no one answered.

"That's strange. She said she would be there. Never mind. Here." The doctor reached into her office desk drawer, handing Luz several folded Bolivianos. "Take this and get a cab. I have other things to do today."

The young mother watched as the woman stuffed her hands in her jacket pockets and briskly walked out of the room without saying goodbye.

Luz cradled her daughter, who was swaddled, and once again sleeping deeply with a soft hum, as infants recovering from fevers do. Her cheeks were pink, where the long lashes of her resting eyes nearly brushed with a gentle arc. Luz raised the child to her nose, smelling her neck -- the perfect, crisply clean smell of baby. It brought an instant smile to her face.

"La Doña will just have to help me care for you. The bees will care for us all. One day, mi querida wawa, I will teach you how to place the hives in right fields. How to gather honey when it is at its sweetest. And how to sell when the market needs it most. Right now, I would guess they need my honey more than ever." She ran a hand over the infant's head of hair.

Outside of the hospital, one cab after another passed without stopping. She tried waving differently, but it had no effect. She was a poor highland colla. The city drivers couldn't be bothered. Frustrated and tired, Luz considered her options.

Carefully placing her daughter to her chest, she trudged back to the Americans' house. She owed Ruth an apology. Luz considered what she'd say, even practicing the words out loud, drowning out the sounds of her own hunger. It had been more than a day since she'd eaten anything warm, and Luz's stomach growled as she passed one restaurant after another opening for the evening meal. The smell of warm, yeasty bread covered the avenue like a fog. Luz held the baby closer, putting her head down against the wind and the city that constantly reminded her how far she was from home.

As she rounded a corner from a side street into the central square, not far from the Americans' home, Luz looked up to see Ruth exiting a small building across the park. It was certainly the housekeeper, with her short, bobbed hair. Outside of the kitchen, Ruth didn't wear her characteristic apron, but instead a modest, navy blue dress. It was the same dress Ruth wore the day they had met in the market.

Ruth didn't have her market basket, and the fruits and vegetable stands were long since closed for the evening. She also didn't have a hat, or a coat. It seemed to Luz Ruth must have rushed from work without thinking.

Families walked past Ruth, on their way into the nearby church for evening mass. Men carried children on their shoulders. Teenagers held hands and snuck kisses as they entered the church with bells tolling. The park cleared, and Luz started toward her friend, the baby still sleeping fast against her chest. A lone cyclist rode a few feet before her sending a cloud of gray pigeons into the air. Then, Luz caught a glimpse of who was standing in the shadows on the other end of Ruth's conversation.

Carmen?

Carmen.

It couldn't be. What was her sister doing here?

Luz took one step closer. Her eyes must be deceiving her. Keeping a safe distance, she watched as the two women chatted. With eyes wide, Luz saw her sister throw her arms around Ruth's neck and let out a cry. The girl moved quickly to hide behind a large tree in the plaza. The wind whipped and she felt the hair rise on the back of her neck.

How could these two know each other?

Luz considered running into her sister's arms in that moment, she would beg for forgiveness and plead to return to La Doña. Her sister would understand. The thought of holding on to Carmen was almost enough to propel her forward. She could tell Ruth the truth and be free of the weight of these lies. She could find a way to pay the Americans back, and go home with her sister and her daughter. They would have to understand!

She followed the pair as they walked down a city street, noticing they were traveling away from the Americans' house. Carmen was leaning on Ruth, who had a hand wrapped around her sister's waist.

What could possibly be going on?

Sure to stay in the shadows at a distance, Luz followed until the pair entered a small building together. Her heart pounded like a drum. She focused on forcing the sick feeling growing in her stomach back down her throat.

Small white cars, most dinged and one missing a front bumper, lined the front of the building. Luz didn't need to be able to read the sign above the door to know Ruth and her sister had just gone to the police.

27. ESCAPE

Holding her wawa with more determination than ever, Luz carefully crept away from the police department to a busier street. Men pushed carts full of thick slices of cake and sugary drinks. Others sold balloons. A woman called out from a stand with hot ears of corn and grilled meat. It was Friday night and families were gathering for dinner at the central square. Church would soon be out, and the plaza would fill with those looking for a glass of Argentinian wine and fillet of steak, both inexpensive this close to the international border.

Luz considered her options. What could Ruth and Carmen tell the police? She had abandoned her own baby and returned to care for the infant. But Carmen thought the baby was dead, and Ruth didn't know this baby was her daughter. Was it illegal to abandon a child? It was certainly wrong, but her other option was worse. She would not sit by in the village and watch her child die of something that could be fixed by the city doctors. She would just have to explain this to the police.

Luz clutched her daughter with one hand and her stomach with the other. She felt the tiny heartbeat ring against her chest. The baby was still soundly asleep. Luz's hunger dissolved into dizzying anxiety. Her stomach stung with its emptiness. She swallowed again and again, fighting tears and walking as fast as she could without waking the child.

Would they send her to prison? What would happen to her wawa?

She considered returning to the Americans' home and leaving the infant in her crib. At least then she would continue to get the surgeries she needed.

Someday, she would find her daughter. Someday, she would tell her about how she had tried to be brave. Luz would have to explain why she had gone to jail. Why every mistake she had made was worth having her daughter—something perfect, something entirely her own.

Her tears were hot, and her hands shook. It was the right thing to do, Luz knew. Yet, when she reached the Americans' street and passed their dark house, she kept walking.

It was hard enough to abandon her child once. She simply couldn't leave her twice.

Instead, Luz stuck a hand into her pocket to find the folded Bolivianos Doctora Claudia had given her. It was far too much money for a city cab; the doctor had been generous. Luz looked at the bills, studying them for the marks that she memorized to teach her illiterate mind how to use currency.

Walking under a flame tree in bloom, she stopped to smell the fragrant red and orange flowers. She had been walking for several hours, unsure of where to go other than farther away from the city center. The night was full of stars, visible even in the city. Luz looked to the heavens, noticing a few late-night bees still sucking nectar from the flowers in the tree above.

Bees. Her bees were waiting for her. La Doña was waiting, too. Did her mother have enough power to send bees to the city to find her daughter? It was possible. Luz stood for too long, staring at the creatures as they gathered their nectar.

She stuck a hand in her pocket; reviewing the bills once more, Luz walked to the bus station on the edge of town, saying a silent prayer. To the jaguars, to the God of the Catholic nuns. To whomever was in those starry skies willing to listen to her, she repeated a simple prayer:

Please help me keep my daughter.

"One for Entre Rios, please," she whispered to the ticket counter attendant, trying to keep an eye on the police officer at the busy bus depot entryway. She slid the bills across the counter.

Would they already be looking for her?

"You are six Bolivianos short." The attendant rapped her knuckles on the glass, getting Luz's attention. "Six short."

She rocked on her heels. There was no more money. She had no one else to ask for help.

"Please, miss. My baby is hungry. This is all I have. Please. Let me go home and I promise you one day I will return with the money."

"Six. Either get out of my line, or give me six more Bolivianos." The attendant had a lazy eye, which made Luz wonder which one to look at.

"Please. My child and I just want to go home. Please?"

"Here, here." Luz turned to see a small man behind her in line dig a hand into his woven bag. He handed her several coins. "Take a few extra and get some food for the trip." He winked at her, patting the baby's head. "Hello," he whispered. She noticed his hands were calloused. The few Bolivianos were a fortune to this laborer.

Luz's face crumpled at the unexpected kindness.

"Now, child. Go on. Pay her. We are all waiting." The man's smile revealed two missing top teeth.

"Thank you, abuelo. Thank you."

"It is nothing, mijita. Buen viaje."

Luz hugged the man, promising him she would do a good act for someone else as soon as she could in return. After asking several other young women for directions, mindful to stay as far away from the lone police officer as she could, Luz took her place on the bus to Entre Rios. She pushed in toward the window and lifted her blouse. The baby's blue eyes stared back at hers. The infant began to fuss.

"Oh, you. You and those eyes! That is what started this all. Why didn't your father leave you with anything other than his eyes?"

While this baby wasn't supposed to breastfeed, and her milk had long since gone, her nipples were the only thing she had to soothe the child until vendors came by selling bits of food. Even then, she was doubtful her daughter would get much more than a dribble of water before they reached home.

Home. What would she tell La Doña?

Resting her head against the glass, Luz felt her daughter suckle. She stroked the baby's head. Soon, the heavy diesel engine started and the bus filled with villagers headed to the high plains. Many women had children on their laps. An old man sat next to her, pulling a ball of rough wool from his satchel, he began to finger knit. Another woman carefully ate a handful of hot baked potatoes, round and purple.

Luz had what she wanted most.

As the bus pulled away, she watched as the lights of Tarija faded into the dark distance. Closing her eyes, she dreamed of one day returning to the city to explain to Ruth. To find the old man from the bus station. To give the Americans honey in thanks for providing for her daughter.

Luz leaned her head back on the seat, took a deep breath and closed her eyes. Her heart rate calmed and her breathing became even for the first time in hours as her hive of anxiety quieted. She whispered a simple prayer:

"Thank you."

Luz and her wawa were headed home.

28. FLAMINGO

The news of Ben's employment made it back to Gloria's compound before Macy did. Like the smoke of cooking fires blanketing the high mountain village, gossip seemed to travel with the wind. This wasn't surprising. Macy knew the Bolivians in these high plains had long been entertained just as her own European ancestors had: a hot fire, close friends, and the juicy details of someone else's life.

"Señora Camera, venga por favor!" Gloria rushed to the road in the dark, carrying nothing more than a small candle. She had been waiting. Pacing, even. "No sabes que has hecho! No sabes! Qué vamos hacer?"

"Gloria, you have to slow down. It has been a long day and I don't understand. You are speaking too quickly!"

"Ah! Señora Macy! Estas en peligro. Tienes que regresar rápido a la cuidad! Qué vamos a hacer?" The woman's tone was frantic and her grip on Macy's wrist impressive. Before Macy knew it, they were inside and Gloria was creating a makeshift front door. She pulled several of the compound children, two goats and a handful of the chickens inside too. Macy noticed a line of buckets of well water in the kitchen and one of the neighbor women stacking firewood in the corner.

"What in the world is going on here? What is this, the OK Corral? Whatever you are afraid of, I am sure we are going to be okay. Gloria!"

The woman turned at her name.

"Please, Gloria. Cálmese!"

Gloria pulled Macy with her to move a heavy kitchen table against the makeshift doorframe. Once the matriarch was convinced her brood within the home was as safe as it was going to get, she pushed Macy into the plastic kitchen chair.

"USAID?" The way the Bolivian woman pronounced it, the acronym came out WHOSAID?

"Who said?"

"Sí! WHOSAID?"

They went back and forth for a moment before Macy realized this emergency was of her own making. Quietly, at Gloria's insistence, Macy did her best to explain that yes, indeed, her husband worked for the American government. Hadn't her cousin mentioned this when he arranged her visit? She thought everyone in Tarija knew. They were in Bolivia because Ben was working on a farming project. Something to do with coca leaves.

Macy knew little of coca, other than what she'd read from the travel books. She knew the leaf was controversial at best, with Bolivia's indigenous president boldly chewing mouthfuls at any international meeting he could muster to stir further trouble. Evo Morales was raised using the coca leaf as a natural medicinal. A treatment for soroche. A stimulant. There was nothing illegal about the pinch of green leaves Bolivians may be seen holding in the sides of their mouth.

In these parts, coca was life.

Across an international border, and rumored within their

own, labs buried under the canopies of rainforest jungle turned the centuries-old green leaf remedy into the ever-desired drug of choice in the western world: cocaine.

Macy had overheard Ben and Raleigh discussing this issue more than once, but she never bothered to pay careful attention.

She could have pinched herself for the number of days she spent in that dark bedroom, or in that stupid rusty bath. What she wouldn't give to see her husband in this moment. To understand the full danger she'd put herself in by unwittingly mentioning her allegiance to one of the greatest villains of South America: USAID.

Gloria pulled Macy into a back bedroom. Through a plastic tarp doorway, she entered the dark space where her hostess slept. Gloria produced a recycled coffee tin from beneath her rope cot, opening it slowly to reveal a stack of dried green leaves. To Macy, they looked like bay leaves— something her mother would have thrown into the spaghetti pot. Macy smelled the container: pine needles and dry grass. This was the formula for the magic tea that had eased her altitude sickness.

"USAID quiere quitar nuestra manera de vivir!"

Macy ran fingers under her eyes, trying to gather her thoughts. How could she show her hostess that her husband's work and politics were not her own?

She took Gloria's hands and motioned for a cup of tea. With a bit of prodding, Gloria let Macy photograph the process of making the tea. Creating the fire for the boiling kettle, placing the leaves in the cup, and the final green product, displayed in a chipped, mismatched teacup and saucer.

Macy slowly and deliberately brought the cup to her lips and took a long, steamy sip. She couldn't care less if they grew, brewed or chewed the leaves.

The last photo was taken with the camera's timer: Macy and the women stood proudly with their cups of tea, the steam rising to reach their smiles, and a lone goat wandering in the background.

The next morning, Macy was nudged awake by her Bolivian friend. Gloria handed her a warm boiled egg and motioned for her guest to follow her. Macy didn't hesitate. She dressed quickly, grabbed a new battery for her camera.

The makeshift door and emergency water were nowhere in sight. The camera display was still smudged from the night before. Gloria and her neighbor had giggled like schoolgirls at the magic of the digital display. Seeing their joy at holding the camera, inspecting photos of themselves, was the happiest moment Macy had experienced in Bolivia.

Now, with only a few hours of sleep, Macy raced after her hostess. She had no idea where they were walking, but the morning light was perfect for photographs. Macy stopped as she could to capture the colors of the highlands as the sun crested the eastern hills. She was thankful to have at least an egg in her stomach.

It didn't take much more than an hour of walking before Macy was ready to collapse. Gloria, strong as an ox, held on to her elbow, pushing her guest farther. Soon, Macy realized where they'd arrived: the penguin boy's house.

This piece of gossip must have arrived too.

In front of the mud home, the boy's mother beat a rug with a stick, sending a cloud of dust into the light blue morning sky. Other bits of laundry were pinned to a line that ran from one building to an outhouse. Macy couldn't help but remark how optimistic it was of this woman to hang laundry when the wind blew in spurts and gusts. The boy wasn't visible as they approached, but this was without a doubt his mother. Two goats grazed on yellow grass nearby.

"Buenas," Gloria said, rattling off another greeting in Quechua. Macy remained silent, fighting the strong itch to photograph every detail of the scene. The deep web of dark brown creases on the woman's face connected with a constellation of freckles across her red, wind-chapped cheeks. The sliver of smoke from the morning meal crept eerily from two missing bricks in the front wall of the house. Macy couldn't tell if their removal was intentional design, or if they were haphazard windows. And there was the landscape. The hills were inching toward summer, with shades of golden and orange flora and fauna that seemed to roll from one hill to the next to the sun above.

As a young photographer, she had the same experience in Greece, where the azure sky seemed to bleed into the sea.

Macy kept her distance, watching with curiosity as Gloria took the mother's hand and eventually brought her into an embrace. The two were deep in conversation for several minutes, their whispers carried away by the winds with the cooking smoke.

Without explanation, the mother pulled away, wiping tears from her eyes. After another quick embrace and big smiles from both women, the mother walked into the home; Gloria returned to her guest. In patient, slow Spanish, she told Macy with gestures when necessary that this mother was somehow a relative. A cousin or second-cousin. And the penguin boy was inside sleeping. They were willing to be photographed.

"Click click, Señora Camera," Gloria said, her smile wide and full of self-satisfaction at having brokered the situation.

"Oh, Gloria. Gracias! Gracias!" Macy didn't hesitate. With the mid-morning sun low on the horizon, she shifted between landscape and macro lenses to capture the exterior before her human subjects were to come into the frame. The stack of logs on the side of the house. The goats. That golden hillside. A nearly dry well. The exterior of a rudimentary latrine much like the long drop at Gloria's.

Soon, the woman appeared in the doorway with two cups of steaming tea. She motioned with her chin for them to come, enjoy. Macy took a quick sip but was preoccupied with the opportunity at hand. The boy sat on the edge of a bench inside; he looked downward with slumped shoulders. Macy crouched in front of him.

"Buenos días," Macy began. The boy didn't respond. "Yo me llamo Macy." She smiled. Swinging her backpack off her shoulder, she continued, thinking of Ruth and her basic Spanish lessons over oatmeal. She continued rooting around her bag until she found a package of chewing gum. Carefully she showed the boy, removing a piece from the silver wrapper and placing it in her mouth. The peppermint provided an immediate sense of home and comfort.

He looked up with raised eyebrows, sniffing.

Gotcha, she thought.

"Quieres?"

He thought about it, eventually nodding.

By noon, her new friend Alfredo was doing his best to run around the yard and play with the farm animals, as she learned he did most days. Gloria explained he wasn't able to go to school with the other village children. Alfredo had instead taught himself to move with incredible dexterity, considering his burns. When he tired, his mother, who had been outside doing chores with Gloria's help, produced a small wood platform with caster wheels. It was a rudimentary, homemade skateboard. Alfredo sat on it, leaning forward and pulling himself with the worn and calloused heels of his hands.

The boy knew how to maneuver around his mother's busy kitchen, the animal pens outside, and even the chicken coop, where Macy watched with wonder as he gathered and delivered more than a dozen eggs safely to the kitchen table.

Alfredo was a creative, determined boy. Macy captured it all, including the kitchen fire. Just as the community health care worker had described, the fire burned on the floor, kept in place with a circle of stones. There was no protection even today from things, or children, falling into the flames. A sooty kettle cooled on the edge, having been placed among the coals to boil the water for their morning tea.

Macy noticed the interior of the woman's home was a different color from Gloria's. The lack of chimney explained why the walls had a gray film. The only opening other than the front door was the two missing bricks. With summer coming, the home didn't need a fire all day. But come winter, Macy couldn't imagine how much smoke Alfredo and his siblings had to breathe to stay warm.

She wished her Spanish was stronger, and that she could get answers to even one of the dozen questions bouncing around in her head. She and Gloria hiked home by mid-afternoon, where the pair dug into the day's chores they'd postponed due to the field trip. Gloria continued her quest to teach her guest Quechua. Macy continued her quest to keep up with the activities of rural life without once again passing out from exhaustion.

"Paykuna sapa punchaw hatarinku ancha timpranu."

"Llamkanku tukuy punchaw."

"Mana llamkasanichu samanaykipaq punchawnintin!"

Macy had her head down, filling the llama's water trough as the afternoon sun began sinking. They were interrupted by the trill of a straining engine.

First Macy scanned the sky, looking for a small airplane. Then to the hills, absent of tractors. Then to the road, where to Macy's great surprise the rising dust announced a vehicle's passing. To her even greater surprise, the small truck stopped.

"Well, hello!" said the driver, leaning out of the window with a goofy grin.

"Pedro!" She ran, hugging him like he was her oldest of friends. "Oh! Why are you here? It is so wonderful to see you! How in the world did you find me?"

"Hola Señora Gloria!" he said, waving at the hostess and other neighbors who stopped their work. Visits and private vehicles were rare.

"Hola Padre!" Gloria waved back, immediately returning to her chickens.

"You know Gloria?"

"Of course I know Gloria. She's Don Campos' cousin. He told me you were here."

"Oh, right. Don Campos. Did you bring bread?" She smiled. She was so delighted to see him. Remembering their last visit, she wondered if he too was glad to see her. The thought of warm, sweet bread made her mouth water.

"I can't come all this way without bringing an entire truck of supplies from our baker friend. If I hadn't asked him to stay behind to care for the children, he'd likely have stowed away too."

"So, how are you?" She wiped her dusty hands on her pants and pulled off a bandana that released a spring of unruly, wavy hair.

"Well, that's a longer conversation. How are you? I heard there have been some conversations about USAID?" He raised an eyebrow.

"How in the world?"

"I made a couple stops to see other friends before getting to Gloria's this afternoon. You are the talk of at least two villages. I would say I arrived just in the nick of time."

Macy blushed. "So? What are you doing here? Oh, God. Oh God! Is it Ben? Is Ben okay?" She took him by the arms, feeling her heart surge.

"Ben is fine. He hasn't had the best month, but he is fine. That's why I am here. Let's go inside."

Macy followed him quickly, unsteady on her feet and grateful to find a plastic kitchen chair.

"The riots were more than any of us could have expected. They canceled our annual meeting of clergy in La Paz. They have essentially shut down the capital."

"But where is Ben? What are these about?"

"There is no easy way to say this, so just remember he is fine." The priest cleared his throat. "Ben and his Australian colleague were apparently jailed."

"Jailed? What do you mean jailed?" Macy stood, and let out a wail. Gloria poked her head inside, motioning for her guest to return to her seat. Macy did as requested.

"They have targets on them constantly because of their foreign employers. Bolivians want coca leaves. They consider this part of their heritage. The US and many other countries want the coca leaf to be replaced with another cash crop to reduce cocaine production. Really, what they should be doing is figuring out why so many Americans want the drug. But that is neither here nor there." He took off his Yankees baseball cap and ran a hand through his graying hair. Macy noticed how exhausted he seemed; dark circles gathered under his eyes. "This is a big political mess. It splits the population . . ."

"Is he safe?" Macy interrupted. Her toes wiggled in her boots. The assistant must have known he had been jailed when Macy called more than a week ago.

"He is out and safe. He should be on his way back to your home in Tarija. The ambassador got them out of the city as soon as possible. When I heard he'd been arrested, I tried to find you. That's why I am here -- to bring you home."

"Is he home?" The tears poured down her cheeks.

Oh, how she missed him! He wasn't angry with her—he hadn't been able to reach a phone.

"He is on his way. I thought you would want to be there as soon as possible."

"Oh, Pedro. Thank you. I will go pack."

"There is no way we are making that drive at night. Plus, I need some sleep. We will leave first thing tomorrow morning. Okay?"

Macy wiped the tears away and nodded. "Thank you."

"Wait to thank me until you see what I've brought. I know a week in the hills can be rough. You could use a drink."

The red wine didn't sound good, but she sipped a glass, keeping him company. The man could drink, as could Gloria. They sat at the kitchen table for the next several hours, eating plates of seasoned lima beans and llama jerky. Gloria kept their mugs of tea full, too.

Soon enough, Macy reviewed another day, tucked under her

blanket, thankful for the comfort she found in its heaviness. The priest snored with the rumble of a hibernating bear from a spare rope cot near the kitchen. She looked across the small home at the chimney, happy to be warm and without a cough.

She was thankful for so many small things she'd previously taken for granted. Toilets. Washing machines. Clean drinking water, straight from the tap. Central heat. Clean air.

Her husband.

Her friend, the priest.

She whispered these to herself, rolling on her side to let the tears of anxiety fall away.

The morning came too soon; a rooster crowed and a teakettle whistled at daybreak. Macy was thankful she didn't have a hangover. Padre Pedro moved at a considerably slower pace, drinking more than a full pot of coffee from the beans he brought with other household luxuries from the city.

Macy packed her things in the truck, returning to the kitchen for an uncertain goodbye. She hoped there would be a chance to return, to introduce Ben to Gloria and to see this community.

"Señora Gloria." Macy took the woman's rough hands into her own. Gloria giggled, her red cheeks bouncing up and down. The bolero hat on her head looked like it would topple at any second, with braids uncoiling. Macy cleared her throat.

"I can translate if you'd like." Pedro chomped a sweet bun, yellow and pink sugar crumbs clinging to the edges of his smile.

"No, thank you. I'd like to try this myself." She rocked on her heels. "Señora Gloria, gracias. Gracias por todo. Usted es muy generosa y linda. Soy contenta porque usted es mi amiga."

Thank you for everything. You are generous and lovely. I am happy because you are my friend.

"Well done!" Pedro smiled. Gloria raised both hands in the air with victory. It wasn't fluency, but after less than two weeks of intensive language, she was able to string together a basic sentence she'd memorized and practiced in the early morning hours.

Gloria embraced her. "De nada, amiga. Con amor."

Macy waved from the front seat as the children of the neighborhood chased after the truck. She suspected her hostess was relieved a bit to be free of her controversial houseguest.

"I know you are anxious to return to Tarija, and I promise we will arrive tonight, but I have one thing we have to do before we leave the altiplano."

"What? Errands, really? My husband was arrested, Pedro. I would really rather go home." She gripped the side of the seat. "Please take me home."

"Trust me."

"Look, I have barely slept. I don't feel well."

"He is fine, Macy. And we will probably beat him home. Trust me, okay? I came all the way up here just for you. Remember."

She pouted. "I don't have a choice, do I?" She wrung her hands.

"No. And I suspect you'll even appreciate it."

Macy rested a hand on her stomach, which continued to churn with nerves. She was hungry, again. She ignored the growls and let time pass, hoping the priest was right and Ben was safe. After nearly an hour of watching the odd high plain landscape pass, including tiny black dots of grazing llamas on the horizon, Macy looked to her friend.

"So you aren't mad at me anymore?"

He laughed. "American women. I forget how direct you can be."

"Well?"

"No, I am not angry. But I am embarrassed to confess I had too much wine to start the day with this conversation." He pulled a thermos of coffee from the car door and produced a handkerchief full of hard-boiled eggs, still warm from Gloria's kitchen. "Let's just drive for a while. We have plenty to discuss."

They sipped black coffee and let shards of egg shells fall to the earth from cracked windows. Macy pulled sunglasses over her face and tried to keep the small breakfast down as they bounced and shook in the small Toyota pickup truck. Some of the road was grated. In other areas, Pedro had to come to a near stop to navigate boulders or potholes. In the most terrifying times, he pulled the truck as close to the side of the canyon wall as possible when other vehicles tried to foolishly pass, narrowly avoiding catastrophe.

Macy groaned. They would be lucky to reach Tarija by nightfall at this pace, if they got there at all. Even the roads in this country were frustrating.

"You know, some of the families up there don't have ovens. They cook on the floors and their children fall in the flames." She pointed toward a hillside where several huts clung together, surrounded by yellow grass. A lone Bolivian flag blew in the wind, attached to a stick propped up on the roofline.

"We have a few foreign teams who come each year to operate at the Entre Rios hospital. They usually bring pediatric burn specialists for that reason."

"It's awful. I couldn't believe the cooking fires."

"Did you notice the smoke?" he asked.

"In the homes? Yes. No chimneys," she said.

"Exactly. Can you guess why?" He looked at her, raising an eyebrow.

"They don't want a hole in the roof? More cold air coming in the house?"

"There was a belief that smoke was the spirit of ancestors. The smoke kept in the home provided good health and luck to the inhabitants. Gloria is one of the champions in her community to fight this. She works on a campaign against selfishness."

"Selfishness? You lost me."

"To keep your smoke inside is selfish. To spread it out over your roof, and your animals and your garden and even your neighbors spreads the good luck and health to all."

Macy laughed. Gloria was a genius. "Does it work?"

"Did you notice all of the homes on her hillside have chimneys? And the children look healthier?"

She considered her new friends. The children certainly didn't cough the way Alfredo's mother did. Macy smiled at her friends' cleverness.

Before she realized they had taken a different route. Pedro turned left instead of right toward Tarija. They crested to a large, high plain, with the warm noon sun in the center of the sky. In the distance, purple and brown mountains were dotted with tall, spiny cactus. The land was otherwise void of animals and plants. The view changed from one curve of the road to another, the slow drive crawling upward from the yellow highlands to stark, blinding white.

"Where are we? What is this?" Macy pulled off her shades, alarmed. She felt her chest tighten.

"Just wait. We are almost there." Pedro navigated the truck off the road, slowly crawling across the flat land toward what Macy thought was a heat oasis. The wavy heat lines in the distance grew closer.

Parking the truck, he motioned for her to follow. "Go slowly."

She remained in the truck for too long, giving him a head start. By the time she caught up, she felt her lungs banging in her chest like a radiator struggling to work. Her heavy camera swung around her neck.

"What? Where?" She gasped.

"Go slowly! We are at nearly 12,000 feet. The air is thin. We aren't in a hurry."

She followed, remaining silent to conserve air. The ground was white, and cracked—like a dried riverbed. When she looked up, she was shocked to see a flash of neon pink resting on a large lake.

"Flamingos." He flashed a wide "I-told-you-so" smile.

"Flamingos?"

She sat in the dirt, steadying her hands to try to capture the scene. She felt like she had climbed into a Dali painting, searching the camera crosshairs for melting clocks.

"I've never seen anything like it." This scene was a photographer's gold mine. If *National Geographic* wasn't interested in her humanitarian feature, they'd certainly publish these. She shot for more than 30 minutes, rising and resting as necessary.

"They start arriving this time of year from Miami and the tropics. These salt flats"—he stopped to take in a deep breath—"there are brine shrimp in the lake. The flamingos love them." He smiled. "They call it Salar de Uyuni."

Perhaps it was the thin air, or the flooded senses, but Macy felt a calm climb up her body from her toes to the top of her head. Her anxiety was gone and she felt safe. For the first time since arriving in Bolivia, Macy felt like this is where she was supposed to be.

"I try to get up here to see these beauties any time I'm in the area." Pedro rattled between deep, difficult breaths.

"You were right." She grabbed his shoulder, steadying herself from whatever was happening in her head. "Thank you for showing me this. I wish Ben could see it."

"So bring him. I'm sure Gloria would love to see you again."

The pair sat on the hard, sun-baked earth to watch the surreal scene before them.

Eventually, Macy relented and climbed back into the truck, stopping only for empanadas at her request in Entre Rios when driving through. She felt at peace, her anxieties and depression gone. Not in the flash of a pink flamingo wing, but in the weeks of reckoning Jacob's death and the perpetuity of life.

She made a point at nodding at the same old men on the park bench in the central square when she paid the vendor. They nodded back. She was thankful to no longer feel dizzy.

"I do owe you an apology," Pedro said, with a mouth full of pumpkin and pastry. She waited, hoping he would finish his food before continuing. "I was rude to you when you requested the mothers' information. I am not angry with you. I'd just heard that morning from the diocese. As you would say, it was 'shitty news.' They are closing my church." He took a long swig of warm Coca Cola from a sea-green bottle.

"What? How can they do that?" she asked.

"Easily. So few go to church anymore these days." He let

out the heavy sigh of one whose determination was starting to weaken. "And when they do, they go to the fancy churches in the central squares. With the silver and gold statues, not rows of kids who need surgery and a home. There is no money for my kids, and they'd like me to go home. To retire."

"Retire? Like golf and buffets?" She laughed.

"Retire like I no longer have a job."

Her jaw dropped. "God, I can be such an ass. I am sorry. We will just fight it. Right?"

He laughed. "My family has been supporting the orphanage for years. They'd prefer I retire too. Maybe it's time."

"What about all of those kids? I can't believe you are going to give up!"

"I'll figure something out. I've always known this wasn't sustainable. It isn't like there is a team of young priests in the US clamoring to take my place." He sighed.

"Jesus."

"Precisely." He laughed.

"So, what happens now?"

"I have a few months, but I have to wrap things up at the orphanage and find a way to get community members to adopt. And I have to get the word out that women from these villages can no longer bring me their children. That's why I made a few stops before coming to pick you up."

"Where will they go?"

"Santa Cruz. It is farther, but the northern province has a good system of orphanages. There is a new Japanese mission there that has offered to help." His voice was quiet and she could feel his sadness like a passenger sitting between then.

Macy shook her head. "I am so sorry, Pedro. I thought you

were angry with me all this time. You and my husband." She grabbed his arm.

"You couldn't have known. It isn't every day you hear you are getting fired from the only job you've ever had." He cocked a half smile.

"Will you go home? New York?"

"Yes. I have been given a post at an urban church in the Bronx, in a limited capacity."

"You don't have to take it," Macy said.

"Yes, Macy. I do. I don't do this work for myself."

"Oh." She paused. "Of course."

"What about that baby at your house? What are you going to do with her?" He raised an eyebrow and smirked. It was obvious to Macy he'd been waiting for the right chance to continue this conversation.

She'd thought about the baby girl with the cleft palate every time she'd seen a child in the altiplano. And every time she fell asleep. And every time she awoke . . .

"The baby I lost, his name was Jacob."

"Was he your first?" The priest's voice was gentle, but curious.

"He was the first to get that far along. We'd had others, but none made it to the third trimester. Jacob. Well, he had a name and nursery. It was different."

"Of course it was." Pedro nodded, grabbing her hand. I could tell when we first met you were in deep pain. It seems that may be a bit better today." His voice was comforting.

She wondered if this intense empathy came with the job, or if it was what made him perfect for the role.

"It is. I can't explain it, and it isn't that I don't miss him or feel the loss . . . I just am different today than I was a few months ago. I . . ." She stopped. They climbed back into the truck and continued their voyage. Pedro remained silent. "I can't feel him like I once could. I loved to feel him moving inside of me. It was so strange, but it made me feel like my body was doing this magical thing." She faced the window, her face wet with tears. "Since I left for the village, I haven't been able to feel that ache where he used to be. It still hurts to say his name. And it feels like I've been slapped when people ask if I am a mother. But it is getting easier."

"I am glad to hear it. I don't think we ever fully 'get over' such sorrow. The children who have died at the orphanage haunt me at times. I worry I could have done more."

"It was my fault. My body failed him."

"I thought Ben said he was stillborn?" He said this barely above a whisper.

"Yes," she gulped. "He was."

"You didn't fail him Macy. It doesn't matter at what point he went to heaven, you didn't fail. Your body did exactly what it was supposed to do."

"Do you think he is in heaven?"

"Off the record? Of course. Purgatory for unbaptized babies sounds like the work of a madman Pope, not a loving God. On the record: no comment."

She laughed. "Thank you for that. I hope you are right."

"All we have in this life is faith. Have faith you'll meet your son in the next life. And do what you can in this one to make it a place of love. That, I know, God approves of."

"So you think I should keep the baby?"

"I think you should consider it. Babies don't just fall from the sky. You arrived in this country and almost immediately were given the greatest gift anyone could receive. I can't imagine that was coincidence." He paused. "I know you say you don't believe in God, Macy. So, I am trying to explain this as your friend. But know I think this child's arrival at your door was a great blessing."

"What does that mean? 'Blessing?' All these churchy words get thrown around so much. They lose their meaning for the rest of us."

"Gift from God. That baby girl showing up in a basket at your doorstep, when you were most in need for something to love, when your heart hurt its most. She is a blessing for all of us."

Macy remained silent. She nodded, closing her eyes.

"I am glad you seem to not be in so much pain anymore. I am glad you are starting to feel the grace of forgiveness. I know. More 'churchy words.'" They both laughed. "You have to forgive yourself."

29. CHASE

The report had been filed. Of course Carmen didn't have a photo of her missing sister, but Ruth was glad they'd gone to the police department anyway. It was during Carmen's description of her sister that she felt her stomach sink with a certainty she hadn't wanted to face.

"She is fourteen. Or is she fifteen now? She is young. She has long brown hair and is probably wearing my favorite green sweater, which she took before leaving. Also—she had a baby recently who died."

The police officer was young, in a tight uniform with dusty black dress shoes. He couldn't have been older than 20. Ruth watched him scribble notes, rarely raising his eyes above Carmen's chest when he did manage to look up.

The report was useless, but the exercise was not. Ruth knew that green sweater. It was the same one Luz wore when she'd met the girl in the market. It was the same sweater she'd mended and was currently hanging on a hook on the back of the girl's bedroom door.

Luz was definitely the baby's mother. Ruth needed to get home and find the Americans. She had to tell someone before something happened to that child.

"Thank you for your time," Ruth rushed the officer, pulling Carmen up by her arm. "We must be going."

They walked quickly to the Americans' house. Ruth let Carmen ramble during the walk, deep in her own worried thoughts.

When they entered the empty home, Ruth led Carmen to the kitchen. She put on the kettle.

"Wait here for one moment." Ruth returned with the sweater from Luz's room, still dark. "Is this your sister's?"

Carmen stood, raising the sweater to her nose. "Yes! Where is she?" Carmen took off like a madwoman through the empty house, throwing open doors and screaming, "Luz!"

"Carmen, come sit down. I know where your sister is. Please come sit down."

She calmed Carmen and led her back to the kitchen.

"Your sister is alive and well. As is her baby. The baby did not die. I can explain, but you must give me a moment."

Carmen kept her face buried in the sweater, shaking her head with disbelief.

Ruth called the hospital. Eventually, through a series of mishandled transfers, the doctor was summoned to the phone after Ruth insisted it was a personal emergency.

"Doctora Claudia, this is Ruth. Can you please tell me when Luz and the baby will be ready for their ride?"

Ruth tapped her foot.

"She left hours ago. She is already home." Ruth thought she misheard the rude physician.

"No, I am here and no one else has yet arrived. When did they leave?" Ruth felt her heart in her throat.

"Five hours ago. I am certain she must be home now. I gave her money for a taxi when you didn't answer. We called."

"If you see her again, please call immediately," Ruth stammered. The doctor hung up before Ruth could mutter a goodbye.

Hours. With money. These were two advantages Ruth hadn't considered. Where else could she be? She knew the baby would need additional surgeries.

How stupid she had been for buying the girl's story.

"Carmen, your sister left a baby here some two months ago. She left a little girl with a cleft palate at the front door in a basket. My boss found her, and the baby needed immediate surgery." Ruth put her hands in her apron and looked at the floor. "About a week later, your sister approached me in the market looking for work as a nanny. She said she had just lost a child. She'd overheard me speaking with a few vendors about hiring a wet nurse. I believed her. Foolishly"—Ruth now waved her hands—"I believed her."

"Are you sure this is my Luz? But her baby died? Can it be her baby?"

"Yes. They were just at the hospital, but left a few hours ago. I am not sure where they are now, but yes." The housekeeper paced. "They were both living here. I didn't realize Luz was your sister, or the baby's mother, until you described that sweater. I had some suspicions when we met earlier and you described her because of the honey. She told me she kept bees."

"That's my sister!" Carmen jumped out of her seat. "Oh, Doña Ruth. Thank God you found me! Thank God. La Doña will be so happy. And the baby is alive!"

"Yes. Luz is a clever one. She tricked me. She tricked us all."

"We thought the child was dead. She said she buried her."

"You said she disappeared for several days to mourn?"

"Yes."

"I'd guess that is when she actually left her daughter at the door."

Carmen wept into her hands. Her shoulders shook with obvious relief. Finally, the kettle whistled and Ruth put together a tray of tea and stale French bread with aji. They ate in silence, drinking several pots of tea, waiting for the door to open.

Eventually, in the middle of the night when both women were dozing folded over on the kitchen table, the front door did open. Ruth hopped to her feet, rushing forward in the darkness.

"Luz? Luz?"

"It's me, Ruth—Señor Ben."

Ruth found the light switch, flooding the entryway with light to reveal thinner versions of Ben and Raleigh. They looked like they'd been kept in the dark for weeks; the purple bags under their eyes revealed exhaustion and dehydration.

"God mate, let's get her to make us some food already. And wine. You have to have some wine in here, right?" Raleigh dumped a dirty backpack on the floor, the personal contents falling every which direction.

"I'm sure we can find something. I need a shower. And bed." Ruth watched as her boss slowly and painfully climbed the central stairs toward his bedroom. His pants were barely sitting on his hips. His blond hair had grown in curls over the top of his ears.

"Is Macy here?" he called down.

"No, Señor. Ella toma fotos." Ruth motioned a camera and pointed toward the mountains.

Ben struggled forward to his bedroom, too tired to respond.

"Food please." Raleigh motioned bringing his hand to his mouth. If he hadn't seemed so pathetic, Ruth would have rolled her eyes. Instead, she pulled out a dining room chair and motioned for him to rest. She made yet another platter of sandwiches and opened a bottle of Señor Ben's wine. The Australian was asleep at the dining room table after finishing his first helping. She heard Ben snoring upstairs too.

"Who are they? What happened to them?" Carmen stared at the sleeping heap of a man in the dining room with a strawberry blond beard.

"Señor Ben is my jefe. The other is his impolite friend. They haven't been here in weeks. I'm sure there is a story." Ruth waved her hand toward the snoring heap of a man at the dining room table. The two watched the man's back rise and fall with his deep sleep. His cheekbones were pronounced and his hair was greasy and needed a good trim.

"Should we move him?"

Ruth had to stifle an exhausted giggle. They wouldn't be able to move him with a wheelbarrow and a crane. Ruth would have climbed under the table to remove Señor Ben's shoes, but left Raleigh alone.

She led Carmen to Luz's room and helped to tuck her in.

"We need a good night of sleep before we explain what has happened. We will do so over breakfast. With any luck, Luz and the baby will join us all at the table. In the meantime, I have to find the right words. Sleep well, Carmen. Your sister is lucky to have you."

Ruth rested, but was unable to find sleep. She worried about her boys, the strained friendship with Myrna, and if she would be able to keep this work once the Americans discovered what was happening under their roof. How had she been so naive to help a needy village girl?

She had just finished tying the brown polera skirt and buckling her sandals when there was a heavy knock at the front door. The sun had yet to rise; it was far too early for any normal type of visit. By the time she reached the entry, Ruth was surprised to find the door open, and a drowsy Raleigh speaking to a young police officer.

"It is too early, mate. What do you want now? We got released!"

Ruth rushed forward, trying to control the situation with a smile and open palms.

"Buenos días, señor. Entra, por favor." She made the greeting in a hushed tone, shutting the front door against the noise of the city.

The bustle woke both Carmen and Ben, who soon joined the group in the front room. Ruth looking from one to the other, unsure of where to start. She watched with panic as Ben looked at the visiting woman, recognizing she wasn't the same one he employed as a nanny, and then at the young police officer, who tapped a small pencil against the side of his starched pants.

"Ruth, why is there a police officer in my living room?" Ben was wearing the same clothing as last night, too tired to have showered. One of his eyes was circled with a sallow bruise.

"Señor Ben, no sé todavía."

"She says she doesn't know yet," Raleigh translated, scratching himself in the rudest way a man can.

"Estoy aquí para hablar con la señorita. Pensamos que sabemos donde está su hermana," the police officer rattled.

With rough translations when necessary, the young police officer described a girl with a baby who had boarded a bus to Entre Rios the night prior. She fit the missing person's description.

"Who is missing, Ruth?"

The translations and gestures continued as necessary.

"Señor Ben, the girl Luz who I hired to care for the baby. She has taken the baby and we cannot find her. This is her sister, Carmen."

"What do you mean she took the baby?"

Ruth took a deep breath, gathering her wits. "The baby is hers."

The words hung in the air long enough. Ben's eyebrows raised after Raleigh's translation and she watched as her boss put together the pieces of the last few months.

"It is a long story," Ruth stammered on, worried about her own culpability, "but it seems she left the baby so someone could provide the infant with the necessary surgeries."

"What?" he shouted. "You mean to tell me that kid had a mother in this house the entire time? Fuck. And, where, the hell, is Macy?"

Ruth handed him the note Macy left taped to the refrigerator. "Great. Just fucking great. This is the last thing I need. She went to the village by herself?"

Ruth stepped back. She hadn't witnessed Señor Ben so red in the face.

"Actually, Padre Pedro has gone to fetch her. I called the orphanage late last night and Don Campos told me the priest had gone to retrieve her in the parish truck. Don Campos told me you had been in jail?" Ruth responded in a near whisper.

The whisper in times of trouble was a tool she'd developed with her boys. When they yelled, she refused to yell back. Instead, she'd startle them by responding with a whisper. It nearly always got their immediate attention.

"Yes, Ruth." He stuffed his hands in his back pockets. "That is a story for a different day."

"Jesus, mate. What a mess this is. I thought being in jail would be the headline. Leave it to this crazy house to add a missing nanny and baby."

"Shut up, Raleigh. Just shut up. Let me think." Ben paced the living room. "Damn it, I wish my wife was here. Three weeks in that cell I spent thinking of all the things I need to say and where is she? Gone again."

The officer described the girl and both Carmen and Ruth agreed, it sounded like Luz. It was enough of a lead to follow.

"Shit. Shit! Let me think."

Ruth, Carmen, Raleigh and the police officer stood in silence as the American paced the entryway. He rambled to himself in English.

After an uncomfortable moment of silence for the group, Ben ran his hands through his hair and then clapped them together. "Raleigh, we have to go get that kid."

"No, we don't." Raleigh didn't hesitate. "This is not your fight. It never was." He rubbed the side of his face where the dining room table left a deep crease.

"That kid was left on my doorstep."

"Yes," Raleigh rolled his eyes. "By her mother . . . who now has her back. End of problem, mate. Don't make this bigger than it is."

"That kid is sick." Ben paced. The women and police officer stared on. No one bothered translating for them.

"It sounds like they are both fucked." Raleigh rubbed his eyes. "Again: this is not your fight. We could get these betties to make us some bacon and eggs."

"Ruth, put some food together for us, please. We'll head up to the mountains and try to catch that bus."

"Who is this we?" Raleigh's words were slow. Even his sarcasm was tired.

"Get your bag, mate. You are coming along. If I went to jail in a foreign country because of your smart mouth, you can take one more road trip with me. And maybe if you are nice to Ruth —her name is Ruth, not Betty—she'll throw in some bacon."

Ruth bit hard on the inside of her mouth to keep from laughing.

"Can she come?" Raleigh motioned toward Carmen. Ruth instinctively put an arm around the girl's waist. Ben raised an eyebrow. Ruth had responded to the Australian's English, without translation.

"I would guess, yes. She'll need a ride home anyway, won't she, Ruth?" Ben asked.

Ruth considered her options. Sending Carmen with the pair to find her sister was likely the best bet. Would they return with the baby?

"Señor Ben, and when you find the bus?"

"I don't know. We just have to find it. Find them."

"Sí, Señor Ben. Carmen can return with you," Raleigh translated. By the time she had the food, and Carmen was convinced it was best for her to go with the men, Fernando arrived in his little truck. They were off in the early morning light, on the one road from the city toward the altiplano and Entre Rios before Ruth had taken her first sip of coffee.

"Ay, Dios." Ruth laid her head on the small kitchen table,

closing her eyes to the silence of the house. "Ay, Dios." She repeated her prayer until mercifully drifting to sleep to the crowing of roosters and taxi horns, as the city of Tarija awoke to a new day.

30. CIRCLE

"Oh, God. No! Not again!" The truck dragged to a halt, as rocks and dust filled the air.

Macy awoke in her seat to Pedro braking hard. The small truck shook violently to a halt. Unexpectedly, the pair had spent the night in Entre Rios with a flat tire. Having left before daybreak, they had made their way toward the desert floor, although the most dangerous turns remained on their descent to Tarija.

Specks in her vision made Macy blink hard. Was she really seeing this? Was she still asleep?

Pedro parked, slamming the door behind him and running forward to a yellow school bus, turned on it's side, most of it hanging off the cliff. Traffic backed up behind the bus with those available helping to pull bodies and survivors from the mangled wreck. The few travelers who had arrived behind the crash had been working for hours to pull those from the bus to safety. They wore shirts on their heads or mouths, undershirts circled in sweat, pants covered in dust.

Macy unbuckled her seat belt and resisted grabbing the camera. She ran after the priest.

"What happened?" She shook her head, unwilling to accept the apparent truth in front of her.

Pedro bent over a man, applying pressure to a deep leg wound. He'd already taken off his shirt. A puddle of dark red blood gathered under the man, who lay with his eyes rolled back in his head and his jaw grinding in pain.

"Tear this into pieces for me. We have to bandage as many of these folks as we can. Move! Macy! Move!"

She tore and did as he commanded. The air was full of screams and agony. Somewhere, in the wreckage, a wounded animal bleated for relief. The bus radio continued to sing Tejano ballads. The accordion, guitar, and singer wailed again and again in a loop Macy would never forget.

"What do we do?" Her chest tightened.

"Run back to the truck and pull out any cloth that can be torn into pieces like this. Then go see if you can get around to the other side of the bus. See who is on the other side and if there is an ambulance yet."

She turned, running to hear the priest call out after her, "And Macy! Be careful! That bus could fall at any moment."

She didn't let herself look over the steep cliff. She knew they were still hundreds of feet above the desert floor. She grabbed her backpack and rummaged through the glove box to find anything that would be of use. She found a flashlight, a large bottle of emergency water, and a small plaid blanket. Dropping everything at Pedro's feet, she ran toward the edge of the bus. The vehicle had come down at an angle and on its side, blocking the entire road. She carefully put one foot on a window edge and used the root of a yucca plant sticking out of the dirt above the bus to pull herself up and over.

Macy didn't look inside the vehicle. The windows were speckled with blood and smelled of human waste.

A queue of cars a dozen long trailed down the mountain on

the other side of the bus. She watched as travelers held strangers, comforting them and concocting splints and braces as they could. Men carried wounded women to the back of the queue, resting those who couldn't walk in the beds of trucks until help arrived.

"Macy? Macy!" She turned, certain she heard her name.

"Macy!" the voice continued through the sea of people. Glass crunched under her feet as she spun, shading the sun from her eyes.

"Ben?"

"Oh, Macy!" He picked her up, hugging her so tight, she couldn't breathe.

"Ben! Ben!" Macy kissed him, and continued to kiss his neck and eyelids and cheeks until Raleigh appeared, clearing his throat. "I tried calling you. You're so thin!"

Ben smiled, grabbing her in an embrace and kissing her once more. "We are fine. My God, I am so glad I found you." He grabbed her hand and started pulling her toward the masses. "We have to find the baby."

"What baby?"

"The infant left at our house. The nanny is actually the mother. She left, and took the baby. I think she's on this bus.."

"What? She kidnapped her own child?" Macy shook her head. Before she could ask for more detail, a guttural howl caught everyone's attention.

"LUZ!" Carmen's cry rattled the canyon.

Her wails reached the hawks circling above; her immediate, intense pain made several strangers hang their head in sorrow. "Ay, Luz!"

Macy, Ben, and Raleigh ran toward the woman, who cradled her sister's body. Luz's neck was broken. The young girl's braids were covered in dust and a dark purple trickle of blood ran from one ear.

"No! No." Carmen tried shaking the girl, with no effect. "No, mi querida hermana. Por favor, no!"

The three stood back, watching the horrific scene. Carmen's tears covered Luz's face, washing away the dirt in streams. Macy bent to the woman, holding her shoulders as she shook with grief.

"Who is she?" Macy whispered. Ben leaned over, taking Carmen's hand.

"This is Carmen, Luz's older sister."

"Where is the baby?" Macy asked.

Ben and Raleigh both looked toward the wreckage.

No one had heard they cry of a child. Macy spun around, trying to place Pedro. She could hear his voice in the distance, barking orders on the other side of the bus. It felt like he was a hundred miles away.

"I'll go."

"No, Raleigh. It isn't safe."

Before Ben or Macy could stop him, they watched the blond, lumbering man pull himself in through the hole where two windows had collapsed. As they waited, Macy reached for Ben's hand. He held her close. Neither of them breathed until finally, two hands emerged from the same dark hole, revealing a bundle. Macy and Ben ran forward. Raleigh carefully handed the baby to Macy. Ben pulled his friend through the windows.

"It's a disaster in there, bloke. You wouldn't believe what I've just seen." Raleigh became sick on his shoes, adding to the stench of the scene. "Like a battlefield! That bus driver must have been going far too fast." He lifted the back of his hand to his mouth in embarrassment.

"You were so brave, Raleigh. Thank you!" She didn't look up when speaking, instead focusing on her shaking hands and what they held. The bundled baby was wrapped tightly in a blanket covering her face. She froze.

What if the child was dead?

"Well?" Raleigh strode over. "I didn't just throw myself into there for nothing. Look at her. Nary a scratch." He beamed.

Macy and Ben pulled the yellow blanket back to see those bright blue eyes framed in black lashes blinking back at them.

"Waaa."

"She isn't hurt?"

"She's solid." Raleigh smiled as though he'd created the child himself.

"God, she is perfect." Macy ran her pinky carefully over the scar on the baby's upper lip. It was healing nicely. "She is so beautiful." She carefully turned the child over, bending her arms and legs with a gentle stroke and watching the reactions. The baby whined, but seemed otherwise fine.

Ben stood back. Macy could feel his eyes on her.

"Oh, Ben. If I hadn't left. If I had just loved her from the start, that girl wouldn't be dead. None of this would have happened!"

"Shhh . . ." He wrapped his arms around them both, holding his wife and the child. They stood in the embrace. Finally, Ben leaned back. "We can't look back."

She nodded.

"I'm sorry. Forgive me?" she whispered.

"There is nothing to forgive." He kissed the top of her head, and she felt tension she'd been holding in her shoulders and stomach for months mercifully release.

Raleigh had recovered from nausea. Soon, he was directing traffic on both sides of the bus, organizing supplies and communication back to the cities on either end of the route.

Fernando managed the arriving medical services on one side of the bus, while Pedro did the same on the other. The four men saw that the most wounded were shuttled to waiting hospital rooms. Macy cared for Carmen and the baby. She looked to the sky, wondering how long the gossip of the crash would take to arrive to Gloria's village. Or Carmen's.

"Vamos a casa," Macy said to Carmen, who continued to shake. She wrapped the woman in a blanket and returned her to Pedro's truck. Carmen didn't ask for the child, and Macy didn't offer her either.

Eventually, Pedro drove the women and Ben back to Entre Rios. Luz's body was wrapped in a sheet someone produced when they'd heard her sister's lament. Carmen had been the one to wrap her, tucking the edges of the sheet with care and kissing her sister's forehead before gently covering her face. The girl's head dropped at an odd angle, telling of her injury.

Carmen wept in the back of the truck during the winding voyage up the canyon to Entre Rios. Macy sat in the front, cradling the baby. Ben and Raleigh hadn't known how to comfort the grieving sister. They all remained silent out of respect for the body they transported. The ride seemed to last for days, not minutes. The light was hazy, the sun dispersed behind thin, high clouds. They could all feel the weight of Carmen's loss, and the uncertainty of the infant's future.

When they arrived at the small regional hospital, they delivered Luz to the morgue. Macy hesitantly handed the still-unnamed baby to a nurse for a cursory exam. Family members from nearby villages were beginning to arrive on foot, crowding the hospital entrance. They rushed to each approaching car, seeking their missing loved ones who had been expected to arrive at the local bus depot late in the prior evening.

The word of the bus accident had arrived in the early morning when a baker, headed to the city with regional breads, had to turn around. Ruthlessly, his daughter now sold the loaves to those waiting family members, hungry from their long walks.

The hospital did not have an ambulance. The health care workers paced the tile hallway, waiting for those who survived to reach their care. They had called the larger hospital in Tarija, but without the equipment necessary to remove the bus, those ambulances were blocked from bringing the injured to Entre Rios. Instead, they were forced to return to Tarija, a much longer route.

"I have been to this town before," Macy told Ben. "This is where I shot the photos of the young mothers. It was so different. Everyone was so happy!"

"The ones that ran in the *Times*. I remember." He smiled.

"We have to keep her."

"I know."

She looked up at him and smiled.

"I knew, but I am glad you know now too," he continued.

They were interrupted by a nurse. She returned the baby girl, who she held upright while feeding a bottle. Macy took over the feeding, smiling through her tears.

EPILOGUE

Ruth grabbed a roll of hot bread from a basket on the edge of her desk. Next to the old rotary phone, and a framed photo of Padre Pedro, sat a stack of bills and mail she'd avoided for more than a week.

She'd washed the orphanage windows and weeded the small, under-producing vegetable garden. The laundry and mending were done. The children's shoes shined. The desk was otherwise tidy.

The warm afternoon sun cast a golden glow over the room. Ruth took a big bite of bread. There was a pat of butter and cinnamon inside the roll, just the way she loved it. Ruth looked outside to see her boys playing soccer alongside Padre Pedro's children.

Her children. *Their* children.

Ruth took a deep breath, sliding the mail and a letter opener toward her, wiping her hands on her apron. Even though she wasn't in a kitchen much these days, she felt most at home working in the faded gingham garment.

She felt the knot in her stomach tense; they were running the orphanage on love and crumbs. Twisting the simple gold band on her ring finger, Ruth shuffled through the stack, surprised to see a blue and red international envelope stuck between the final notices on phone and water service.

How long had this been overlooked? Her eyes danced. It was from Macy!

Ruth tore open the envelope:

"Querida Root,

Hello from Flagstaff! I am sorry it has been so long since we've reached out. As you can guess—we've been a bit busy. Esperanza is a handful, and her new sister Luz is finally starting to sleep through the night.

Did you know, Ruth? I wonder, sometimes. You always seemed to know what was happening in that house. (Maybe I would have known more if I'd bothered.) I had no idea I was pregnant until we returned to Flagstaff. I thought I was tired from having one infant.

You must think I was clueless. Perhaps I was.

Luz was born screaming, with black hair like her namesake. She's a healthy, fat baby with rolls on her arms and legs and a smile you'd love. Today, her hair is the color of honey and her eyes are blue like her older sister's.

Please tell La Doña, if you can send word, that Esperanza is doing well. She's had a small surgery on her ears, but she is a strong one. She's walking and is saying three words (non-stop): daaaa, ma and more. We call her Hope.

How is Don Campos? Pedro told us the great news of your marriage. What a surprise! I bet your boys are happy to have a baker around, too. It makes me smile to think of you all together.

Now, to business: please find enclosed the information from the Banco Central. Ben spoke with the head banker, Señor Octavio Norte. He's waiting for this document to release the funds to you. I sold a few photos from our time in Bolivia. We've included that, and a bit for a honeymoon too. I hope you can find someone to stand in for a week at the children's home and take your family to the beach. You can thank the flamingos. Of all the photos, can you believe those were the ones that ran in National Geographic?

We miss you, Root. Tell that Don Campos hello for us.

Ben and the girls send their love.

Fondly,

Macy

Ruth wiped the tears from her chin, and happily patted her apron pockets for a tissue.

The church bell began to chime. Her attention drawn outside, Ruth watched as her husband poked his head from the bakery across the street, pointing to his watch and then the culprit's.

Francisco laughed, running off with the other children as the bell continued to ring in the wind.

ACKNOWLEDGMENTS

Special thanks to Lighthouse Writer's Workshop of Denver, Colorado.

To Melissa Griggs, for being a generous writing group hostess and the many ladies of the Griggs' writing circle for providing kind, constructive feedback. Also, to the Moriarty writing circle for helping with the final details.

To Adam Wright, Sagar Gondalia, Bert Rock, and Alma Celaya for being good editors and great friends.

To Esperança, for nurturing my burgeoning career in public health, providing thousands of Bolivian families safe homes and raised ovens, and being a beacon of hope to those in need internationally. www.esperanca.org

And of course, to Rex, Karel and Cody Donley—my best cheerleaders.

J—I love you more.

ABOUT THE AUTHOR

Kelli Donley was born and raised in Arizona. She has been an avid reader and writer since childhood, which led to studying journalism in college. After volunteering in west Africa with the Peace Corps, she returned to school to study public health.

She is the author of two novels, *Under the Same Moon* and *Basket Baby*. Inspiration for both stories was found working in the developing world in international health.

Kelli currently lives with her partner Jason, two children, three dogs, and a bunny in Mesa, Arizona. She continues to work in public health for the State of Arizona, and blogs at www.africankelli.com